Death Rattle is published quarterly by Evil Cat Press PO Box 238, Blacklick, Ohio 43004
www.evilcatpress.com

ISBN 978-0-9828389-3-8

DEATH RATTLE
A Magazine of Dark Fiction
Volume 1
Issue 1
Fall 2010

Carolanne Patton
Editor

Cover art by Carolanne Patton

Table of Contents

A Note From the Editor:

Welcome to the first issue of *Death Rattle*. Just in time for Halloween. How fitting. The first issue is a mega issue, packed to the brim with short stories and poetry by both established and new authors.

If there is a theme to this issue, it would be diversity. I was surprised to get submissions from all over the world. In this issue are authors from Canada, New Zealand, Great Britain, Slovenia, and of course the USA.

I tend to like my horror with a bit of irony or humor, and you will see that in some of the stories and poetry in this issue. Enjoy!

Carolanne Patton
Editor, Death Rattle

Comfort Food
By Matthew Quinn Martin

"It only takes nickels," Liza said as she and Grace rounded the corner onto 45th.

"I know how it works." Grace patted her overstuffed hip pocket. "Look, another one," she said, catching a glint of silver. "Must be my lucky day," she said, noting a warmness blushing across her heel, spot on the junction of strap-buckle and tendon. Even the short walk from Grand Central had her damning the stiff new sandals.

Blisters would soon have her wincing for her comfy clogs—the ones she wore every ten-hour shift at the wine shop—but this was her day to be girlie. Grace needed to be girlie, even if just for Liza who never had a hair out of place, never had to pay for an appletini.

Liza halted in front of a toneless gray door. Sunk three steps below the cracked sidewalk, tagged with scratchy graffiti and fading stickers, it didn't look like much. A flat faux-stone facade jutted out on both sides by a full yard, sloping back to a ropey black-tar join halfway up the mismatched brick.

"This better be worth it."

"It will," Liza said, pressing the buzzer. "One for The Book."

The Book: a still-hazy notion, a cloud grudgingly coalescing around a dust-mote idea in Grace's mind, something to take the sting from a Manhattan that had beaten all the big dreams out of her with years of ceaseless mundane pragmatism. She'd been inspired after stumbling through the false back wall of a phone booth at Criff Dogs and into a hole-and-corner country of password pro-tected speakeasies, of recondite lore the barest strata beneath familiar, of that hidden city lurking in the crenellated facets of the island the center of the world. The alleys and byways of which formed a warren where even the most jaded metrodenizens could once again touch wonder.

Between its still hypothetical covers, The Book would hold tales of FDR's top-secret train platform below the Waldorf Astoria; of how a bucket of sand tossed into the bowels of Grand Central could have lost the Allies WWII; of bowling alleys beneath the Frick; of a specter haunting the Belasco's elevator shaft; of ticking clocks embedded in sidewalks for over a century; of whispering galleries and abandoned pneumatic transit tubes.

Of all this and more. All she had to do was start writing it.

—*mmmclickt*— The magnetic door-lock hummed open.

Liza pushed through and into a small gray room facing a door even plainer than the first. She stopped glossing her lips long enough to wink, "Chase sent us," at a security camera mounted high in a corner.

"Who's Chase?" Grace asked.

"Just some guy."

There were scads of 'just some guys' at Liza's lovesick lunch counter. She was spoiled for them, Grace thought

And as the door swung open there it was. All complaints of a blistered heel, or neglected heart, shifted to the rear of Grace's cerebral queue by the sight. Threshold tiles snagged her eye first, inlaid hexagons of scuffed ruby spelling out a single word: AUTOMAT. Row after row of tiny steel and glass doors stretched out beneath milky art-deco signs for sandwiches, dinners, desserts.

"Tres retro-chic? Non? Chase says the pastrami's—"

"I'm getting pie," Grace said, striding for the nearest door bank, hand thrust in pocket. "Cherry pie and coffee."

"Yeah, coffee's supposed to be good. Guilty or something."

"Gilt-edged," Grace corrected as she pulled a lever. Coffee and cream poured together from a dolphin-headed spout.

"That's it. And in ceramic cups," Liza said, clinking the handle with a slightly bent metal spoon. "Only five cents too, can you beat it? That's like a hundred to one frappichino ratio."

"How long has this been open?" Grace asked, feeding nickels into the machine.

"Not sure. Rumor is, it's always been, since the 30s."

That's silly, Grace thought. The last Manhattan automat closed in nearly twenty years prior, just more hipster hype to go with the secret location and nickels-only policy. She twisted the knob, then reached for the pie she'd dreamt about tasting again for almost twenty years. She jammed her fork through the pie's steaming crust to spear a plump cherry. Lifting it to her mouth, she was hit with the buttery sweetness of pie and memory both.

At five her father had treated her to an automat lunch one weekend. She'd stared wide-eyed at all the doors, waiting for Daddy to decide, but he'd said she was "a big girl now," and she should pick. She could still feel that cold steel counter under her chubby hands as she pushed up on Mary Jane's to catch a glimpse of what lay inside the shiny boxes, but all she could see was the bottom row. She wanted Daddy to lift her up. But he'd told her to be a big girl, and she'd make him proud. Those top choices were out of reach.

She'd settled on a slice of pie—cherry—and a coffee. Odd choice for a five-year-old, but Daddy had said she could have what she wanted, and what she wanted was to have the same as her Daddy. Feet dangling from the chair, she dug into her pie, fork clutched in her tiny fist and smiled at him. And he smiled back, wiping red-smeared crumbs from her chin. And she laughed. And ate more pie. And sipped at the nasty coffee. And it was the last time she'd see him. A week later he'd split for good.

"How was it?" Liza asked. "The pie."

Grace looked down at her plate, empty but for the thumb-edged rind of crust. "This place is going in The Book—page one. Think I'll get another slice."

Grace sauntered back to the dessert section, lifting a fistful of nickels to the tilted slot.

"What've you got?" a broken voice rasped in her ear. A wiry arm shot past her face toward the nickels. "Come on, show it to me. Show it to me!"

Grace jumped back stunned, but managed a confused, "Back off," at the thin, feral thing. "What's your problem?" Grace yelled, then slapped the woman across her cheek.

The woman snapped still, retracting her arm as a look of shaking realization swept her face. Her eyes clear for one moment before welling up with tears. "I'm so sorry, I don't know don't...my—" She turned, head in hands, to collapse at the nearest table.

Grace couldn't peel her eyes from the

thin crying mess. She leaned in. "Are you OK?"

The woman gushed a blubbering flood, interrupted only by mucousy snatches of breath, "I'm sorry so sorry—he the nickelman—he won't give me any more and I thought maybe maybe you had some—I don't, I mean I tried—I didn't think it, you know, it could be so—"

"It's OK, OK, just calm down. What's your name?"

She gulped a deep, wet breath. "Shelly."

"OK Shelly. Did you want something to eat?" She looked like she could use it. Grace could see now that she was a year or two younger than herself, but worn. Her skin hung loose on her frame like a weather-beaten trash bag. "A cup of coffee maybe?" Shelly shook her head.

"What then?" Grace asked resting a nickel-laden hand on the table.

Instantly, Shelly's eyes flicked to it, then to her lap, then back again. Back and forth like someone watching the final seconds of a tight game. "These?" Grace asked, twisting her palm up. "You want these?" The cables of Shelly's neck tensed. A cicada sound of teeth-gnashing rung from her mouth. "Here," Grace pushed the nickels toward Shelly. Whatever had brought this woman to such torment, it wasn't worth a pile of nickels.

Shelly pounced, fanning the coins across the tabletop. "Okay, okay. I just want to look, really—I doubt—I mean what are the odds right?"

Each nickel was put though an examination with exponential desperation, then flicked back to Grace rejected. With just three coins remaining, Shelly found something. She double-checked it, triple checked it. Then put it aside—close to her—as she relaxed, giving the rest a cursory inspection. Content, she pushed all but the single elected nickel back to Grace.

"That's all? Just the one?"

"Yes, yes, thank you," Shelly said, neither her eyes, nor her hand straying from the coin. "One's all I need. One's enough."

"Is it valuable?" Grace asked inching forward.

"Yes." Shelly answered, pulling back. "No. Not really. Yes I suppose. Sentimental."

That word, 'sentimental,' echoed in Grace's mind. Sentimental was something she could relate to, even if Shelly was, perhaps, more 'mental' than 'senti.'

"May I see it?" she asked, pointing to the coin.

Shelly's face flashed no way, but after a moment, she relented, holding it out; holding it tight, thumb and forefinger ringing the entire edge. Above the dome of Monticello, Grace spotted a capital "A" stamped bold. Shelly flipped it to reveal a blurry Thomas Jefferson, almost twofold, as if viewed through a few too many cocktails.

"Double-die," Shelly explained.

Grace thought that a funny name for a coin, and was about to say so when Liza interjected, "Come on Kittens; I see moseying in our future."

Grace wanted hear more, but sensed Shelly folding further into herself, eyes darting from side to side to Liza to side to her to the automat doors. Grace shook her head and turned to go. As the duo hit the exit, Grace caught a flash of Shelly bounding across the cafeteria floor, nickel extended. "Liza, I'll meet you later.

"What's the deal?" she said, barring Shelly from reaching the automat knob. "You act like that nickel's the Holy Grail and then you just spend it? WTF? I could have bought you a—" she cased the door, "toasted cheese, if that's what you wanted."

Shelly gripped Grace's shirt, pulling her close, her voice a hoarse whisper. "Please don't make a scene," she said, unnervingly calm. "They're watching."

"Who's—"

"Please!" Her grip tensed. "I'll...I'll share it with you." Shelly nodded toward sandwich tucked behind the automat's beveled glass door.

"Fine," Grace said, turning the knob. "We'll share." She felt a clicking resistance as the toasted cheese blinked away; in its stead a plate of. . .of something else.

"But that isn't—"

"Doesn't matter what it was," Shelly snapped. "Could have been anything, any door. Just take it and don't make any more scenes."

Grace did as she was told, following in Shelly's wake to a table shadowed in the corner.

Grace gazed at the grayish patty swimming in goopy gunpowder gravy. She poked it with her fork; an acrid aroma rose to scratch the inner walls of her sinuses. "What, exactly, is this supp—"

"I didn't have to share with you, you know," Shelly spat, mouth half-full, gluttonous eyes already devouring Grace's share.

"Fine." Grace clipped off a triangle with the side of her fork, popped it into her mouth, and chewed. The texture and taste were both lighter than she'd expected, like feta laced with lemon and electric rust. Silk and graphite.

Then it slid away, caroming into all the flavors she'd ever tasted. All the special ones; the cast-iron smoke of her father's long for-gotten navy bean soup, the yeasty cake of her grandmother's Halloween donuts. And all the tastes she'd missed; the crisp middle-school lunch line fries she could rarely afford, a slice of cheesecake she feared might show on the beach, the tangy apple pie she viewed through tears as it slid down duplex steps, peace and crockery smashed to bits by her mother's third husband.

Those, and every flavor she might someday savor; six course decadence served nightly as she cruised the globe, a surprise birthday breakfast in bed of blue-dyed pancakes brought by her precocious seven-year-old twins with help from daddy, the buttery finish of lobster bisque and chardonnay still clinging to her palate as a dream date got down on one knee, diamond ring glinting in the Manhattan starlight.

All this in a simple bite. And in the next, the same.

Swallowing the last of it, Grace looked up at the clock; three hours had passed. She turned to Shelly, "Wow! Where can we get mo—" but the sound died on her lips. Shelly was gone.

# # #

The next morning the strange meal's effects still clung to Grace. Even hours later, feeling but a fraction of what she had at first, the world was new-scrubbed, making all her yesterdays as dark as a dismembered dream. She wasn't sure how it worked, or why, and didn't care. The mechanism, the mumbo-jumbo, the magic, all of it paled in view of the thing itself. Of what it could do.

She wanted more.

A web search netted nothing about double-die nickels. Flummoxed, she dialed a dealer in rare coins, the metallic taste still

4

lingering on her tongue, her mouth watering in anticipation.

No luck.

She dialed five more dealers. "Listen lady," the last one told her. "I been in the coin biz fifty years this spring, and I tell you there ain't no such nickel. No A on the back. That's a mint mark. P, S, D, sure, but no A."

"But I'm sure I've seen—"

"And my cousin Myron seen a UFO once. Ask him about it. Bend your ear right off. Look, you find another, happy to take a gander. Probably fake, or from Canada maybe."

Seemed the A-stamped double-die Jefferson wasn't just rare, it was mythical. She shook her head. What were the odds of one winding up in her change jar?
That's when it hit her.

It *hadn't* been in her jar. It was the one she'd found on the automat stoop, probably dropped by some customer in the know, maybe even Shelly. That left Grace no choice. No choice but to go back with fingers crossed, hoping Lady Luck would smile on her.

The Lady, however, didn't.

Grace spent hours searching the stoop's every nook and cranny--as well as half the block--throwing sidelong glances at the folks entering the secret eatery, her x-ray imagination prodding their pockets for magic nickels. But she found nothing more than bottle caps, gum foil and, of course, a few normal nickels.

She'd almost given up hope when she spotted something. There, next to the top buzzer of the automat building, almost totally curled over, hung a small label. Smoothing it out, she read: *Vadszlav Coins, Rare & Unique.* Beneath the name, in ink faded to a near imperceptible brown, someone had added, *the nickelman.*

Grace pressed the button.

—*mmmclickt*—

Grace ascended a creaking staircase to face a ribbed-glass door emblazoned with that same moniker, *Vadszlav Coins, Rare & Unique.*

She twisted the knob.

Yard after yard of black-rubbed wood grain greeted her as she entered. Red velvet cushions topped spindly benches, the only color to slash the monochrome. Across a threadbare oriental, at a high Dickensian desk, sat and old man behind a crib wall-like portcullis, jeweler's loupe clutched between a massive overhanging ledge of gray eyebrow and equally solid hawk-like beak. He scratched an upturned bowl of hair sitting lifeless on his head, the color and texture of a scoop of dryer lint, as he slowly flipped a coin end for end.

"You catch draft, Miss. Come in," the nickleman said without so much as looking up, his accent thick as Hungarian goulash.

"I'm looking for a nickel," Grace said, as she approached him.

The nickelman raised his eyebrow, an invitation for Grace to continue twisting in the wind.

"A certain kind of nickel," she added.

"Well, we certainly got nickels. Certain kind and uncertain kind. What you look? Buffalo? Indian head?"

"Double-die."

"Ahh…that certain kind. Perhaps with big "A" on back?" Grace nodded. "Very popular this nickel." He squinted, his blue eyes misted by cataracts. The nickelman rubbed his jaw, scrutinizing her as thoroughly as if she were a coin beneath his loupe. "No," he said setting back to work. "Big sorry Miss. For you, I don't have."

She moved closer, wrapping her hands

around the thin waxy bars. Close enough to see the frayed seams and pilled fabric of the nickelman's sport coat. "I have money," she said.

The nickelman sighed, folding one liver spotted hand over the other. "Someone send you perhaps? Someone not smart?"

"No."

"Is bad this, for someone to do. You stand-under?"

"I just...I read the label on the door. I've been, you know, down there. In the automat. I know what it's like."

The nickelman split his desiccated lips in what might have been a smile. "Oh... you know what is like." Hooding his eyes with vein-riddled lids, he leaned forward. Grace could smell his breath—stale cabbage and rye bread. "Why you no say? For you, Miss, maybe I have." Reaching under the worn wood counter, he produced a stack of five nickels. "Special price. Twenty dollar. Each."

A hundred bucks. That seemed reasonable for five rides. She pulled a mixed wad of twenties, tens, and singles from her pocket, then slapped it down in front of the nickelman, who pushed the coins forward under the bars, but kept them under the cup of his hand. "Are you sure Miss, that you want?

"Yes. I'm pretty sure."

"You are pretty?" he slid through another gash of smile.

"I'm sure," she answered and was down the steps within minutes, standing before the automat door, the precious nickels still cold in her sweaty hand, anticipation dancing a victory jig around her heart.

# # #

"What'ya think?" Phil asked as he put the finishing touches on the wine shop's Father's Day display.

"Looks great," Grace said without so much as a glance up from the register. She needed to concentrate, needed to keep the numbers in her head.

"What'ya getting your dad?"

"Scotch," she answered, not remembering if she'd even mentioned to her boss that no father, not in any sense other than biological. "Single-malt, I guess." She hoped that would shut him up. She needed to focus on the math. The sixteen bottles she'd "sold" while hitting the 'no sale' button meant she could safely pull $276.55 from the till.

"My kids'll probably get me another tie."

"That's nice.

—bzz—bzz—

Grace answered her phone with a curt, "What?"

"Settle kitten," Liza said over the ether. "Drinks tonight?"

"No, I've got stuff going on."

"Working on The Book?"

Grace hadn't thought about The Book in months, not since that first trip to the automat, which had since become daily if not twice daily. "No, not The Book. Look, gotta jet." She clicked the phone closed without waiting for a reply.

Forget the damn Book, she thought. The world can find hidden treasures on its own. If it can't see the precious things right under its nose, it doesn't deserve them. She turned back to the register.

—thud—

Phil set a green glass bottle down on the counter in front of her. "Take it," he said. "Single-malt, for your dad, for Father's day. 25 years old. That's how old you are, right? I know it's not polite to ask a lady—"

"No, no. Thanks," she said pulling the bottle toward her. It was worth a hundred bucks, easy.

Phil nodded and turned back to his work.

Grace looked back down at the register, not quite ready to believe she was about to rip this man off. Had already been ripping him off for weeks. Had gone from searching for double-die nickels in the till, to pulling twenties from it. All of it to feed the automat, which just made her hunger for it stronger.

Grace took a deep breath, then slipped the money from the drawer and into her pocket. "Mind if I split early?" she asked Phil. "Not feeling great."

"Stomach again?" he asked, concern still outweighing the annoyance that edged into his voice.

"Yeah," she answered. "Yeah."

# # #

"Miss," said the nickleman, hands in the air. "I no have more."

"Look, you rhinoceros-nosed creep," Grace said, rattling the portcullis bars. "I know you've got more back there. I know you're in it with the people downstairs. I don't know what kind of game you're running, but I'm sure the IRS and the health department, and the police, and the Better Business bureau, and the newspapers…and the…a lot of other people would love to hear about it. I'll shut you down so fast! I'll make such a stink! I'll—"

"Calm please, calm," the nickleman said slipping from behind his desk. "We can work this. You come in back, maybe I have some…somewhere. But calm, please."

"Fine." She followed him through a sliding oak panel into a small apartment, just as dingy as his shop.

"Could take time," he said, tugging out a long drawer from a nearby cabinet, and flipping through square white cardboard pouches. "Sit. Sit."

Grace did, fidgeting.

"I am old man," he said. "Just want to make happy people."

"Happy people?"

"Yes, happy people, but can't make all happy. Only so many nickels," he said half to himself. "You seem nice girl. But this…what downstair is, for some, much. Too much. You eat, but then it eat. You eat, but then it eat. You stand-under?"

Grace nodded, wearily. She didn't need a sermon, just more nickels––and this b-movie reject had them.

"You should maybe just go to home," he said, a deep kindness whispering from beyond his cataract-frosted eyes.

Grace didn't care. "I'm not leaving."

"Ho-Kay," he said clapping his hands together. "Is going to take time though. I make tea." And with that, he slipped into the kitchen.

Grace took a deep breath. Maybe the nickelman was right. In three months she gone from drifting dreamer to thief, liar, and loser. She stood up. She'd go through that door and break it. Forget the automat. Forget the nickelman. Forget they even existed.

Right after tonight. Right after this one last time.

The nickelman came back with a cup of tea. "Have. Good for nerves." Grace sipped. It tasted faintly of licorice. "Old recipe, very old. From back across water."

"It's sweee…" She started, before her lower jaw went slack. The cup slipping from her limp grasp as her eyelids sealed her in

7

black.

# # #

Grace felt a metallic coldness beneath her body. She tried to sit up but found her arms held fast. Pain ricocheted around her head as she squinted in harsh fluorescent light. Her lips cracked as she ran a cottony tongue over them. Shifting her eyes she caught sight of pots bubbling away atop a grimy commercial range. Beyond that, she saw open metal cubes. She was in the automat. Behind the doors.

A man's back came into view, dirty chef's pants and the knotted string of an apron. She watched as he pulled credit cards and cash from her wallet, then consigned the rest to the trash.

"Mister? What's going on?"

"Shh," The man said. "Should not have said to call cops," he said turning to face her. "Is bad this."

Grace should have recognized the dull gray bowl haircut from behind. The nickelman. He stepped forward and she felt a numbing throb as he tightened the screws pinning her head.

"Are you going to kill me?" she asked, barely able to form the words.

"No. Not exact. Not at first. Is better if awake."

"Awake?" she managed.

"Yes," the nickelman said pulling a black Sharpie from the sleeve pocket of his chef's coat and uncapping it with his teeth. She felt the cold wetness of dotted lines as he drew it across her forehead. "Is better if awake. For recipe. Is old recipe. Very old."

"Recipe?"

"Of course. What you think in that food you like so much?"

He picked up a tiny surgical saw. At first Grace couldn't even scream--her voice frozen--but she did. A sound lost to the echoing whine of the saw's tornado teeth as it bit into her skull.

The End

Matthew Quinn Martin is an MFA candidate in Popular Fiction writing at the Stonecoast Program, University of Southern Maine. He is also the writer of the crime drama "Slingshot", a feature film starring Julianna Margulies, David Arquette, Thora Birch, Balthazar Getty and Joely Fisher. Available on DVD from the Weinstein Co. www.matthewquinnmartin.com

Rumpletstiltskin

By Donna Burgess

Memories of that day have grown soft with time
Facts are just facts—the stink of blood in the air,
The clock ticking too loud, the pot boiling over

He does not remember the feel of the moment, nor does he wish to
Mother singing a pop song—that was a fact also,
Partridge Family song and that tune makes him sick to this day

She was to sell the boy, or maybe give him away
To a wretched gnome with a ghost face and a long coat
For what?

He did not know, at the time,
But she changed her mind, like moms are apt to do.
Changed her mind so he changed her body, too.

Opened up, flayed, filleted,
Scattered, torn, splattered
Onto the smooth and round two-year old face.

Rules are rules shouted the little man
He left the child just where he was.
Could not take him without agreement.

Suggestion of night forty years on
And he believes he sees the little man,
Beneath the streetlamp at the end of the drive

In the crib his own tiny boy slumbers
Thumb screwed into the rose-shaped mouth
In front of the mirror, his mother has made a deal

Something about losing the lines around her eyes
Or maybe it was dropping the
Last ten pounds of pregnancy fat on her bottom

But deals are made to be broken and
He waits for the little man to come through the door.
He will be ready. Unlike his mother, he will be ready

Donna Burgess is the owner/editor of Naked Snake Press, which is starting new, after a three year hibernation. Her work has appeared or is forthcoming in many genre publications such as *Weird Tales, Brutarian, Albedo One, Chizine, Sybil's Garage, Neon Magazine* and others. When she is not writing, she enjoys running and surfing. She is also currently back in school, after a nearly twenty-year absence, pursuing an M.F.A. in creative writing, with plans to move into teaching.

Morning at the Night Market

By Todd Bowes

I watched from the bookseller's stall as the husband's face twisted from shock to rage. His wife's shrieking, directed at him but heard by the whole esplanade, had caused a boy eating sweets to loop around them, even as the more dutiful crowd shuffled past. She pointed at the ornate package dangling from a shiny ribbon in his hand. The old bookselling man yawned.

Under the rosy glow of paper lanterns and signs strung across the esplanade, I saw it: a black flash streaked with crimson criss-crossed the husband, releasing the scent of old coins moulding somewhere forgotten. A blood scent. Pungent though it was, it would not rise above the more pervasive odors of shrimp and squid, rice cakes and potato treats. I fished a butter candy from my pocket and popped it into my mouth.

The husband whirled around, howling about his girlfriend, and stormed off in the opposite direction. The shrieking began again, and they vanished into the throngs of the Shida night market, here in Taipei. The boy finished his loop, and moved on. He did not see the three other boys that were eyeing his candy bag, and did not notice when they followed him.

I followed the screaming married couple. The crowd was parting to give them as big a margin as possible, though such outbursts were easily swallowed by the noisy crowds that always came to Shida.

I came up behind his wife first: a coifed and elegant woman fashionably dressed in something expensive. She was not unattractive, and in another time I would have stopped her screaming short with a mild touch, talked her down, bought her some dinner, invited her to my Spartan apartment, and seduced her. It made me smile just to think of it, and I thought of Yi-Swan in San Francisco, the way her lavender scented hair fell into my face, in that moment before I gave in to her.

Sliding my fingernail just under the woman's ear, barely enough to break the skin, I placed my lips close, and got just the tiniest taste: her blood was hot and metallic, but spicy like coriander and cayenne. And in that other thing I take, that silver line in the blood, I stole her rage as well. Her screaming moved from her throat to mine, but I held it in check. She relaxed and slowed, and saw me for the first time. I smiled at her, and her eyes softened, turning blue from the completed Exchange, the emotion transfer, as my calmness spread through her. There was a quick flash of a distant argument about a female co-worker with whom her husband had had dinner.

I spun to follow her husband and, invigorated, shifted past the crowds until I was at his shoulder. He was an office type, dressed in black slacks and matching jacket, and moving in a line, ignoring his wife. His pace was quickening though, his strides becoming longer. The package no longer dangled from the ribbon but was clutched tight in his fist. His eyes glittered as he stared ahead, as if assured of his destination, and with every confident step, his smile grew wider. That glitter – yes, I'd had about enough of that. The scream was rising in my throat again, so I grabbed his shoulder and wrenched him around.

"So tell me, Kei," Sheng-Qi demanded, "did you come here to die?"

I reared back. This was not her husband! But someone else's husband...I shifted again, away from the office man and his wife, trying to shake off the vision. I moved until I was between stalls fifty-one and fifty-two. There were crowds but no one watched me; I fetched the paper sack from my jacket pocket and ate a candy. That couldn't have been Sheng-Qi. I was not ready for him yet.

Stall fifty-two had the good *lu wei*, so I bought an order of the vegetable kind. It took the cook a few minutes to boil it in the broth but I didn't mind. As I ate them, I smelled her lavender, and saw the azure mist from the Escapement, the memory transfer. High above San Francisco Bay, Yi-Swan cuddled in my lap. "Why couldn't you come to my photo shoot today? I wanted to see you."

The Golden Gate bridge traffic zoomed beneath my hotel window, an unending string of white and red lights. I sat up a little and stroked her hair. "Aren't you glad to see me now?"

She smiled with half her mouth. "Of course," she said with a little laugh, "but you would've liked the bikini I wore."

"No doubt."

She got off my lap, trotted over to the window to watch the traffic, still wearing her street clothes. "So will you tell me?"

"Just business."

"Liar," Yi-Swan retorted, half smiling. She'd only been in the United States for a few days but had already picked up their penchant for bellicosity. "You were doing something nasty. I can smell it on you." She sat in front of the false fireplace; the electric flames threw ripples of lurid light over her skin.

I leaned back on the couch. The hotel room was huge and spacious, the furniture modern and free of affectation. "I told you: I had to look at the proofs from another model's shoot."

"I still don't believe you," she replied, rolling over and laying on her stomach, stretching her long body in front of the fireplace.

I put the phone on speaker, then dialed room service, and ordered two bottles of champagne, charging it to the Taipei Stars Modeling executive account. Her jaw dropped.

"I can't believe I'm here with you: Kei-Chen Liu, the president. and CEO," she said.

"Then you shouldn't be calling me a liar," I said.

She screamed and flew at me, landing in my arms, entwining me like a nest of silken serpents broken free of gravity, and we sunk deep into the plush white velour of the hotel couch. I tasted the sweet dates from her lunch, and a metallic aftertaste.

"I want to be better than anyone," she enthused, running her fingers through my longish hair, "Can you make me the best? The most famous?"

I looked away from her. "But you have so much," I whispered.

"I need more," Yi-Swan replied, "Just show me how to get it."

I locked my eyes on her. "You're arrogant."

She grinned and said, "I know."

I felt the pulse of her heart drum a cadence so rapid it burst away from my own. I chased her bloodstream in kisses and tracked her veins with my tongue. Her corpuscles expanded under my fingernails, and her skin blushed wherever my teeth found her naked. She took in a sudden breath like a backdraft at the first piercing, then wrapped her arms around my ribs and crushed herself against me, letting the red tide wash me away, far away from her and everything else.

The Escapement faded, and I came back to the smell of lavender and copper.

"You bastard."

Yi-Swan was leaning against the stall frame, fingers thrust into the tiny pockets of her tight black pants. She looked the same as she did in San Francisco: tanned skin, black hair parted over her right eye stopping just above the shoulder, and that cocky half-smile over perfect, straight teeth. Her eyes gestured up, and I looked up above her to a poster adorning a building's façade across the street: the same face grinned back at me. So she kept modeling.

I pushed the candy to the back of my mouth. "So it was you that I saw with that office guy," I said, "I saw that black flash of shifting but I couldn't place it exactly."

"Yes, and you ruined my fun when you grabbed him." She snorted. "Even that horrendous tramp of a wife gave up. It totally bombed." She heaved a sigh, glancing in the direction of the couple.

So...she hadn't seen me cut the woman. "You mind-tricked him?"

"This is not the woman you are looking for," she quipped in her best Obi-Wan, and waved her fingers from right to left. Then she laughed. "The irony? He bought that necklace for his wife. Now all he can think of is his 'girlfriend.'" Her smile faded as she gazed at me. "It's been what? Four years? A long time."

"Not really," I answered, "That night in San Francisco seems like just a few hours ago to me."

She grinned. "Yeah, I guess so." She took my hand in hers and led me off. We shifted above Shida and perched on a rooftop overlooking the esplanade. She leaned back against the edge, stretching her lithe body out, and asked me, "What are you doing here? I've never seen you here before, and I've been prowling here for a while."

I said, "Appropriate choice of words."

I felt the air part before she was upon me, but let her torso slam into mine, and her hands press on my shoulders as she forced me down. Her eyes had gone black and savage – the Enraging sign. I smelled blood on her breath, and her voice boomed so loud and deep that for a moment I thought for sure someone on the esplanade would hear, or get flattened by the masonry surely plummeting earthward.

"What am I?" she bellowed, "Why did you do this to me?" She hurled me across the roof, scraping my back on the tar. I hit the opposite side and slammed my fists down, shoving myself upright.

I cracked my neck. "I gave you what you wanted."

She launched herself at me, her fists swimming in blue air, sparked with anger, tinged black, the Escapement swelling, invading my memories again. "Shut up," I hissed, "and tell me why."

Sheng-Qi grimaced, shutting his eyes tight, squeezing out bloody teardrops. "How else?" he screamed, "The army was chasing us into the sea! We needed it! How else could we survive?"

It was then that he opened his eyes, and saw two others hovering above the concrete floor. The caked blood and drool flaked and fell from his face. His eyes expanded and jaw slackened. "Bei Fong, Shui Lan..." He slumped to his knees, and his grimace spread into a smile. He laughed, long and loud. "So, that's who you are? I can't believe you remember! But..." He raised his head and took in the full sight of me. I was wearing a black suit with a red tie, but my hair was short. "You are not old."

I rolled up the right sleeve of my jacket. "Your father," I said, "brought a package to my mother." My knuckles cracked.

"It makes no sense," Sheng-Qi stammered, "You were not that much younger than me."

"I'd heard the stories of what those left behind endured from Mao's armies," I fumed.

Sheng-Qi moaned, "Why are you not old?"

I raised my hand and leveled it at Sheng-Qi's neck. His body rose from the ground, and I clenched my fingers. "It was for the whole nation," he choked, sputtering wet gasps. His eyes widened, red veins bulging like swollen rivers. "Please." His hands stretched out, short of my hand by a few meters. "Stop."

I opened my hand, releasing the pressure on his windpipe. He dropped to his knees, clutching his neck, hacking ragged breaths onto the cold concrete.

"Remember this place, remember this face," I said, "In twenty years' time, at the top of this hour before dawn. You will see me again."

Yi-Swan released me, and the last ephemeral strands of the Escapement disintegrated to pixie sparkles. A thin carmine line slipped across her collarbone to curve around the rise of her right breast. I grinned back at her. Unsmiling, she wiped away the streak with her finger and turned away, her unmarked skin glowing auburn from the cold cadmium lights radiating down on the night market. She strode across the rooftop, placing her elbows on the rail overlooking Shida. She shivered even against the heat, and looked down on the night market. The street moved. Some stalls had closed up, including the lu wei stand, but many remained open. The married couple was now talking out everything. Argument, evidence, reconciliation; argument, evidence, reconciliation – their conversation spun in spirals like two fish in a vortex.

Only a couple hours to go.

"I would have, you know," Yi-Swan muttered. She swept her rogue locks away from her right eye.

I touched my neck where her lips had left a bruise, now fading. "It was arrogant of me," I began.

She scoffed. "Please, I'm the one guilty of arrogance."

I relaxed my shoulders and the bruise vanished. "So do you still want to know?"

"You don't have anything to tell me now." Yi-Swan scraped her fingernails along the plaster rail.

I folded my arms across my chest and gazed at her. Her slenderness and beauty were intact, pristine, made even more glamorous by what I'd done to her. But her posture was steelier. "I received nothing either," I muttered, "More than fifty years ago, I was left on the other side of death over a pylon at Dadaocheng." I glanced in the direction of the harbor. From up here, the inky water slid along the perimeter of the horizon, cupping the rooftops in its soft, blue-black grasp. "No explanation of it. It was over and done in seconds. It was a man, and not nearly as erotic as—" Her glance, like a phalanx of spiky, rotating columns, stopped me.

Then she looked toward Shida. "Near as I can tell," she said, "there are no answers anyway." She turned and faced me. "Tell me: Does the past hurt us more?" Her eyes had turned to ocean water.

My arms drooped, feeling empty. "I was left to figure it all out on my own too." I wanted to add, *Even as a child*, but didn't. "All the answers are in the past. That's all I know."

Yi-Swan clutched her elbows, her jaw quivering and tears falling fast. A wicked wind slashed across the rooftop, whipping her hair into her eyes. Though she whispered, I heard clearly, "I would have stayed with you, that day, and every day after." She looked over her shoulder at me. "And you could have told me what you should have, about the fire lashing us in our bellies, the wind in our legs, and everything else we take from those on whom we feed."

I couldn't reply, couldn't tell her it was the loneliest I'd ever felt, until today.

"That boy is in trouble," she said, "I'll show you."

She didn't have to, but I let her. We shifted across the rooftops until we spotted him. He was being taunted by three bullies who looked a little older. We watched for a minute, and Yi-Swan smiled not the cocky half-grin, but like the girl I knew in San Francisco. She murmured, "I saw it in that last Escapement, you know. You were only a kid. There was nothing you could do back then." Her arms wrapped around my midsection, she kissed my cheek, and whispered, "Remember what you said," and then disappeared behind my back, leaving only a blue Escapement.

There was no noise from behind me. The houses were stark and quiet, but the Dadaocheng pier bustled while the grumbling diesel engines hurtled ships across the strait, then powered down to coast into the harbor to dock and unload. I wasn't interested in the cargo vessels – just the passenger ships. Ma had lent me two dollars and told me to go and wait for my father and brother to come across from Fuzhou.

"They'll be on the last night boat. Get something to eat and wait." She shoved coins at me.

"Can't I stay here until they come?" I pocketed the money.

"No," she spat, and she returned to her ledger.

I snatched a picture book on my way out; it was filled with images of happy kids playing with dogs, playing by rivers, playing in sunshine. At the pier, I spent a dollar on a bag of candies and the merchant hid his face for taking so much. Even I knew that it was too much, but Ma had said to get something to eat.

Buttery warmth saturated my mouth as I rested against a shack stuck into the hillside, reeking of pigs and gunpowder. The paper bag was clutched in my hand; each candy was stickier than the last. I sat up straighter as dusk crept in, scanning the sea for the sleeker boats that shuttled passengers, rather than the floating boxes hauling goats and grains from the mainland.

Then the shack behind me shook, and a brace of boys came over the fence. I was only eight, and the eldest, whom I didn't know, looked only a couple years older than me. He wore an olive jacket with Chiang Kai-shek's emblem on the sleeve, and stopped the other boys with his arms when he spotted me.

"You," he snapped at me, "Where'd you get those?" He pointed at the candy.

"I bought them," I said. I regretted it.

"Give me one," he ordered, "I'm a refugee, your older brother. So give me one."

I stuck two fingers in the bag and produced a candy. He snatched it from me and devoured it; his hands were stained with motor oil and his fingernails were black. I could smell the mud and pig shit on him. Then he glared at me. "Now," he garbled through the sweet, "one for my friends. Each."

I weighed my bag in my hand. I began to protest, "But I can't..."

"Do it!" he screamed. His face turned bright red and his skin shook. Those oily hands turned into fists. I gave a candy to each of his friends. They slammed it into their mouths, glancing at their leader, but he was still breathing hard, his jacket trembling. "Now give us all one more," he commanded.

I looked at him and pulled the bag close to my chest. "No, these are mine!" I yelled.

"Asshole!" he screamed, and his big sticky hand invaded my chest, clawing after the bag. I let it go for fear it ripping, and his booted foot kicked me in the shoulder. I twisted over, and I smelled dirt, tasted pig shit. My book was smeared by filth.

The boys laughed and ran away, eating my candy. I coughed, spat, and then vomited. A little piece of candy came back up to sink into the muck.

I ran home, crying, afraid to touch my eyes for the dirt on my hands. My tears cleaned huge pink canyons on my face. I wanted to tell Dad, or brother, but only Ma was home. As I approached our house, I saw four heavy men walk out the front door. They were talking about Dad and my brother, but I didn't understand what they were saying. I ran through the back door, but stopped short. Ma was at the table with her ledger, and a pile of gold bars and coins.

I walked in and Ma stared at me, saying nothing for several seconds, before asking, "What are you doing here?"

I couldn't reply.

"Did you get something to eat?"

I nodded.

"Did you find your Dad and brother?"

I shook my head. She looked away.

"Maybe tomorrow," she sighed, tapping her pen against the ledger's edge.

I ran away, because I heard her lie.

Blue clouds of Escapement parted, and the bullies ran away with a small sackful of candy and a few purloined dollars. The boy had taken a serious slug to the eye and was unconscious between hefty bags of garbage. I floated down the building's side and touched down next to him. No one followed him in; no one intervened as three larger boys cornered him like a diseased rat and bludgeoned him all the same. He was all alone to face them, and now, unconscious, a broken being, what exactly would he remember? Their jeers? Their fists? The stink of this food trash and petroleum-based garbage?

I slit his wrist with my fingernail and sucked out a pint of blood; an Exchange of this magnitude required such. The memory will stay, the pain will stay, but the endless mourning of hatred and grief will not. Not this time.

Morning approached and Shida had closed. The stalls stood bare, husks of wood and paper. In the charcoal tinted edge of dawn, all the square lanterns hung like veiled guests at a funeral, their eyes pointing down as the casket crept by. Dawn howled at the urban horizon of half-shattered rooftops, the light screaming its baleful warning. I walked back to the old bookseller, who stood stone-like with his hands folded behind his back, head down and gazing at an open book on top of the stack. As I drew near, he said, "I was so glad you told me when I'd see you next. I could prepare."

"Sheng-Qi," I said.

He smiled, adding, "I brought you a present," and gestured to the book before him. I looked at the book; it was the same as the one I soiled that night by the docks. "Over the years," Sheng-Qi said, "I'd found and lost copies of it, but after we last met, I saved this one. It's funny, about what we save, what we lose. Things we do. If you're here to kill me for that night, if that's why you killed my friends, then go ahead. I've nothing to lose." He slid the book at me. "Just this to give."

I raised my hand, summoned the telekinetic energy to crush his throat. But Sheng-Qi, his grizzled face creased by the ravages of time, his hair snowy and thin from weather and wear, did not move. His eyes gazed at me, sad but compassionate. There was no fear, nothing of the frightened boy from 1949, or the new grandpa of twenty years ago. The energy twitched at my fingertips, sputtering like a faulty engine, fading like a lonely song from the radio. There was nothing, nothing in my heart left to push that energy out. I turned the other way, and strolled down the street's center, the bare rim of light chasing me, precursor to the heat swelling at my back, the safety of darkness getting edged out.

What we save, what we lose.

Yi-Swan called my name. Her soft eyes were welling up. She held the ornate package in one hand, the office man slumped over in another, her face streaked with blood, his body limp. The wife was nowhere, except for her scent, raw and pulsing, still moving. Yi-Swan beckoned me into the doorway of the building, to go with her, and the inevitable bloodfeast. Her mouth moved and formed words that had no language. I slowed my pace, and she retreated into her refuge, escaping the light.

In the end, when you kill someone, you are all that's left. When you let someone live, they are all that's left.

All the answers are in the past.

The heat burst on my back, flames lashing off my clothes and curling my skin. I spread my arms wide to accept ignition. I guided fire along the esplanade's edges, lighting lantern strings and scorching the walls. At last, my skin ash, and eyes plasma, I turned again and bared my fangs to the sun.

The End

Todd Bowes is a recent graduate of Manhattanville College's Master's of Arts in Writing program where he also served as the fiction editor for *Inkwell*, the Literary Journal of Manhattanville College, for the spring and fall 2010 issues. His short story *Down Time* has been published by sffworld.com, and he recently released an album of original music with his band Dared the Knot, available at their website www.daredtheknot.com.

This Thing of Darkness I Acknowledge Mine

By Thomas Zimmerman

Such darkness bleeding down. The stars revealed,
mere holes punched in a tragic mask. Festooned
with rheum, the swamp-fog like a drug congealed
of ague-dreams to numb the still-raw wound

of conscience in my gangrened thoughts. I haunt
the lawn. The yew tree burning black. My jaw
a vise that mangles prayers. What makes me want
to set my neighbor's house on fire? The law

of man that bludgeons yin with yang? That, or
the feminine in me I love but fear?
Inside, my wife with froth and hound before

the hearth, those books of spells upon the shelf.
My window-mirrored face a monster's, dear
to hags and succubi. Hell is myself.

Thomas Zimmerman teaches English and directs the Writing Center at Washtenaw Community College, in Ann Arbor, MI. His poems have appeared recently in *Paper Crow* and *Eudaimonia Poetry Review*. Three of his poetry chapbooks are available at GenreMall.com.

For Love of the Echo

By Christopher Butera

"I'm sorry Mr. James, it seems as though there's nothing we can do," the young doctor began to rifle through David's medical report, a disconcerting look imprinted into his freckled face. "The deterioration is simply progressing at far too rapid a pace for us to try and control, least of all stop completely."

Following a prolonged pause, David James, his long dexterous fingers tapping rhythmically upon his knees, managed a weak smile. "And here I thought I might be getting some good news today," he tapped his fingers a few more times, breathed a sigh and lost his smile. "Nothing you—we can do? No medications, surgeries? Something? Anything?"

Doctor Edwards took his eyes from off his clipboard and they slowly found their way to meet David's—bright and desperate. "Dave...I'm afraid at this point nothing seems to be working. We've given you most of the proven medicines that we could, yet your body rejects them. Even the hearing aids didn't help in the slightest. I'm sorry to say...it may just be a matter of time now."

David could feel his stomach drop. His mouth was dry and pasty, yet his hands were slick with sweat. His voice was choked as he spoke, and on his lips not even a shadow remained of his former smile. "How much time are we talking...?"

Doctor Edwards' eyes flew directly back to his clipboard, his brow furrowing, and his hands moving swiftly. "It's not that simple. I mean, you'll probably lost the left ear first and who's to even know if—"

"Paul, please. As a friend... how much longer?"

"A few days, Dave," he swallowed hard, his Adam's apple rising and falling. "We mapped it all out. You've got four at most. Then total hearing loss."

#

Elly James paced forward and back in the small sunroom, listening to the rain drip onto the window and cascade down the glass in rivulets like hundreds of watery veins. Her eyes spied out through the streams every so often, the nails from her right hand each taking a place in her mouth as she bit down nervously. David had never taken this long coming home from the doctor's.

Outside the street was hushed, frozen in time. Nothing moved besides the silent swaying of the trees in the October wind, the red and yellow leaves taking flight from off the cracked branches turning the sky into a peppered inferno. Behind her windows Elly felt as though the outside world was miles away, as if the glass and painted frames kept the natural beauty *just* out of her reach; kept David *just* out of reach.

She began to pace a little faster.

Once during her pacing she thought that she could hear the sound of a car speeding down the boulevard. She imagined David hurtling down the slick streets and avenues of their small town, his little Ford kicking up the rain runoff as he sped, splashing fallen leaves against the street curb like fiery ships crashing upon a cement shore. She held her hand to her chest and she could feel the heat rising to her face, but her gaze fell once more as a different car flashed past and left her alone once more to worry about her husband.

I have to calm down, she thought. It may not be so bad if his hearing was gone…

But looking around, her heart knew this to be false.

For some people, it's their sense of sight that they cherish most. To be able to see the sun in all of its splendor lit up like a Christmas ornament, or shimmering like a ripe orange against a clear sky. To see flourishing green trees or a lover's face as they slept peacefully at your side.

For others, it's their sense of touch they relish: to feel lush grass between your toes and underfoot, to feel the wind slide between your fingertips and rush around your body, or the soft touch of a child's hand grasping your own as you walk the cobbled streets.

For David though, life would not be worth living without his sense of hearing, without sound or melody. He couldn't fathom a world without the whisper of a summer breeze on your neck or the howl of winter's wind at your door. An existence without laughter on everyone's tongue, or birds singing in the highest boughs, or his own whistling as he kicked his way down the boulevards—such, to him, was a world without purpose.

Elly began to run her hand over the picture frames resting on the window-side table. There David was, smiling in nearly every picture, his sharp face caught in moments of elation and gaiety, so wild and almost illegally happy. There he was with Stevie Wonder, with Paul McCartney and Ringo Starr. Here he was with guitar in fist, or piano key underhand, with a drum in his lap.

Each picture—his eyes danced, his smile shone. Yet behind each frame a willing ear soaked beautiful music in like a sponge until it came away sopping wet, dripping bass notes and treble clefts, fueling his heart.

And finally there was the last picture, their wedding picture, with her smile becoming his twin. She could recall the day he proposed to an exactness—him down on one knee with his acoustic guitar, eyes brimming with tears, his tongue dripping sweet honeyed words formed perfectly just for her.

She knew he loved her unconditionally and without question, but she also knew there was no lover he cared for more than song.

Elly was pulled from her daydream at the sound of the jiggle of the lock and soon enough David was walking through the front door. His eyes red and rough, and there was a slight shake to his hand that Elly knew all too well. She wanted to run to him, to kiss him, to throw her arms around his neck and tell him everything would be okay, but she couldn't move.

David took off his hat, then his coat, shedding each layer of sopping wet clothing. Finally he placed his key on the hook by the door, walked to the living room doorway and looked to her, his eyes telling her everything she needed to know.

"Four days," he looked to his wife's face, his eyes blinking furiously. "At most. There's, um…there's nothing they can do." His eyes seemed to glaze over and suddenly he wasn't looking at her anymore.

Ohh baby. She moved to him in two

steps and held him tight. David kept his gaze where she had been standing moments ago and he didn't move to hold her as well. Slowly he disengaged himself from the embrace, muttered an apology, and moved out of the room—his eyes vacant and unresponsive in shock.

Watching as he disappeared around the corner, Elly James began to weep. David, she realized, could not exist in a world without music.

#

Dr. Edwards came on the third day following David's consultation. He arrived early in the morning, racing rain clouds all the way to James' house. By the time Elly had answered the door however, the rain had finally caught up with him.

"Morning, Elly," He was huddled under his black overcoat, smiling at her as an old friend would as the rain pummeled his back. "Is he in?"

"Yes, please won't you..." She motioned for him to come in, slamming the door as he entered, barring the way from the angry gales that slipped between the door cracks and raised goose-bumps across her bare arms. Elly began to lead him through the house, the good doctor close at her heels, his hat pressed hard to his chest.

"How is he?"

She stopped walking in the narrow hallway that led to the kitchen and faced the man, finally granting him the chance to take stock of her face. She was gorgeous; there was no doubt about it. From her high cheekbones and startling grey eyes, even down to the tiny gap between her two front teeth—she was a delicate beauty in anyone's eyes. But there was a sadness there, a longing behind her stormy iris, a loss of hope.

She couldn't meet Edwards' gaze.

"He's kept mostly to himself in his studio, only coming out to use the bathroom or find another instrument around the house, or a CD. He's in the bedroom now though. I've been looking in on him from time to time, and it's always the same story: he's just lying there on the bed with his head phones on, listening to music."

"He's trying to get the last of it in?"

Elly nodded, her storm clouds of eyes finally breaking, sending the rain to pour down her face in plump turquoise drops. "I can hear his headphones all the way across the room, the music is turned up so loud," she finally caught the young doctor's gaze. "I think he's at his limit. He won't even come out to eat, Paul! He's been at it for days!"

And suddenly she was nestled against Edwards' chest, her sobs muffled against his coat, the rain pouring and pouring in torrents. "I just want my husband back, Paul! I just want him back..."

#

David was lying on his back as the doctor slipped into the room, lost within Beethoven's Fifth, drowning in a sea of violins, bass, and flute. He stared at the bare white ceiling and could see the notes falling in quick succession across an imagined music sheet—a quarter-note here, a rest, sixteenth notes. Sharps, flats, and naturals rose and subsided across a bold black guideline, flowing like a typewriter, ebbing this way and that like the tide.

Edwards could see his puffy, red eyes darting back and forth across the ceiling, a somber smile upon his lips. His shadow fell across David's face, breaking his melodic reverie.

"Dr. Edwards, making house calls now?" He sat up, slowly drawing the headphones from over his ears.

"Heard you could do with some cheering up, Dave. How are things?" Edwards pulled a chair over to the foot of the bed and sat, folding his hands over his lap.

"Oh you know, just peachy. Just sitting here, enjoying some Ludwig, thinking about how I'm going to topple him."

Edwards' laughed. "Sounds like you've got your work cut out for you."

"Ludwig's a hell of a man." David squinted, almost painfully. Edwards' noticed how long it was taking for him to respond, seconds maybe, but the practiced doctor knew it was those precious few seconds that it took David to read his lips and decipher their words. His hearing was almost gone.

Edwards' looked to his shoes. "How's the ear, Dave?"

A few moments passed. "Couldn't be better."

Their eyes met. "The left's gone, isn't it." It wasn't a question.

David nodded, looking down to hide his unbidden tears.

"And the right...?"

David now looked to the ceiling again, his voice cracking, trying to hold back a shudder that threatened to capsize him. "It's almost gone," he chuckled. "You doctors... really know your estimates...four days, right on the money." He began to weep silently.

The good doctor looked to his long time patient, his friend, and he felt something break within him. His mind was made. "David. I've come here as a friend, not your doctor. When I walk out this door you need to forget I was ever here."

The musician looked up from his seat on the bed, eyes bright against the light. "What are you talking about, Paul?"

Doctor Edwards reached into his coat pocket and withdrew a yellow pill bottle, it's inside filled to bursting with small neon green capsules. "You need to listen to me very, very carefully, Dave. Now I can't guarantee this will work, it's still in the experimental stage, but all early test results are positive—over 87% effectiveness."

David James couldn't move. "What are you saying...?"

"Just *one* a day. One pill a day could give you your hearing back. It won't be a hundred percent, but it'll be better than zero. Take it until the bottle runs out and we'll go from there." Doctor Edwards stood, placed the pills on his chair, and put his damp hat back upon his head.

David couldn't speak, his eyes went from Paul, to the pills, and back again.

Edwards' hand was on the door handle, his gaze on David, his free hand pointing. "Remember Dave, *one*, just one. Good luck."

"Wait!"

And with that he was gone, leaving David alone once more surrounded by a sea of sour notes, Beethoven faintly heard in the distance, and the small yellow bottle resting upon the empty chair.

# # #

The pill felt weighted in his hand, its green coating stark against his peach skin, stolid upon the crisscrossing creases of his palm.

"Just one pill...what could one pill possibly do?" David sighed.

The muted light of the bathroom was flush across his bare chest as he stared at

22

the curious pill in his hand. The lights were dimmed as to not wake Elly, shrouding the modest lavatory in an eerie blue-black aura that cast a strange pallor upon his skin leaving him almost corpse like.

David looked to himself in the mirror. Stubble had begun to wreak grey-snowy havoc across his cheeks and there were bags under his eyes that he hadn't noticed before. He tensed his jaw watching as the muscles tightened on either side of his face just below his cheekbones. His hand sat outstretched with its curious prize within his peripherals, seeming to look almost as if he was offering the pill to himself. *'Take it.'*

There was nothing to stop him from swallowing the pill. No harm could come, no foul. Paul had never turned him in the wrong direction before, had he?

With his free hand, David turned the hot water faucet on to a low steady stream without looking down. Immediately he could feel the heat rising from the pooling water, warming the underside of his hand. He could even feel droplets bounce from the edge of the sink and land just below his naval. Steam rose from beneath his gaze, yet still he looked forward, his eyes locked on with his doppelganger's. He refused to look to the pill, to the water. For, if he looked down his eyes would be one last sensory detail to tell him what his ears did not register—that the water had indeed been turned on.

He couldn't hear the water.

He took the pill dry.

# # #

Underfoot, David could hear the purr of the car's engine as he sped along the lighted streets of his small town. Just outside his window a gentle rushing filled the car as he passed by the blurred shapes of pedestrians and cars as he navigated the curved grid of his neighborhood. Idly he flexed his fingers around the steering wheel, his ears, although still slightly muffled, received the sound with tender acceptance. And beneath his smile, David thanked his good friend the doctor—him, and his miracle pill.

That pill, the lifesaver. Its shape, its wonder, everything about it so non-descript, so absent of extraordinary descriptions had become the vessel towards the renewal of life as David had known it. That neon pill was the catalyst of his rebirth.

Over the few days since that initials dose, laughter had found its way back into his lungs and filled his home with melody. He awoke not only to the sun on his face but bird song at his bedside window. He would roll over to the rush of the blankets shifting about and hear the wet smack of a kiss as he placed it on Elly's lips. Then there was the gentle rain of the shower on the marbled floor, the steel-sliding of toast popping from the toaster, the ruffling of newspaper pages, coffee slurps—he soaked it all in.

Then it was off to the studio where would spend the day listening to mixes and the chuckling of the musical friends he'd invited to play along with him in his reverie. The halls would be filled with a chorus of instruments: there a trumpet, here a guitar, followed by flute and snare. The hiss of static would spike, the squeal of feedback would pierce, the click of a plug into a socket would arouse anticipation.

It was all harmony in his ear, all *life* incarnate.

As he turned onto Breckenridge Road and caught sight of his house in the distance, he turned the radio dial to the off position and slowed his car almost to a standstill. As the world drifted past in a lazy idle he rolled his window down even further allowing for the lush sounds of autumn to fill his car and mind with flashes of drizzle and the crescendo of wind in the trees.

# # #

It wasn't until the end of the week that trouble began.

Elly found him sitting at the kitchen table in the middle of the afternoon, a pill bottle's contents spilled in a neat pile in front of him looking much like a collection of green jelly beans. His head was hung low as she entered, hiding his face from his wife's gaze.

"Honey, can you show me—" Her words were cut short, her entire being caught midway between the doorway and the half-empty table.

David lifted his face to meet hers, his cheeks puffed and red, his eyes glistening. "It's going away, babe. I had it again and now it's going away…!" His hands swept along the remainder of his pills, nine in all, never touching one almost as if they radiated a heat that was much too hot to be felt. "He said take one a day and I'd be fine. Not 100%, but *fine*. I was better! I could *hear* again! I could *listen*! Now it's all going away again…."

"David, what are—"

"I went from 80%, to 40%, 30%," his eyes shot to hers once more. "The left is almost gone again, Elly! I can't take losing it twice, not again, not again…" He began stammering and running his hand through his graying hair, pulling at the roots. He broke down and began to weep, his tears falling from his eyes and splashing upon the pills.

Elly came to his side in seconds, calmly placing her loving arms around his neck and nuzzling her nose against his right ear as he shuddered and gasped for breath. "*Shh… shh* baby."

She led him through the silence of their home as though he was on crippled legs, all the while his tears running unbidden and hushed down his face. In their bedroom she pulled each article of clothing from off his body one by one and lay him down on the snow white sheets.

From where he lay on the bed, David could see Elly's lithe silhouette painted from the afternoon sun against the window as she drew the shades closed, and he could hear a soft murmur in his good ear as she whispered him a goodnight—but none of this registered in his mind as his exhaustion drew his eyes to a close. All he could see, all he could think about were those green capsules frozen in time upon the kitchen table.

Waiting for him.

# # #

When David opened eyes again it was dark. Elly lay beside him in bed, a curious frown etched on her pale face as her chest rose and fell with each breath. She didn't stir as he rose from the bed, nor as he padded along their hardwood floor, not even when he scraped the chair in the kitchen across the linoleum in earnest.

He sat at the table, eyes wide, staring at the pile of medicine exactly where he had left it. He scooped each green pill into his hand and waited.

"*Just one. One pill a day could get your hearing back.*" Edwards' words echoed within the silent confines of his skull.

"It's not enough." He whispered as he emptied the contents of his palm into his mouth and swallowed.

#

He woke with a start to full daylight, his eyes tearing open before his mind could even comprehend what was happening. There had been a noise. A throated humming that had filled his dreams for mere moments before propelling him back to reality. David lay for a moment, hearing nothing.

It had to have been near the afternoon, the memory of his midnight snack falling to the wayside of his subconscious much like his sullied dreams. The windows had been closed, shutting away all the outside sounds and the thick walls of the bedroom shut out all the normal sounds a house would make. The room was as quiet as a graveyard. David closed his eyes once more.

His eyes flew open as the sound, the horrible sound that permeated the bedroom with a cacophony of buzzes and warbles, cracked at his head like a steel hammer. David's hands went to his ears, his eyes closing again—this time in pain. He could feel himself gasp rather than hear it over the noise as he rose to a sitting position, gritting his teeth.

His eyes began to rove around the room attempting to pinpoint the origin of the sound. It was so loud…so strangely familiar. It was like a jackhammer on the wall, a chainsaw grinding its teeth upon the headboard—always gunning, piercing his eardrum.

And then it stopped. Ending almost as if building to a climax and falling just short.

David, confused and cautious, allowed for his hands to fall from around his ears. Soundlessly swinging his legs over the side of the bed, he stepped onto the lush carpet and rose to his feet, his eyes running from this end of the room to the other in anticipation of the noise.

And there it was again, erupting at almost the exact time of his rising, causing him to cry out.

Once again his wrinkling hands cupped immediately over his ears, and he half stumbled half walked aimlessly across the carpet.

He noticed the fly almost immediately making its way across the nearest wall. Its minute black body bobbed this way and that as it flew away from David. Unsure of why he noticed the insect, David allowed for his eyes to follow it's descent towards the dresser, the pain coursing through his ear from the maddening chugging almost doubling him over onto the floor.

The fly changed course, working its way to the corner of a movie poster on the wall and landed.

And almost as if by trigger, the noise stopped and silence reigned once more.

Relief crashed over David, his breath bursting from his mouth as if he'd been released from a vice grip. He lay on the floor gasping for a few moments before the curiosity of his conscious took hold.

The fly sat unmoving upon the poster, its beady eyes seemingly staring into David's, waiting, watching.

David rose from the floor, his eyes locked with fly's. He inched forward towards the poster, strange interest rife on his face. Less than two feet from the poster the fly leapt away.

The noise exploded once more, almost twice as loud as the first two instances threatening to destroy the musician's eardrum. Fighting back the urge to fall once more, David's hand groped at a magazine resting at the foot of the bed, and took aim at the fly. The culprit had worked its way to the far side of the room and was just about to settle upon the wall when David came out swinging.

The moment the magazine struck the wall smashing the fly a blare like a shotgun blast brought David to his knees, blinking back tears. The buzzing had stopped, what remained was a ringing, the remnants of the report still lingering within his ears.

David lay in a daze, eyes wide, his mind working a mile a minute. His lips mouthed the words that he could not comprehend, that wouldn't come out. 'It was the fly…the noise…the fly…how?' Realization dawned upon him, setting terror deep within the pit of his stomach: the pills.

He worked his way to his feet. At the door, he turned the knob slowly and pulled the door open as gentle as he would handle a baby. He stood in the doorway staring out, not knowing what he was waiting for, his breathing heavy in his chest and his ears.

A clacking like magnum shots suddenly poured through the hallway, practically knocking him back into the bedroom. David knew the sound immediately: Elly and her high heeled shoes cracking on the kitchen floor as she made her way to leave for work. Again he moved to speak but each gunshot step beat him further backwards as if he indeed was becoming riddled with bullets, incapacitating him.

Soon he could tell Elly was moving away, the clicking of her shoes beginning to dissipate leaving only echoes to pummel his ears. Finally there was one last succession of clacks, followed by a reverberating sonic boom of the front door closing as she left.

'I have to catch her,' he thought, not daring to speak. 'I need her. I have to catch her before she leaves.' Struggling to his feet, he began moving down the hall as quietly as his feet would permit, supremely conscious to the noises his body would make on the en-vironment to betray his progress.

But once he entered the kitchen, he could go no further. As he rounded the corner into the afternoon glow of the sun on the marble countertops, he was met with a wall of sound. Away from the comforts of a sound-proofed bedroom, out here he was exposed to the elements.

The creaking of pipes sent shivers down his spine. The automatic cycle of the dishwasher churned a thunderous sea. The hum of the refrigerator's cooling fan blasted like a roving bulldozer. Even the gentle slicing of the fan cut like a tornado through his conscious.

David fell to the floor, screaming. His mind threatened to cave in upon itself, his ear drums assaulted over, and over, and over as an infinite pulse. His veins swelled in his forehead, his forearms, his neck. His eyes bulged, his faced turned scarlet.

He ran, bursting through the kitchen door to the back yard. A mistake.

Song bird trills tore through his brain like jelly. A woodpecker fired mortar round against his head. A car horn burst like a foghorn. A roving thunder cloud erupted as if the earth itself had cracked in half.

Screaming, his hands stamped to his ears, David ran far away from sound.

# # #

The center of town was quieter than normal due to the threat of the storm clouds, yet still couples roamed the streets for a midday stroll, shoppers searched for pumpkins for their children to carve in anticipation of Halloween, and shop owners went about their normal routines.

Around three o'clock, just as St. Luke's bells began to peel, a curious sound split the air. It began quietly but slowly built in force and volume as it neared the town square.

David came bursting into the square from between two store fronts, his eyes bloodshot and wild, his mouth opened wide reverberating with screams of terror.

"MAKE IT STOP! PLEASE!"

He ran between a pair of wanderers, looking to their eyes but not entirely seeing their faces. Tears ran steadily on his cheeks, his hands clutching and falling away from his ears in haphazard rhythm.

The townspeople stared after him in horror, their hands reaching either towards mouths to gasp or phones to call the police.

As he neared the edge of the square, David's stumbling course ran him straight into a couple, acting as spectators, standing by a light pole. The man placed his hand out in an effort to impede David, but in his crazed state David drove forth like a wounded animal, straight into the man's wife. A scuffle ensued as David bounced back and forth between man and woman like a pinball, his screams reaching glass-shattering heights. The man lashed out blindly with his fist, catching David in his ear, hurtling him towards the ground.

And then the street was silent.

Thunder peeled over head and the first droplets of rain began to fall from the sky in random patterns about the square. In moments a crowd had gathered around David, forming a perfect circle around where the wounded man lay. No one moved to help, nor even to speak a word, the pedestrians simply stared on in mute horror.

David lay flat, motionless on the ground. His eyes were wide, staring far above at the roving black clouds in a trance. Blood dribbled from his ears in a thin steady stream and the virgin rain kissed his cheeks.

"It's nothing now. I hear nothing..." He spoke in a whisper as the crowd pressed in. Smiling, repeating:

"It's quiet now. Finally quiet. Quiet..."

The End

Christopher Butera has been published in Columbia College's *Slick Black Book*, and has conducted interviews with such individuals as Sam Weller, author of *The Bradbury Chronicles* and *Listen to the Echoes*, and Dustin Kensrue, frontman for the band Thrice.

The Monsters' Trick-or-Treat

By Elizabeth Creith

If you go out on the street tonight, you're in for a big surprise.
Not everyone on the street tonight is going out in disguise,
for ghosts and ghouls are all on the prowl
and every werewolf's out for a howl.
Tonight's the night the monsters go trick-or-treating!

No crucifixes to make them flinch, no garlic to make them run;
Tonight's the one night out of the year when they look like anyone.
And all the kiddies out for a treat
Just look to them like something to eat.
Tonight's the night the monsters go trick-or-treating.

Zombies lurching everywhere!
The werewolf's combed his hair; he looks like a regular guy tonight.
Vampires standing here and there;
they turn their spooky stare on kids who don't stay beneath the light.
Maybe they'll take one or two
Of children just like you who wander from door to door.
But when sunrise comes they'll have to get off of the streets again and scurry
Back to tombs, crypts and lairs once more.

Elizabeth Creith's work has been featured in several publication since August, 2008, including *Flash Fiction Online, Grey Sparrow, The Drabbler, The Verb, Random Eye, Silver Blade, Goblin Fruit, Dog Oil Press*, and others.

Ghosts in the Jungle River

By Coy Hall

Rain fell in huge drops, splashing in the dark river, and drumming against overhanging palms. The *Father's Farewell*, a British diesel-powered fishing vessel, cut through the water towards a sharp bend. The Congo jungle closed in on all sides. Trace McReynolds, a small man with a thin mustache and sharp, hardened features, stood beneath the boat's tarp ceiling, his thoughts drowning in the din of heavy rain. This was his seventh expedition into the Congo. He made a comfortable living from poaching elephants, then selling their tusks on the black market. It was a lucrative business while it lasted, while he lasted.

As was his habit, two familiar associates accompanied him: Stein, the *Farewell's* captain, and Otto Cordingly, or 'Howl' as he preferred it. Howl had hunted big game for the better part of thirty years, and his mind was keen, though somewhat unbalanced, from long years in the solitude of the jungle.

Like so many others in the trade they were a group of social pariahs. McReynolds had worked in the circus throughout his teenage years and into his late 20s. He'd ended his career as a fortune teller—and not a bad one. He'd always had a mind for money, and for giving people what they wanted in order to get it. Poaching was that type of business—a business he could wrap his mind around.

The boat took the bend and opened up into a narrow stretch of water, no wider than 40 feet across. A large crocodile slithered from the bank at their appearance, disappearing beneath the rocking water.

Howl stood from his seat under the tarp, moving to the edge of the boat. "Mac," he shouted above the noise, "there's a market for those fellers too, you know." He turned and flashed a smile dominated by three silver teeth. He had a glass eye as well, which looked eerily past you at all times. Howl'd led a hard, violent life. He had a desire to hunt the lazy river crocodiles and he never failed to remind Mac of their worth.

Mac laughed and brought his hand up, rubbing his fingers and thumb together. "Not enough money in it," he said. In a way, Mac was the financier of the group, and therefore his word on what they hunted was final.

"Still, we could throw one on the back of the boat. Get somethin' from it." Howl moved back to his seat, his expression unchanged.

Mac watched him go. He wondered how Howl would fare in an actual job, how he'd fare in real life. He couldn't imagine him in a suit, or clean-shaven, or bathed for that matter. He was a white savage as far as civilization was concerned—a position proudly reflected in the necklace of ape teeth he wore around his neck.

After the initial downpour, the rain passed quickly. It left huge clouds of steam, which rose like ghosts off the water, in its wake. The air grew in humidity, and the heat was enough to boil the river.

The boat's engine buzzed steadily as

Mac joined Stein at the front of the boat. The captain was soaked to the bone, his old, grizzled features drooping. He was a gaunt man, his face almost skeletal. Once, he claimed, he'd been a ferry captain on the Thames, but that was another life. He'd been in and out of Africa since he was 32; 29 years had passed in that time. He treated the *Father's Farewell* like a child, because, as Mac guessed, that was the only family he knew—and the only family he cared to know.

"Mate," Stein said, watching the water intently.

Mac wiped the rain and sweat from his brow, replacing his hat which he'd been protecting through the storm. "I'd say we're close, don't yah think?"

"That we are, boy," Stein said curtly. He was hard to talk to sometimes.

Mac looked out on the steamy river. Another bend lay ahead, the last before they'd finally dock. From the back of the boat, cleaning his rifle, Howl shouted out. "What are you two fruits squawking about up there, huh? You know," he said, standing, "I was thinkin'. Wouldn't it be somethin' if we could get cash for takin' native scalps? Like in the old days with the Indians. I bet a guy could make a fortune doin' that." He grinned, flashing those teeth.

"You wouldn't last," Mac said. "They'd scalp you the first day out. They'd know your kind a mile away."

Stein chuckled.

"Hell," Howl said. "We could pick 'em off right here from the boat. Like we could with the crocs if you'd ever get a mind for it."

"I've never seen a single native from the boat. Not a damn one," Mac said. "Hell, there isn't a tribe for 50 miles around."

"You're just not lookin' hard enough.

I see their eyes sometimes, lookin' out when we pass by."

Stein broke in. "You got shit comin' out your ears," he said. "Even if they were around, they'd be slicker than that."

"Still think I could make good business of it," Howl said, and let it drop there.

Stein steered the boat around the jutting growth of jungle, and let out a shout at what greeted him on the other side. "Boys!" he said.

Mac and Howl rushed back to the front of the boat, looking out. On the shore beneath a dense canopy of tree vines rested a grounded boat. It looked old and weather-beaten. Vines crept along its exterior.

"I'll be damned," Mac said, confused and a little pissed off about the possibility of someone taking his hunting ground. But, as the boat inched closer, any hint of jealousy fled his mind. The ship was a small cruiser, the kind tours were sometimes conducted on. "We're awful far out for a safari, don't you think?" he said.

Stein raised his eyebrows. "I'd say. Even if a safari had a river leg to it, I don't imagine it'd be out thissa way."

"Get up beside it, Stein," Howl said. "I'll board her, see what she's got."

Stein eased up beside, then killed the engine.

The sounds of the jungle once again drifted down. Birds squawked loudly in the distance, freed from the burden of the passing rain.

Howl reached out, grabbing the edge of the small cruiser. "You comin' Mac?" he asked.

Together they boarded the ship. It was open in the front and back, and a small room occupied the center. It was a simple structure, sturdy though, meant for moving

30

people short distances.

Mac moved around Howl towards the control room. The paranoid thought crossed his mind that this was nothing more than a set-up by the authorities. But he couldn't believe it for more than a second. This was too elaborate, too real. If the authorities possessed that type of ingenuity then poachers would find eking out a living much more difficult than it actually was.

Howl rummaged through several bundles which were stuffed under the front deck. He barked out his meager finds to the waiting Stein.

Mac opened the door, which was ajar on rusted hinges. For a man that's lived the life of a guy like McReynolds it took something especially strange to catch him by surprise. But, upon opening the door, Mac stood momentarily speechless. Lying on the floor, curled in a fetal position beneath the controls, was a middle-aged white man. He had no life in his face as far as Mac could tell, but his back heaved a little under a sudden breath.

"Howl, come over here," he said finally.

"Hold on a minute, Mac. I think—"

"Get over here," he said again.

Stein looked on curiously.

Howl plodded along the plank deck. "What the hell do you ... I'll be god damned," he said quickly, his eye falling over the strange man.

"What is it?" Stein shouted impatiently across the boats.

"There's somebody in here," Mac said, removing his hat and wiping the sweat from his forehead. "And he's still breathing."

# # #

There wasn't much in the way of first-aid in either boat, just a few bandages. The man still hadn't spoken when Mac and Howl laid him out across the worn jungle trail along the bank of the river. Water was the best they had to offer him. In the meantime, Stein had docked and secured the boat and presently joined his comrades at the strange man's side. He carried the anemic first aid kit, but it was of no use. There wasn't a single cut or bruise on the man's body that Mac could find. Regardless, he lay on the ground like he'd suffered a sound beating. He was around thirty-five, dressed in white cloth, matted to his perspiring body, the pants ripped up the left leg. He hadn't shaved in three weeks and his face was nearly hidden beneath the massive black beard.

Howl passed around damp cigars which he'd found in one of the bundles on the derelict ship. Mac stuffed his in his front shirt pocket, his mind too occupied to think about much else. He watched the man and tried to speak with him. "You understand English?" he asked, looking back and forth between Stein and Howl.

The man's eyes opened and closed long enough to show that there was consciousness about them.

"I think that's a 'yes'," Howl put in, letting out a cloud of cigar smoke.

"Can you speak, mate?" Stein asked.

The man made no gesture, no indication that he even heard the question. Mac pressed an open canteen to the stranger's dry lips; he swallowed the water without strain or force.

"Mates," Stein went on, "I don't mean to rattle your Good Samaritan consciences but we only have a small window, you'll remember, to do our business."

"He's right," Howl said.

Mac shook his head. It wasn't that he worried about his conscience, he just imagined this fellah as himself. He didn't like the prospect of Stein and Howl's reaction to such a situation if it were him involved, though it didn't surprise him. Money came first. "What do you suppose we do? Leave him here at the mercy of some man-eater? That's just fine of you two."

"Put 'im back on the boat," Stein offered. "We can put him on mine even. If he lasts the week, then we'll take 'im back with us. If he croaks, then we'll send 'im down the river."

Howl disgustedly tossed his cigar into the lapping river water. "Wet and stale," he said, "take my word for it. Mac, you're still green in this business. Stein and I've been at it for over half a century. It's like the frontier. If a man's down, you gotta leave him behind. He either walks or dies, you know that."

"There's no two ways about it," Stein agreed.

"Damn it, fellahs. Would you just let me think? Let's get the gear out. When we're ready to head on, if he ain't moving, then ... well we'll put him back on the boat. Fair?"

"Whatever suits you, mate" Stein said.

Howl grunted his reply, waving the entire situation from his mind.

It took less than 30 minutes to assemble the gear. As was usual, the three men took nothing more than they could carry on their backs. In a way Mac sympathized with Stein and Howl about the strange man. In the jungle one took only what was essential. Anything else was a burden, a liability. It could be the difference between life and death. If they took the injured man along his weakness would become their weakness.

Greed, of course, was the ultimate root. After all, the problem could be solved by heading back up the river to the nearest village. But that meant time lost, money lost. As Mac shouldered his share of the load, his final decision on the matter settled. If the stranger could walk he was welcome to come along. If he couldn't then God help him.

To Mac's disappointment the stranger hadn't moved an inch. He lay still across the trail. "Howl," Mac said stoically, "you wanna help me get the fellah on board."

Without a word Howl coldly walked around, grabbing the stranger by the ankles. Mac took his shoulders and they lifted. They placed him where they'd found him: on the small cruiser, within the feeble protection of the control room. Mac gave him an extra canteen, nearly full.

Stein waited, balancing their rifles with his own.

Mac took the door in hand and gave one last look to the stranger as if to offer an apology. His guilt was immense. If it was up to him, he wanted to believe, they would've forgone the hunt, taking the stranger to safety instead.

But it wasn't up to him, not completely.

It was occasion to reflect on things. The type of moment when a man realizes his strength is with others' strength. His decisions are others' decisions. The idea depressed him and he moved to slam the door shut, to put a final lid on the matter. But just as the door reached the frame Mac saw the stranger lift his head. He opened it again. "Can you move?" he asked.

Stein and Howl conferred back on the trail, wondering what the holdup was.

The stranger looked at Mac, moving his eyes with the last strength he possessed. His mouth framed a single word which froze in his throat, leaving him silent. His eyes closed again, then his head fell to the floor in exhaustion.

Mac waited for a moment longer then shut the door angrily. That's the last thing I needed to see, he thought. We're as good as murderers. The man's breathing and moving. He's alive enough to suffer. And I'm turning my back on him, walking away.

Mac gained the trail, making an effort not to look back. He adjusted the pack on his shoulders then moved with Stein and Howl into the sweltering heat of the matted jungle.

A large bird beat its wings against the green overhead. Creepers snaked around trees and across the jungle floor, rivaled only by the massive vines that hung seemingly everywhere. The path was beaten by the travel of elephants, shared by the apes, lions, hyenas, and panthers. It was unseen and unknown by most humans—even the native villages were far distant.

Howl led the way, a rifle over his shoulder, a busy machete in his right hand. Mac, who usually kept pace, lagged a few steps behind. His heart simply wasn't in it. Stein occupied the middle ground, his old body accepting the weight of his pack less and less with each step. He wasn't one to complain, though. And one could hardly tell except for the hint of pain in his eyes.

They set up camp four miles inland, northwest of the sprawling Congo River. The tarp tents were erected quickly, mosquito nets pulled tight, a fire pit constructed, all in silence. Mac contemplated heading back to the river several times but always he kept on. He wondered what kept him from putting his foot down; why he let their decisions become his own. Like it or not his greed was as great as any of his companions. There was simply too much money to be made—a weakness he couldn't overcome.

That afternoon they did their preliminary scouting but saw nothing of the local elephant population. Howl made a big deal about a trail he uncovered, insisting that it would prove gold the following morning. Mac and Stein believed it; Howl knew the jungle as good, if not better, than anyone.

The harsh edge of the heat faded with the evening—an annoyance replaced by the bite of mosquito hordes. The sun fell quickly from the sky, leaving their camp in nothing but the glow of firelight. A plume of smoke rose into the trees as Howl roasted several slabs of antelope meat.

Mac sat back from the fire, in front of the tents, avoiding the worst of the heat.

"That stranger's still gettin' to you, ain't he?" Stein asked, taking a swig of scotch, his gaunt face bathed in the orange firelight.

"I just wish it wouldn't've happened. The whole thing," Mac said. "I'll get past it, though."

"Sure you will," Howl said, taking the Scotch offered by Stein. He filled a metal cup. "Especially if you stick in this business. That ain't the first time I've left a man behind," he bragged. "Not under those circumstances of course."

"I wish he coulda told us what that cruiser was doin' out here," Stein said. "That's the thing botherin' me. I don't want our hunting ground to become an expressway."

Mac listened but his thoughts were lost in the darkness of the jungle beyond their camp. He watched it, looked into it. The moon was nothing but a sliver in the sky, revealed by a break in the tree tops, offering little light. Animals moved unseen through the shadows, no doubt curious about the burning meat. Every now and then one would slip up, trailing its foot along a clump of dry leaves, or snapping a dead limb, making itself heard. Mac rested his rifle across his lap. Even with guns, though, the men weren't guaranteed of safety. Anytime they stepped into the Congo wilderness they put their lives on the line. They weren't guaranteed anything—out here, Mac knew, chance ruled.

"Aren't yah gonna have a drink, Mac?" Stein asked, offering the bottle. "It ain't like you to turn down a chance to get soused!"

"Sorry fellahs," Mac said, returning his gaze to the fire. "I was just thinking."

"Well have a drink, boy. Relax," Howl said, handing out the dinner he'd fixed.

Mac took a long swig, shaking his head against the pain from the fiery liquid.

Howl mused about what they'd find along the trail the following morning. His eyes lit up as he talked, wrapped in the fantasies that ran through his mind.

The three ate quickly.

"I hear ivory's gonna plummet soon," Stein said, wiping grease from his mouth.

"You say that ev'ry time we're out," Howl waved him off.

"You do," Mac said, and laughed.

"The hell, I never..." Stein stopped, raising his head, listening.

Mac heard it too. He gripped the butt of his rifle, moving his hand to the trigger. Something heavy stirred in the forest beyond, something with clumsy footsteps. Mac's eyes searched the darkness. The sound continued, unabated.

"Whatever it is, it ain't makin' a good effort to keep hidden," Howl said, pulling a pistol from his side.

"That it ain't," Stein whispered.

All three men, armed, tensely combed the darkness in the direction of the sound.

Whatever it was, it was coming along the trail they had used. The trail that led back to the river.

The anticipation made Mac's heart race. It was a necessary nervousness, though—it fed alertness, brought it to concert pitch.

The sound came closer; but, as it did, its ominous nature seemed to fade. It was much too open to be threatening. A bout of curiousness replaced any fear that had been in the three men's hearts. Mac stood to get a better look.

Out of the shadows stepped a tired, ragged man: the stranger.

Mac couldn't believe it. Neither could Stein or Howl because all three remained in shocked silence. The stranger spoke first, his voice low and forced. "You left me to die," he said, then collapsed, crumpling to the ground.

Mac jumped over to the body, dropping his rifle and hat in the process. Stein and Howl were at his side.

"You tellin' me that boy walked four miles, part ways in the dark?" Stein asked, searching for a pulse in the man's wrist.

"If he comes to, he better count his blessings," Howl said. "I can't say I've ever seen anything like it," he laughed.

Mac pushed the stranger onto his back then pulled him through the sand, closer to the warmth of the fire. It was a miracle that he'd gotten through the jungle being unarmed, injured, and probably delirious. Why else would he chance such a trip? I bet he's been walking that trail all day, Mac thought. It's just taken him that long to get here. The thought of the stranger crawling along the deck of the cruiser just out of sight from Mac, Stein, and Howl sent a shudder through his body. He'd been desperately trying to follow the entire time.

"I guess your conscience can rest easy now," Stein said, taking his seat by the fire.

"Yeah," Mac said. He laughed uncomfortably.

# # #

Surprisingly, the stranger wasn't out for long. The man, Mac noticed, was actually full of surprises. When he awoke he was alert enough to eat and drink and he did a generous amount of both. The night wore on but Mac, Stein, and Howl couldn't tear themselves away from the situation long enough to sleep.

When he'd eaten his fill of antelope meat the stranger began to talk copiously. Maybe it was an effect of his situation but it seemed that everything he did he did in excess. He talked with animated gestures, fueled by some phantom-energy the hunters couldn't understand.

He was English they found out, which Stein appreciated. And his name was Howard Phillips.

"All that's fine," Howl said, now drunk. "But what I wanna know is how you got that cruiser all the way out here."

"And how you got to this camp," Mac said.

Phillips looked around with beady eyes, dark as the beard that hid his face. "The music drove me here," he said in a grave voice. "I stole the boat, of course. It was all I could manage in the time I was given. I took it all these miles, eating nothing and drinkin' only water from the river."

"You're pullin' our leg," Stein said.

"I'm not," he said slowly. "I promise you that. You can't sit here and tell me you haven't heard the drums. I heard them on the trail, I know they're close. I heard them as you left me behind."

"Mate, either you're foolin' or your nuts," Stein said with a chuckle.

"I think he's out in the sun too long," Howl said. They toasted to that.

Mac watched Phillips, wondering. If he is delusional, he thought, I'd rather not be around him during one of his fits. But there was something about the sincerity in the man's voice that intrigued him, frightened him a little.

Phillips let the snide remarks pass without a hint of reaction. His voice remained calm, and now he spoke slower than ever. "It's a horrifying sound," he said, his eyes darting from man to man.

The fire crackled.

"I tell yah, that's why I follow it," he went on, emphatically. "I can't stand it. It drones in my mind, the same hypnotizing beat: again and again. I knew if I didn't come here, it would eat at my mind till it left me nothing but hysterical."

Mac put a question to him which had been on his mind since he sighted the stranger on the shore. "You know, Phillips, one thing I don't get. Why were you in the Congo in the first place? You don't look like a hunter. You're certainly not dressed for it."

Phillips straightened. "It's an unavoidable thing I suppose. I'll tell yah. I was holed up at the prison camp, 70 miles or more up the river."

"You escaped?" Stein asked, alarmed.

The fact that a prison camp existed so close along the river was news to Mac. He wondered if Howl knew, or Stein.

Phillips nodded in the firelight. "I had to. The music wouldn't stop; I told you that. I had to come find it."

Howl spoke in an elevated voice. "You

tellin' me that you're leadin' the prison boys down this way after you? I'll be damned to hell. Mac, if you don't ask this fellah to leave I'll send the nut down the river myself. Head first too."

"They'll be comin' after you," Mac said to Phillips; he obviously hadn't thought of that before but it dawned on him that they could all be in trouble if they were found while Phillips was being apprehended. Phillips would go back to the camp followed by three new prisoners, all of them locked up for poaching.

"What do you three have to worry about?" Phillips asked, with naiveté that, on the surface, seemed artificial.

Stein had a look of disbelief on his face. "Plenty," he quipped. "You're not as dense as all that, mate. The police frown on our trade after all."

"You're poachers?" Phillips shrugged in a disconnected way. The next instant something from within must've seized him because his eyes grew wide, and he cocked his head towards the darkness, listening.

It was a strange sight and Mac watched intently. Phillips really is insane, he thought. Back home he'd be in an asylum rather than a prison regardless of what he'd done. Working in the circus for so many years Mac had come across his share of lunatics. He was more accustomed to it than most. But Phillips was of a different caliber. His mind seemed spaced, distracted, and all in a comically exaggerated way. It was a peculiar thing watching him and listening to the warped things that poured from his mind.

"Did you hear it?" he asked after a moment of silence, his head still cocked. "The drums … they're close now." He looked back to the fire with wild eyes. "There's your evidence. Go on, tell me you didn't hear it. Tell me it didn't chill your heart!" He laughed rapidly.

Mac, Stein, and Howl looked back and forth, straining their ears in the night. Their effort was greeted by little except for the distant cackle of a hyena and the buzzing of several blue mosquitoes beyond the range of firelight.

"Go on," Phillips repeated, "let it out."

"Mr. Phillips," Mac said, glancing down at the rifle beside his seat. "There are no drums."

"Not the hint of one, you bloody maniac," Stein offered, finally reaching the level of intoxication shared by Howl.

Howl, for his part, had a long, unsympathetic laugh. "Oh god boy," he said, wiping a tear from his face, "You're beyond help."

The hysterical expression fell from Phillips' face, replaced by a look of honest confusion. "I see," he said, dropping his voice to a whisper. "May I stay here tonight? I'll move on in the morning."

Mac gave him the only sympathy he could afford. "Sure," he said. "You stay here Mr. Phillips. And tomorrow if you like." It would have to be outside, of course. There was no room in the tent for an extra body.

Phillips nodded his thanks then lay down in the sand beside the fire.

"A nut," Stein said to Howl as they moved past the mosquito net and into the tarp tent. Howl popped his head out one last time. "You better keep that fire goin'," he said. "Those mosquitoes don't have much mercy now."

Phillips turned over, turning his back to the tent.

# # #

36

The morning came quickly, the sun chasing shadows from the jungle floor. Mac stirred with the first of the light, a learned habit. Not surprisingly it was warm out despite the early hour. Humidity swelled within the tent. Mac pushed aside his light blanket, moving out into the morning air. Howl and Stein were soon behind him. Phillips lay in the same position which he'd been in when they'd left him; unmoving like a corpse that had fallen there in the night.

"Bloat's a heavy sleeper," Stein said, stretching his back.

The fire was reduced to a clump of smoldering ashes, releasing small trails of smoke.

While Stein and Howl began to gather equipment for the day's hunt, Mac knelt beside Phillips. He pushed the man's shoulder but got no response. Agitated by the early hour, and frustrated by the stranger's burden, Mac gave Phillips an extra hard shove that turned him from his side onto his back. In the next instant Mac nearly jumped out of his skin. As Phillips turned over a black mamba wriggled out from beneath him. It bared its black mouth and large fangs, curling into a defensive coil. It snapped threateningly. Mac jumped back, prepared to run. He called out for Howl, who quickly tossed his pistol across the clearing. Mac caught it and fired once, blowing the snake's head to shards. The mamba squirmed as its last nerves burned out, then fell motionless to the sand.

Mac rushed over to Phillips' side, giving the snake a swift kick in the process.

"Did it get 'im?" Stein asked, coming forward.

"Phillips?" Mac said excitedly, smacking at the man's jaw. When the stranger didn't answer Mac searched his body for any signs of the mamba's bite. It was a highly venomous snake, and aggressive. He didn't have to look far: a purple wound festered on the inside of Phillips' forearm.

"He's a goner, mate," Stein said.

Howl looked over his shoulder from the tent. "Some people got all the luck," he said with a laugh.

"Poor bastard," Mac said. He looked at Phillips' face, noticing that it was surprisingly calm. His eyes were closed; he looked to still be asleep.

"I don't believe it," Stein said suddenly. "The mate's still breathing."

Howl laughed from inside the tent.

Mac shook Phillips' shoulders violently. Amazingly, the stranger's eyes opened, one at a time. He brought up his hands, rubbing the sleep from his face. Apparently unphased by the snake bite he looked around with his own astonishment. "What's going on?" he asked.

"Mate…" Stein began.

"Phillips, do you feel anything right now?" Mac asked. "Your heart shoulda blown a gasket by this point. It may've just gotten you so rest back."

"What are you…" he stopped, eyeing the wound on his arm. "Oh, I see" he said. Then, amazingly, he stood. His legs didn't even wobble. He obviously felt no effect.

"That mamba over there bit you," Mac said, watching Phillips' face for any hint of a human reaction. There was nothing, not the slightest fear or pain. Instead, Phillips, who should've been dead, cocked his head like he'd done the night before, walked calmly to the edge of the clearing and looked out into the jungle, listening. No doubt he was hearing the drums that terrorized his warped mind.

Stein and Mac looked at one another,

expressing their own fear. It was the first time Mac had seen fear in the old man's eyes, and they'd been through quite a bit together. As Mac dropped his gaze a haunting idea possessed him. It was immediately unwelcome for it conflicted with any reason he possessed. Howard Phillips couldn't be human. It was a simple matter of logic. The venom in a black mamba's bite kills humans but Phillips was unharmed by the serious wound. He reacted to it the way one would react to a mosquito bite. Ergo, Phillips wasn't human. As to what he was, Mac couldn't say, he couldn't begin to guess. It was a cold, deep fear that settled in his mind as he watched the stranger — one that he knew would direct his actions in the days to come.

Howl emerged from the tent, giving a quizzical look to Phillips' rigid frame. "The drums," he said to the others mockingly.

"Howl, you ever seen a man survive a mamba bite?" Mac asked quietly.

"Nah," Howl said, shaking his head. "It must not've gotten him like you think."

"Take a look at the mate's arm," Stein said, nodding.

The purple wound, which had grown outward, was visible from where they stood.

"Probably rolled over on a rock," Howl offered. "We headin' out?"

"We can't just leave him. Not like that," Stein said.

"Oh, now you're joinin' with him, huh?" Howl nodded at Mac. "You two are gettin' a little soft for my taste. You need to go back to ferryin' if that's how you're gonna play it, Stein. And you, Mac, I'm sure you can get back into readin' old ladies' fortunes."

Mac took offence to Howl's brash tone; his stomach twitched with anger.

Howl noticed the change in Mac's face, because he drew a pistol from his side in re-

action. Although Mac entertained the idea for the slightest second the gun wasn't for him. Howl turned on his heels and walked over to Phillips, who was now crouching, but still listening intently. Howl cocked the gun and placed the barrel against the stranger's head. Phillips, not surprisingly, didn't budge, or even acknowledge the threat.

"It's that easy," Howl said. "Just one bullet and problem solved."

"God damn," Mac said, "is everybody losing their mind?"

"It's mercy with that mamba venom in his blood," Howl said sarcastically. "Just one shot."

"Don't do it," Stein said shakily.

"Here's how it's gonna be," Howl said, moving Phillips' head back and forth with the tip of the barrel. "Either you two get your gear together or I'll kill the bastard." He stared at Stein and Mac with wild eyes.

Mac, inclined to believe the unstable Howl, got his gear together and prepared to head out. This is the last time, he told himself. This experience was showing him the instability of his life. One bump in the road and it fell to pieces around him. Death seemed more real to him in that moment than it ever had before. It seemed like it was in the air even, which was a strange feeling to acknowledge.

Phillips prepared himself, drank a cup of the coffee Howl'd fixed, and made his desire to follow the drums apparent. "I'm setting out," he said, and disappeared into the matted growth of the jungle.

It didn't take Howl long to realize that he'd crossed the line with the gun trick. He made light of it, which was his way of trying to make amends. But neither Stein nor Mac had anything of his apology. Their expedition was quiet and tense as they set out.

Mac's mind, exhausted from the

strange morning, still sped on, running over things, thinking back and forth. As uncomfortable as it made him to have Phillips around it made him more so to not know where the man was. As Howl tracked ahead of them he and Stein conferred quietly about the stranger. Mac knew something deep was on Stein's mind and after a mile of tracking he was able to get it out of him.

"It's a story I heard years back," he said quietly. "No man in their right mind would ever put any stock into it, mind you. But this morning after seeing Phillips take that mamba bite like it was nothing more than a flea got me thinking about it."

Mac listened, watching the trail ahead.

Stein went on. "There's a small tribe around here, not too close but near, called the Shaunti."

"I've heard of 'em," Mac said.

Stein nodded. "They had a shaman named Tumwalde who could do some strange things. The story I heard was that he was able to take drums and..." he paused, thinking. "Well, you see mate, they use the drums to communicate things. To talk. To warn and to threaten more or less. He could take the death drums and construct a person out of the magic contained in their sound. Like the sound was an entity and he made a body for it."

"Nuts," Mac said. "What good would that do?"

"Makes the drums travel. Helps their reach, mate. He makes a body for the sound and it searches out enemies."

"You thinkin' that's what Phillips is?"

"I didn't say that. No, I don't. I just said it got me thinkin' about it. I was told you could tell if that's what a person is if the chap can't suffer or feel pain. And that snakebite, with it rotting his arm like it was, made me wonder."

The two men fell silent. Mac raised his machete, slashing a vine from the path. His shirt was soaked through with sweat and clung to his body uncomfortably. Bugs buzzed around the brim of his hat. Insane, he thought. But the story was specific, and it fit Phillips in a peculiar way. Fit him perfectly actually. A question came into his mind. "What do the drums do?" he asked Stein.

The old man squinted in the sun as they stepped into a clearing. "Well the death drum is just supposed to scare you, scare off enemies I suppose. But if it's got enough magic in it then the sound comes to a man that's about to die like the reaper. He knows it, mate, when he hears it. And it... well, he just knows. That's enough to drive a man crazy."

"I s'pose. Why would we be their enemies?"

"The elephants, mate. Same way you'd feel if a chap was getting in the way of our business. They think they got a right to the elephants."

Stein and Mac looked up suddenly as the shattering sound of Howl's rifle blasted in their ears.

Howl stood only 20 yards ahead, out of the clearing, firing his rifle rapidly in all directions like he'd finally gone off the deep end.

Mac ran ahead with all the speed he could manage in the thick undergrowth. He caught Howl with his back turned and grabbed at the rifle, yanking it from his hands with the aid of surprise. Stein was behind him in another second, his own gun raised defensively.

Howl turned angrily. "You can't tell me you don't hear those god damn drums?!"

he shouted, there was agony in his voice. "They drone on all night and day. I can't stand it!" He reached for the rifle but Mac eluded his grasp. "I've heard 'em since that son of a bitch came into the camp."

"Why didn't you say somethin'?" Mac asked, raising his voice to keep up with Howl.

"I didn't want to look like a lunatic! Not with the way we were lampooning Phillips. But I heard 'em god damn it—loud and clear from the first second."

"Well you look like a lunatic now, Howl. And not for what you're hearin', but with that damn rifle. Damn," Mac said, wiping the sweat from his face. "I'm all for making money," he said, trying to reason with Stein or Howl, whoever would listen. "But this trip's goin' to hell. I'd like to leave with my mind intact. Stein, I know you feel the same."

"Sure, mate," Stein said. "I'm ready to head out this second."

"How about it, Howl?" Mac asked.

"Give me the rifle," Howl said calmly. He caught his breath and nodded as if to say he was okay.

"I asked you a question."

Howl kept his hand extended and it shook despite his mental effort. "Just give me the rifle, Mac. You and Stein head out if you wanna. But I gotta find that sound. It'll haunt me as long as I live if I don't."

"As long as you live?" Stein cut in. "You hear death drums don't you?"

Howl nodded. Sweat dripped from his chin and matted the hair protruding from his hat. With a quick lunge he grabbed the rifle from Mac's hands. Mac cursed himself and stood back as Howl raised it to his shoulder. He looked with his good eye above the sights. "You two get outta here. I don't want

you in on it if you can't hear it. Just go back. Go to the river."

"But you'll die out here, Howl," Stein said. "You can't give in that easy."

"I'm already gonna die," he said. Then, without a word, he left the elephant trail and sprinted through the jungle towards the ghost drums in his mind.

Mac watched him go, not tearing his eyes away till Howl disappeared from sight. It was futile trying to follow him. It was just as useless watching him go but it seemed the only apology he could offer his old friend in that moment. As Howl lost himself in the thick jungle Mac knew it was the last time he'd see him. Distant shots echoed, then died in the air.

Mac and Stein turned back down the trail, back towards camp. It was an anxious trip. Both were lost in thought so few words passed between them. Maybe Phillips really did fit in with the story Stein had heard, Mac thought to himself. Ultimately, though, it didn't matter. Mac couldn't care less about the roots of the trouble facing him; he just had to get away from it as quickly as possible. He could live with not knowing. Phillips was stirring something loose in their minds regardless of his intentions or purpose.

A single worry rose above all others, however. As Mac listened to the familiar sounds of the jungle he dreaded the slightest hint of a beating drum. Whether it was in the mind or not it seemed perfectly real to those hearing it. Howl didn't believe his imagination was running wild on him; he believed in the spectral sound of the drums. He believed in it enough, in fact, to sacrifice his life in finding the source. The sound drove him insane. And Phillips, Mac guessed, was a perpetrator rather than a victim.

Stein nudged Mac's arm, bringing him

from his thoughts.

"Look ahead, mate," he said, his voice a whisper.

Standing in the trail, partially hidden by several thick vines, was Howard Phillips. He stood waiting, not threatening, his hands crossed at the front of his body.

Threatening or not, Mac felt dread creep through his body like a capsule in his mind had burst. He white knuckled his rifle, sliding his hand closer to the trigger. The thought to do more crossed his mind but weakened quickly. Rather, he walked stalwartly forward, his chin held tight by gritting teeth. The thought of Howl caused anger to mix with fear.

Stein was bravely at his side. They faced the man together.

Phillips had no malice in his eyes as he watched them approach. He wore no emotion at all. His wounded arm, which he concealed at his side vainly, was black from wrist to elbow, the flesh loose in places as if it was charred. The mamba venom literally rotted his arm, spreading further in purple veins that snaked beneath the sleeve and out of sight. "I heard shots," he said calmly.

"We are hunting, mate," Stein said coolly.

"Where's the other?" Phillips looked around.

"I thought you were going on your way?" Mac asked tensely.

Phillips stared at the gun and then into Mac's eyes. "I believe you gave me the courtesy of staying in your camp today. I'll take you up on it."

Mac's blood boiled, his temper finally breaking loose. He pointed the gun. Not surprisingly, Stein followed his act, aiming his gun almost simultaneously. They both had a bead drawn on Phillips, but the stranger remained unmoved.

"Mac, if you wanna do this, ain't no one ever gonna know it," Stein said, making his wishes known.

"I'll give you one more chance to go," Mac said. The thought that a bullet would have the same effect as the mamba bite crossed his mind, but he maintained his bluff. "I don't know what you want here and I don't care. You had somethin' to do with Howl runnin' off, I know that much. And if you think you can play the same game on Stein and me you're outta your mind."

Phillips suddenly cocked his head, listening to his drums.

"GOD DAMN IT!" Mac shouted. "You're not foolin' us with that garbage. Get the hell," he shoved Phillips into a thick patch of creeper, "out of the trail and let us be!" Mac, fueled by rage, turned his rifle and slammed the butt against Phillips bearded face. Phillips didn't struggle; he lay where he'd fallen, blood oozing from his gashed forehead, his expression unchanging as stone.

Stein followed Mac briskly along the last stretch of the trail.

As Mac's anger subsided it was replaced, once again, by dread. He looked over his shoulder constantly, waiting for Phillips to emerge calmly. That was the worst part of it: the calm look that was always on his face regardless what had befallen him.

At the camp he took his extra canteen and prepared to head out, leaving everything else behind. Stein, he thought, was inclined to do the same. But the old man sat in the tent for two agonizing minutes while Mac waited at the edge of the clearing, watching for a sign of Phillips. When he couldn't take the tension any longer Mac hurried over, pulling the flap aside. "Stein!" he screamed, his stomach rising to his throat.

41

The old man lay back with a hunting knife pressed to his throat. He hadn't done anything yet, but he was threatening to do it. "What are you doin'?" Mac asked, trying to stay calm.

"I can't lie to you," Stein said in a trembling voice. His eyes shone with tears. "I hear them," he choked out the words. "Ever since you blasted him back there. I hear 'em just like Howl."

"Give me the knife," Mac said, preparing to pounce and rip it from the man's hand.

But Stein was too quick. In the next instant the knife slid across his neck, releasing a stream of gore.

Mac wheeled around, his mind racing. His stomach twisted and wrenched. It was up to him now, he was alone. He only had to keep his mind long enough to get to the boat, he reasoned. It would be easier once he was on the river. Mac threw his rifle over his shoulder and turned to the river trail.

Howard Phillips stood there, his arm black to the fingertips and his head smothered in blood. He stared. "Don't you hear them?" he asked calmly.

Mac's first shot hit him in the neck, tearing away enough skin to make his head tilt. Phillips staggered back and fell, but his eyes remained open and alert as Mac ran past. It was an effort not to look back but Mac kept his gaze on the trail ahead, dodging quickly in and out of obstacles. He managed to make it the four miles, his head and sides bursting in the strong heat.

The boat rested where Stein had left it floating. Mac untied it, dropped his canteen and rifle to the floor, then started up the engine. He'd driven the boat before and he maneuvered it into the deep center of the Congo River with relative ease. A blur of thoughts and sensations battered his mind.

Thoughts, sensations, and sounds.

Mac listened above the buzzing engine as the boat moved forward, his mind suddenly pulled back into the jungle he'd tried to flee, which he'd come so close to escaping. Above everything came the horrible sound of a drum, noting a haunting rhythm that pulsed in the air, and hung there without fading. It was a mortifying sound, one that signaled the approach of death. Out of the corner of his eye Mac swore he saw the gory figure of Howard Phillips standing on the bank. Yet, when he turned to look, the shadow had passed. The drums grew to a deafening height.

It was the last sane thought to cross his mind.

The End

Since 2008, Coy Hall's work has been featured in *Arcane Twilight, Mirror Dance Fantasy, New Voices in Horror, And Soon the Darkness Halloween Anthology 2008, Drops of Crimson, Blood Moon Rising,* and others.

A Mere Cackle

By Jane Gwaltney

He says I remind him of a bird;
that I see him coming before *he* does,
legs like cocktail toothpicks
stirring...

He's never heard those cryptic messages,
passengers, transported by wind...
those tender pleas from rotting wood,
stirring...

I'm quite unassuming.

I think the strangest of strangers
deserves a casual preen.
He takes issue, squawking
like a dodo would, if it *could*.

So it's time he was reminded
that my appetite outweighs my body,
yet I can dine on the head of a pin.

I think I'll start with his eyes.

Jane Gwaltney was born on Travis Air Base near San Francisco, but has
resided in St. Louis, Missouri, most of her life. She has received
Honorable Mentions in "The Year's Best Fantasy and Horror" and "Best Horror
of the Year, volume one." Her poetry, fiction, and art appear in *Dreams and
Nightmares, Wrong World, Wicked Hollow, Paper Crow, Redsine, Breath and
Shadow, Champagne Shivers, Simulacrum, Aoife's Kiss,* and more.

Her novella "Darkness, Darkness" (Sam's Dot Publishing) is available in
trade paperback.

Black Dog

By Matt Baxter

Thirty miles to go till he reached home, and for the first time Duane thought he might make it. The overtime paid well, but when he left the warehouse it was two in the morning and the empty world around him felt slightly unreal, as though its soul had been taken from it. He wanted to see some sign of life, some other human being, but at this time in the morning the roads were empty, and he hustled the big old car through the countryside as fast as he dared.

Music, that was the answer. The car might be more rust than metal, but its saving grace was a Blaupunkt CD changer which was worth twice as much as the vehicle that held it. The radio was no good at night, a choice of somnolent easy listening or brain-aching dance music, but somewhere down in the passenger foot well there was a Nirvana CD, where he had chucked it the previous day. Milly might treat CDs as being worth more than gold, and keep her wretched Christina Aguileras and Whitney Houstons in their diamond cases in their own little rack by the bed, but Duane didn't think that was very rock and roll. One wipe on his trousers and it would play again, no problem.

The problem was that he had to find the disc somewhere down there in the no man's land in front of the passenger seat. He swayed his hand down as far as he dared, and touched only empty air. He tried again and his fingertips brushed against an empty crisp packet, a Coke can, and – that was it! Maybe not the right CD, but anything loud would be good right now.

He edged further over towards the passenger side, speed down to sixty now, driving along the white line with one hand on the wheel and one eye on the road. He reached down again, brushed the disc again, and still couldn't quite get a grip on the thing. Duane turned on the dome light and there it was, glinting up at him, mocking him. He leaned over a little further, only the fingertips of his right hand remaining on the wheel, and took his eyes off the road for a second, two seconds, three -

His fingers had just grasped the disc when the car hit something. A massive, metallic thud shook the Vauxhall's bodywork, the windscreen imploded in a billion tiny glass cubes, and Duane looked up just in time to see a large, black object slide upwards from the remains of the windscreen onto the roof. The car was slewing towards the ditch by the roadside now, and Duane grabbed the wheel in both hands, slammed both feet down on the pedals as hard as he could. The car lurched left, then right, swayed, and something fell off the roof onto the road surface. Duane felt sure he would capsize, but the Vauxhall stayed upright, and came to a stop with a jolt that slammed Duane's face against the steering wheel.

Duane stood up on the pedals for a long time, unable to believe that he was still alive and uninjured. Slowly he allowed himself to sit back down in his seat. He experimented with taking his hands off the wheel, but they spasmed wildly in the air and he put them back down until they stopped. He was all right, he had made it.

He had hit something.

Drive on, he thought. Go home and don't tell anyone about this, and don't buy any papers for the next few days.

And in a couple of days' time, answer the door to find a couple of coppers there, asking if he owned a dark blue Vauxhall Carlton. Duane watched CSI from time to time, and he knew they could do wonderful things with flecks of paint these days.

"It wasn't a person." Duane whispered, and he didn't even convince himself. He cracked open his door and stepped into the road on weak, unwilling legs.

The front of the car was as bad as he had feared. The front bumper was hanging on by a single rivet, and one good tug was enough for Duane to take it off completely. The bonnet and grille were dented, and there was a shallow pit in the roof, but the engine was still running smoothly, for now.

Duane put the bumper inside the boot, where it rested on a bed of old carrier bags. Duane didn't look at the road behind him. He didn't think he was ready for that just yet. Instead he reached inside the car and turned the engine off. The road was quiet now. No traffic, not even any birds in the trees, not two hours before the sun came up. There was moonlight, though. There would be plenty of light to see what he had hit.

Finally he forced himself to turn, half an inch at a time, as though he didn't want to spoil the surprise. There wasn't much to see. Just a black, shapeless mass about fifty yards behind the car. It was about the size of a man. It wasn't moving.

Duane walked towards the body, unable to stop himself. He might still drive on, probably would in fact, but he had to know first. At least when the cops came for him and the grieving family screamed at him from the public gallery, he would be able to say that he had made sure, that he hadn't just left the victim to bleed to death in this godforsaken place.

Duane was about twenty feet away when he saw that the victim wasn't wearing a black coat at all, but was covered with black fur. He squinted into the darkness and saw a snout, pointed ears, a black, wet nose.

And praise the Lord and all his little saints and angels; breath was rising from the dog's nose. You had to look hard to see it, but it was there.

"I'm saved." Duane said aloud, and he began to run towards the dog.

# # #

"Milly?"

"Hnnngghh?"

"Milly, are you awake?"

"Of course I'm awake, you moron. You've been prodding at me for the past five minutes."

"Why didn't you answer me before, then?"

"I was hoping you'd go away."

"Milly, there's been an accident."

And just like that she was fully awake, throwing off the duvet, jumping out of bed and opening a drawer to find some clothes.

"What kind of an accident?" she demanded. "Are you all right?"

"I'm fine, not a scratch on me."

"What about the car?"

"Well, to be honest, Hon, the car's not in such great shape."

"Brilliant, Duane. Absolutely sodding brilliant. How are you going to get to work without it? How am I going to get to hospital?"

You could walk, you fat cow, Duane thought. Aloud, he said, "The car still goes OK. It's mostly just cosmetic damage. I, ah, hit something."

Milly's stare could have destroyed galaxies. "What *kind* of something?" she said.

"I think it's a dog."

"You're not sure? You don't know if it's a dog or not? Duane, have you been drinking?"

"Milly, you really need to see this." Duane said.

# # #

Milly was unimpressed. "Yes, Duane, it's a dog. A Rottweiler, in fact. Are you sure you haven't been drinking?"

Duane blew sober breath into her face, and Milly flinched away. She was orange under the streetlights, which was a change from her usual baby-pink, but she didn't look any healthier. Duane was starting to regret having woken her up.

Duane looked at the creature lying on the car's back seat. He supposed it was a dog, all right, but this was no Rottweiler. Back in his student days Duane had worked for a pub landlord who owned four rotties, and he knew the breed well enough. Short, stumpy tail, barrel chest, square jaw. This dog had a long body, a very long tail and an elongated snout. It was covered with thick, black matted hair. It looked about as much like a Rottweiler as a dachshund. It smelt as though it had spent all day rolling around in graveyard dirt, but in Duane's experience most dogs smelt like that.

And then there was the animal's sheer size. It was at least a foot taller and a foot longer than any rottie that Duane had ever seen.

All the same, Duane knew how much good it would do to argue with Milly. If she wanted to see a Rottweiler, she would see one, and no amount of reasoning would change her mind.

"Is he hurt?" Milly asked.

"Not that I can see."

"We ought to get him to a vet."

"Which we can't afford."

"Isn't there an NHS for animals, then?"

"No, there's a bloody great bill for animals. And dogs are supposed to be licensed, and someone's out looking for this bad boy, and wondering where he is."

"Then we should – "

Yes, thought Duane, we should, as he tuned out the rest of Milly's diatribe. We should, only we aren't going to. Because for some reason or other, I rather like this tough old bugger, who can be hit by a car and hardly have a scratch on him. And anyway, I owe him.

On the back seat, the dog made a gurgling, snurfling noise that startled them both. It stretched out its front legs, as though it was waking from a relaxing sleep, lifted its head up and opened its eyes for the first time.

Duane didn't scream, though he did take a large step backwards. Because the dog's eyes were red, a bright scarlet that seemed to be lit from within the creature's skull. The eyes burned out at him, and before he could turn and run, the dog sprang from its seat. Duane had enough time to think that this was it, game over, and then the dog was slobbering over his face with a bright pink tongue that had to be a foot long.

He likes me, Duane thought. That thing with his eyes is probably just an optical illusion, like cats' eyes. And even if it isn't, he *likes* me. Owner or no owner, we're keeping him.

# # #

There was a row, of course. These days, there would be a row if Duane suggested that grass was green and the sky was blue. Milly declared that the police must be informed, and that this creature would eat them out of house and home. And who would look after him? Both of them worked, and they couldn't leave the dog alone all day. Was he even housetrained? And what would Mrs Stepancik say?

That last item wasn't something that worried Duane too much. Mrs Stepancik was their landlady, who lived downstairs and smelled of mulligatawny soup. She always said something to Duane when they met, but he had never once understood a single word she spoke in her Polish-accented mumble. Quite possibly she'd been telling him for months to get the hell out of her house, but as long as Duane couldn't understand her, he stayed. Mrs Stepancik might love dogs or hate them, but he would probably never find out which.

As for Milly, Duane thought he had an answer for her, too.

"You want him out, you get rid of him." he said.

"What? You're the one who brought him into the house in the first place." Milly said.

"Yeah, because I ran him over, and I was trying to do the decent thing for once in my life. If you want to throw him out of the house into the rain and snow – "

"Duane, it's August."

"Whatever. If you want to throw this poor animal out into the night, all alone, you go right ahead. But you can do it by yourself."

Milly looked at the dog, who had made himself quite at home on their threadbare sofa. He sat with his mouth agape, enormous tongue lolling down so far that it almost touched the carpet. Duane didn't know exactly what Milly saw, but he thought the dog looked harmless, so long as you didn't think too much about his eyes.

Milly took one step forwards, and the dog didn't move an inch. But Duane fancied he heard a growling sound, so low that he felt it as much as heard it. It was only his imagination, he was sure of that. Milly turned around and decided to make a pot of tea instead. That was the last time she ever mentioned getting rid of the dog.

# # #

Duane had to admit that dog-walkers were a disappointment. Mick down at the White Hart had assured him that all single women had dogs, and that as a result the park at six in the morning was a sea of pussy. Duane thought that this was true, so long as you liked your pussy around seventy years old and attached to a Yorkshire terrier. With a tartan coat.

Zoltan was happy enough, though. Duane had tried him on a lead, but it was like trying to hold back a freight train, and now the dog was rushing around everywhere, sniffing at everything in sight, frightening the squirrels and barking loudly at other dogs. He was full of joy at being alive, and why not? It's not everyone who can get hit by a car and be running around a couple of days later. Duane felt some of that joy, too. He might be chained to Milly and the warehouse, but Zoltan was free.

"He's a big fellow, isn't he?" came a voice, startling Duane out of his daydream. The voice's owner was a generic old lady, complete with a long tweed coat and a fluffy purple hat. Looking at her wrapped up like that, Duane wondered if he hadn't stepped into January by mistake.

"He's big, all right." Duane admitted.

"What breed is he, a border collie?"

"He's a cross, I think." Duane said. "We only got him a couple of days ago from the dogs' home." As if he knew that they were talking about him, Zoltan trotted over and sat on his haunches, tongue hanging out gormlessly.

The old lady bent down and patted Zoltan's huge head. "He's beautiful." she said. "Almost as lovely as my own little darling." She indicated the dog standing by her side, a dirty-white Scots terrier which was eyeing Duane furiously, as though it was thinking about eating him.

Zoltan noticed the smaller dog for the first time, and stood up leisurely and sauntered over to meet his new playmate. The Scottie whined quietly, but it didn't move. It expelled a jet of urine as Zoltan sniffed its nose, its back and finally its rump. Satisfied, Zoltan emitted a single, short bark, and the Scottie took off.

Technically, Duane supposed, the smaller dog was running, but didn't your feet have to touch the ground if you were running? It shot towards the park gates like a small, furry missile, with its owner trailing unsteadily after it. She was shouting a name that Duane couldn't make out. He did hear the scream of brakes in the street outside the park, though, and heard the bump-bump sound.

When he looked down at Zoltan, he could have sworn the dog was grinning at him.

# # #

"Come on, boy, you've got to eat something." Duane said, as he pushed the plate of Pedigree Chum across the garage's concrete floor, making a scraping noise that Milly's mother could probably hear upstairs. Not that that worried him too much. With a bit of luck the old bat would come down, see Zoltan as he really was and expire on the spot. It would solve a lot of problems.

Milly's mother was an older version of her daughter, and the thought of two of them in the house together was a good part of the reason he was in the garage. That was what he was marrying, that was what Milly would look like in 25 years' time or so. Milly's father had died a few years back, from exhaustion or despair.

Zoltan, unconcerned by mothers, sniffed at the dog food and looked up at Duane with his expressionless red eyes. He was obviously having none of it, but that wasn't too surprising. He hadn't eaten anything since coming to the house. He hadn't drunk any water from the bowl that Duane put on the kitchen floor. And Milly's worries about whether he was house-trained had proved to be unnecessary.

He's just taking time to recover from the accident, Duane thought, and another, treacherous thought said that if that was the case, shouldn't he be hurt? Shouldn't he be wasting away from lack of food? Instead, since the incident in the park, Zoltan looked healthier than ever. And how did a dog recover so quickly from being hit by a car, anyway?

"Duane!" shouted Milly from the top

of the stairs. "My mother wants to see you!"

Duane climbed to the scaffold with leaden feet.

#

Before Duane entered the living room, Milly took him aside. "He's locked up tight, isn't he?" she hissed.

"He's in the garage." Duane said. "You know, the strangest thing happened this morning – "

But before he could finish, the figure of Mrs Belper filled the doorway. Milly's mother was somewhere around twenty stone, almost a perfect sphere with stumpy arms and legs attached as an afterthought. She favoured enormous haircuts that made her seem even larger, and the general effect as she waddled towards Duane was of being approached by a small planet.

"Duane!" she said. "Don't you have a kiss for your future mother-in-law?"

Duane submitted himself to her hairy lips, trying to pretend that Mrs Belper was nothing worse than a drunken auntie, and eventually she let him go.

"Milly and I were discussing plans for your wedding." she said, as she took Duane by the hand and pulled him into the living room. She sat him down on the sofa and sat beside him, far too close, so that he could feel her hot breath on his face. Duane saw with dismay that the coffee table was covered with magazines that were full of brides. All of the brides in the pictures looked terribly pleased with themselves.

"Now," Mrs Belper said, "There are only two months to go, and we must start getting ourselves *organised*. Particularly the guest list, so that we can let the Legion hall know how many they'll be catering for.

Now, our family amounts to no more than forty-one, and including Milly's friends, that comes to a total of ninety-six for our side of the family. So how many do you think you will be able to contribute, Duane, dear?" She smiled at him, and Duane saw her bright scarlet lipstick melt, along with her rouge and mascara. Not just her make-up, he saw, but her whole face was melting and flowing, dripping in rivulets like candle-wax.

Duane blinked, and there was Mrs Belper, old and insane, but very much in one piece. She was still smiling too widely.

"How many?" Duane asked, uncomprehending.

"How many guests, dear? Goodness me, I know Milly says you aren't always too bright, but do try to pay attention." Mrs Belper smiled again, and laughed delicately, like a rattle of china cups. Milly laughed from across the room. Almost the same laugh, in fact.

"I don't know." Duane said. "Maybe about twenty people?"

"Is that all?" Mrs Belper exclaimed.

"Well, there's my mum, my sisters and their families, a couple of aunts and uncles, a few people from the warehouse and the boys from the White Hart. I guess we could make it up to thirty?"

"Hmm." Mrs Belper said, "I suppose that will reduce catering costs, if nothing else. Now, what about your outfit?"

Duane tuned her out as he did so often with her daughter. Mrs Belper showed him catalogues of grooms in black suits, dressed for funerals. They weren't grinning quite as widely as the brides in the other magazine. Duane nodded and smiled at the right moments, but he was sure that Mrs Belper would carry on talking even if he dropped dead right there in front of her.

49

Duane's mind drifted off and he thought about Zoltan. Was the incident this morning really that strange? Any creature that could scare the hell out of small, yappy dogs had to have some good points. And those Scotties were highly-strung, they'd spook at anything.

Like a dog with fiery red eyes, that only you can really see, Duane thought. Maybe you ought to take him back to where you found him and let him go.

I can't. I own him now.

Again that thought. And again, the thought that it wasn't quite right. That, if anything, Zoltan owned him.

Before Duane could wonder about where that thought had come from, Mrs Belper woke him with another rattly laugh.

"Do wake up, Duane!" she trilled. "Anyone would think you were off in your own little dream world!"

"Sorry." Duane said.

"That's all right, dear. Soon to be a husband, soon to be a father, it's only natural that you should be a little preoccupied. Tell me, have you and Milly discussed what to call the baby yet?"

No, Duane thought, we've been avoiding the subject because neither of us wants to face up to it. But thanks for reminding me.

"We haven't discussed it much." he said. "There's still another five months to go."

"Yes, but you must *plan* these things." Mrs Belper said, and she patted Duane's knee. He looked in horror at her liver-spotted claw, which reeked of Oil of Olay, and she withdrew it.

"Our family has a name, going back many generations, that is given to all the first-born boys." she said, "Now sadly I didn't have any sons, but I would be so glad if you would pass the name on."

"What is it?" Duane asked.

"It's Algernon, dear."

"Algernon?"

"It's an old name, very well respected."

Not by kids in the playground, I bet, Duane thought.

"We'll think about it." he said.

#

Duane had never felt comfortable getting his car serviced. He ought to feel at home, being a working class boy and all, but he had always felt intimidated by mechanics and their secret knowledge. All he was good for was shifting boxes from one place to another, and he never felt it more acutely than he did here, standing in the reception area of the garage. Zoltan's presence beside him gave him a little more confidence than usual, but not enough.

He stood three feet away from a short, fat man in greasy red overalls, with a fancy piece of stitching above his left tit that told anyone who cared that the man's name was Mike. The reception area was as greasy and unkempt as the man himself.

"How much?" Duane asked again.

"Seven hundred." said Mike, and this time Duane was sure the man would break out a smile and tell him he was just kidding, of course it wasn't that much, didn't Duane feel silly now? But he didn't.

"I don't have that sort of money." Duane said.

"Won't your insurance cover it?"

"Third party only. It was cheaper."

"False economy, that." Mike said, with no little satisfaction. "Always go for fully comp, you'll thank yourself for it one day.

Or you would do. Bit late now."

"You've only got to knock a couple of dents out." Duane said. "Surely it can't cost that much?"

"Have you seen the size of those dents, mate? It looks like you hit a bloody elephant." Mike said. He squatted down and ruffled the fur between Zoltan's ears with his blackened fingers. "Nice doggie. St Bernard, right? My Nan's got one of these, only about half the size of this bugger, mind." Zoltan's tongue lolled and he offered a short bark as Mike stood up again.

"Yeah," he reflected. "Looks as though you hit something pretty big. I'm kind of surprised that I haven't seen anything about it in the papers, in fact. Because you would have thought, when you reported it to the police, that they would have put something in the press, wouldn't you?" He didn't look at Duane, but kept his eyes firmly fixed on the dog.

He doesn't mean it, Duane thought. He's not really going to go to the cops.

I can't take the chance.

"I'll find the money." he said, "Just fix it."

"That, sir, is a very good decision."

# # #

Standing at the bus stop on the other side of the road, waiting for a bus that had to be a good twenty minutes away, all the frustrations of Duane's life crashed down on him at once. He kicked hard at the bus shelter, putting a satisfying dent in the grey metal. He tried punching it, but that only hurt his fist. Shouting worked better.

"Why me?" he yelled at Zoltan, who was the only one there to listen. "What have I done to be worth this? I knock up some bird on a one-night stand and now her family have got their hooks in me, my landlady plays Mantovani all day at maximum volume, my job's a waste of time, and now that.... person is ripping me off. And there isn't a damn thing I can do about it."

Zoltan watched him with those expressionless red eyes, not moving.

"Just once, just once I want to come out on the winning end. Is that so much to ask?"

Zoltan barked, a sound which elongated into a howl that echoed in the empty street and bounced off the nearby houses. Zoltan sprang to his feet, bounded across the road, and ran inside the garage.

Duane couldn't see what happened next, but he could hear plenty. The screams weren't even the worst of it, nor was the howling that he heard every so often. The worst was the crunching, tearing sounds, and finally a huge cracking noise, like a backbone breaking.

# # #

Milly brought him breakfast in bed. That was surprising, but what was close to miraculous was that the food tasted pretty good. Until he was fifteen or so, Duane had believed that fried eggs were supposed to have a brown crust on the bottom, but these eggs had reached a state of near perfection. He could almost remember what had attracted him to Milly in the first place.

"You feeling a bit better now, love?" she asked, as she bent down to kiss him. For once, Duane wasn't vaguely disgusted by her kiss. In fact, he was happy to return it.

"A bit better, thanks." he said. "You didn't have to do this, you know."

Milly sat on the edge of the bed and

stroked his hair. "Poor, silly thing." she said. "It was a terrible shock to you, what happened. It could have been you, instead of that poor man."

"Yeah." Duane said, through a mouthful of sausage. "It could have been me."

"The police still don't know anything, but they never do, do they? They're still saying it was some kind of dog, but I overheard one of them say he thought it was a wolf. Can you believe that?"

Duane tried not to look at Zoltan, who had wedged himself into the narrow gap between the bed and the wall. As far as the police were concerned he was an Alsatian, of course. That was a big dog, potentially dangerous, but hardly capable of doing what had been done to the late Michael Callaghan.

Two coppers had interviewed Duane at the bus stop, and then again at home. The coppers had been the fag end of the force, the man unshaven and the woman with long, uncombed hair. Neither of them had been able to put their hats on straight.

Duane told them he hadn't seen anything, and neither had anyone else, it seemed. The other mechanics at the garage had vague and contradictory recollections. So far the description they had was: a large animal, probably a dog, possibly black. One of the mechanics had said it looked unreal, like a blur.

"Work phoned." Milly said. "They want to know when you'll be back."

"Soon." Duane said. "Tell them I'll be back on Monday."

"All right. But don't forget we need the money. And I won't be able to work soon, in my condition." She patted her stomach, which was about the same size as always. No bump showed yet, but it couldn't be long now.

"I'll go back." Duane said, "There's something I need to do first."

#

Duane went to the garage on the off-chance, but the place was encircled with blue and white tape, and a uniformed officer stood guard, so he gave up on getting his car back. Instead he walked the two miles to the station with Zoltan, trying and failing to clear his mind. His head felt like a jumble sale, full of confusing piles of junk that had just been thrown together in no particular order.

And that was without the dreams. That night he had woken at two and forced himself to stay awake for the rest of the night, drinking coffee and watching vacuous early morning TV shows. He couldn't remember all of the dream, and he was obscurely glad of that, but he remembered enough; walking through vast, black gates into a great mansion full of creatures which screeched and gibbered and made wet, soft noises deep in their wattled throats. And these things had welcomed him as one of their own.

As he got off the train Duane thought the university had changed in some indefinable way. He had walked past these buildings often enough as a kid, and he had always felt slightly intimidated by the square concrete blockhouses, set on scrubby lawns that never really grew. This place wasn't for the likes of him, and as a kid he had always hurried past.

Now, Duane could see the university more clearly. The blockhouses were grey concrete, but they weren't square at all. They were more like parallelograms, with corners that never quite met at ninety degrees. Windows were placed at odd angles and unreasonable heights, the grass on the lawn was clearly long dead, and the few trees seemed to cower in fear. The students mostly kept their heads down and avoided looking at him, but those few who did meet his eye viewed him with naked contempt. They scowled, they sneered, but finally all of them looked away from Duane's eyes.

Lack of sleep, he told himself. It's lack of sleep and bad dreams making you see things that aren't there. But he knew that wasn't true. He was seeing the world clearly for the first time.

With Zoltan by his side, the world couldn't hurt him. He walked across the blasted lawn and through a door that led into a corridor that smelled sweetly of floor polish. A few doors down on the left was a brass plaque, now going green at the edges. The plaque read 'Dr Cornelius Favell', and below this, 'Sociology Department.' This was where he had been referred when he had phoned up the previous day, so he knocked carefully on the door. The wood gave a little under Duane's knuckles, but sprang back into shape instantly. Duane hardly noticed.

"Come in!" came a high-pitched voice, so Duane pushed the door open and shut it behind him. The room he found himself in was a dimly lit chaos of books, stacked all around the walls and on every available flat surface. Most of them looked ancient. There was a single desk in the middle of the room, with an armchair in front of it, and a tiny kitchenette by the filthy window. A rusty kettle sat on a gas ring, trying to whistle but only managing an asthmatic wheeze.

The owner of this jungle library stood up from the chair behind the desk and held out a hand for Duane to shake. He was well over seventy, nearly bald, with tiny wisps of hair clinging on over each ear. He wore a rumpled brown suit, which matched his rumpled brown teeth when he smiled. Duane didn't mind. This was the first person who had smiled at him all day.

"Mr Wesley, is that correct?" the professor said, and ushered Duane into the tatty armchair. "Would you care for a cup of tea?"

"No thanks." Duane said.

"Oh, that's a shame." said the old man, and shuffled over to the kettle, which he poured into a cup that was held together by brown cracks. "Tea is the staff of life, you know." he said, pouring milk into the cup. White lumps floated alongside brown flecks that Duane assumed were rust from the kettle.

Dr Favell made his way back to the chair behind his desk and made himself comfortable, shifting from one skinny buttock to the other. "Now," he said, "I understand you are here in connection with the unfortunate incident a couple of days ago."

"Er, yeah, that's right." Duane said, as the professor took a long sip of filthy tea. A lump of milk stuck to the professor's upper lip and he licked it away. "I sort of witnessed it."

"I see." Dr Favell said. "And why do you think I might be able to help you? I am a sociologist, not a psychiatrist."

"Yeah, well, you do weird stuff, right?" Duane said.

"If you mean that my particular speciality is English folklore, particularly the legends of East Anglia, that is correct, yes. It would be fair to say that I have investigated one or two cases of what might be termed high strangeness."

"Great." Duane said. "Does a lot of odd stuff happen around here?"

"Well, many people would say so," said the professor, clearly enjoying his subject, "You have the famous UFO case at Bentwaters air base, for example, and the drowned city of Dunwich, there are the green children of Woolpit, the haunted house at Borley Rectory, the last case of plague in England, and the crimes of Matthew Hopkins, the so-called Witchfinder General. And of course there is Black Shuck, who I assume brought you to me."

"That's a big, black dog, right?"

"Well, to be strictly accurate he is a wolf, since the legend is a result of medieval fears. Very few wolves lived here by the Middle Ages, but fear of them was out of all proportion to their real threat, so some people began to see wolves where none existed. They created this demonic, red-eyed dog to both fuel and allay their fears, all at once. It's something of a classic case, actually, in folkloric circles."

"Right." Duane said, sure that he had understood at least half of what the professor had just said. "Black Shuck kills people, right?"

"Well, yes, in a manner of speaking."

"In a manner of speaking? You mean they're not quite sure if they're dead?"

"No, what I mean is that Black Shuck does not kill with a physical attack, but purely by supernatural means. During his famous assault on the church at Blythburgh, for example, people dropped dead from his mere touch, and one man was said to have shrivelled up like a prune. In other cases he supposedly puts a curse on his victims, so that they die within a week of first seeing him."

Duane tried to think how long ago he had run over the dog. Had it been five days ago? Six? The pain in his mind made it hard for him to concentrate.

"Professor, what I need to know is, how do you stop him? What do the legends say about that?"

"Mr Wesley – "

"Duane."

"Duane, then. I really do think you might be better off seeing a member of a different profession. The victim of this recent attack was surely killed by a dog, nothing more than that. The culprit is doubtless being hidden in somebody's garage. I deal in legends, and a legend, by definition, is something which does not exist."

Dr Favell licked his lips, and his eyes darted momentarily towards the door. Measuring the distance.

"Professor," Duane said, slowly, "I can understand you think I'm a bit nutty, but why don't you take a look at my dog, here? Take a really good, hard look."

The professor kept his eyes on Duane instead. They flicked for a second to Zoltan, who was curled up in front of his master's feet, but only for a second.

"You see," Duane said, "Most of us don't look very hard at the world. We just see what we expect to see. But sometimes I think we can see pure reality. And that's what Zoltan here does. Hardly anyone can see him properly, maybe no one except me. And he shows me the world like it really is. He's really helpful in other ways, too. If ever I get annoyed with someone, he'll take care of them. So don't get me annoyed, OK? Look at him. Please."

With great reluctance, as though his eyes were nailed to Duane and he was having to forcibly wrench them away, Dr Favell looked at Zoltan.

"He's just a—"he said, and that was as far as he got. His eyes widened, his mouth fell open and he began to drool a little. He stood up in slow motion, and started backing away even more slowly, as though he really

54

thought that would save him. He began to edge his way carefully around the desk, towards the door.

"You've seen him, I guess." Duane said. "And now that you have, I shouldn't make any long-term plans. Not beyond the next week or so, at least." He got up and walked to the door, and Zoltan followed him.

"Goodbye, professor." Duane said, and he left without looking back.

#

On the journey back, Duane and Zoltan might as well have been invisible. No one looked at them in the twilight streets or at the station, and Duane was glad of that. Instead of the two-carriage electric Sprinter train he had been expecting, he had got on a ramshackle, creaking diesel with slatted wooden seats and windows that were opaque with grime.

When Duane got back to the house he didn't turn the lights on. He could find his way perfectly well in the dark. He crept upstairs in his socks, trying to avoid the step near the top that creaked. Although now, nearly all of them creaked.

Zoltan padded by his side all the time, his constant, faithful companion. When Duane stood in the bedroom, looking down at the shapeless lump under the covers that was his future wife, Zoltan looked at Milly, too, almost expectantly.

God, but she snored! She sounded more like a pig than a human being, and laying there under the covers you could believe that she was just that, a large, unclean animal. What right did she have to take over Duane's life, just because of one mistake?

She's the mother of your child, said a small voice in Duane's mind, and he tried to ignore it. He hadn't asked for a child, and what kind of life would the kid have, between a mother who only loved chocolate and a father with no love for anything? Thoughts like that could make a man angry, and Duane allowed the anger to come, welcomed it as the solution to all his problems.

He summoned up every bad memory of Milly, every time she or her awful mother had slighted him, to his face or behind his back. Her sometimes wilful stupidity, her coarseness, her way of picking her nose and eating what she found there with a thoughtful expression on her face, as though she was contemplating Michelangelo.

But images of another Milly kept on surfacing. This Milly laughed at his jokes, even when they weren't funny. She worked occasional weekends at the charity shop in town, even though they didn't pay her. She had nursed him when he was ill. She was sometimes a decent person, and for all his best efforts Duane couldn't forget that.

Duane's eyesight had adjusted to the dimness by now, and he caught sight of the mirror in the wardrobe door. It was a full six feet high from floor to near the ceiling, and Milly loved to admire herself in it. Maybe she saw a different version of herself from the one that everyone else saw. Duane moved around until he was standing in front of the mirror. He switched on the small lamp on the bedside table, turning the bulb away from where Milly was sleeping.

This, then, was Duane as he really was. His hair was grey, that was the first thing he noticed. It was the same length it had always been, half an inch, no more, but what had been dark brown last week was now silvery grey that would have looked distinguished on a better looking man.

Duane had lost his looks quite badly. His face was creased like a cheap suit, and the eyes that stared out of cavern-deep sockets were bloodshot, their whites turning yellow. Duane opened his mouth and saw that his teeth were the same yellowish colour. One of them had fallen out; Duane tested the gap with his tongue and tasted copper.

"You're an old man, fella." he whispered, and his voice was a forty-a-day rasp. He smiled, and could only manage a pervert's lopsided leer. He looked into his eyes, and a murderer stared back at him.

Duane turned to Zoltan, the one unchanging feature in a world that was decaying by the minute. The dog, who had looked at Milly with such expectation, now gave Duane the same stare. Duane looked into the mirror one more time, at what he had become.

"Enough." Duane said.

# # #

The next morning Milly rolled over in bed, and found that the other side was empty and cold. Duane hadn't come back, then. Hadn't she always known he would run out on her one day?

She heaved herself out of bed, stepped around to go to the bathroom, and there he was on the floor, face down, dead drunk.

"Great." she muttered. "You scared the hell out of me there, idiot." She kicked him in the ribs as she walked past, and his body didn't yield at all. He might have been made of oak.

It took Milly a second to think about what this might mean, and when she did she knelt down and turned Duane's body over. The gap between bed and wardrobe was narrow, but she managed it as much by force of will as anything else.

Duane's eyes were open, lips drawn back. Milly sat down hard on the bed and tried not to cry, tried to think of what she ought to do, and failed in both efforts. All she could think of was how happy he looked. How much his expression was like gratitude.

The End

Matt Baxter is a chef who occasionally runs an online bookshop, and he lives somewhere in England. This is his first published short story.

Green and Grotesque

By Mike Berger

Green and grotesque; shutting my eyes,
I couldn't look. It's single red I had green
veins running through it. It's mouth was
an abyss punctuated with bright yellow
fangs.

Trembling, fearing that I was its next
meal, I watched it slowly advance. The
creature slowly oozed its way along.
A shudder ripped down my spine. The
rotten egg stench made my stomach
do flip-flops.

Eye to eyes the thing stared. Frozen
in my tracks, I couldn't run. It's mouth
gaped open; my knees turned to Jell-O.
It spoke in a high monotone, mechanical
voice, "I am in the mood for some curry,
is there a Thai restaurant nearby?"

Mike Berger, PhD is
bright, articulate,
handsome, and
extremely humble

ARC

By Derek Muk

Jan kept staring at the block of ice. "That thing gives me the creeps."

Albert Taylor studied the cave man encased in the ice, a look of fascination on his face. He felt like a kid in a candy store. The cave man was of average height and stocky, and had dark, shaggy hair, wearing nothing but a piece of animal fur around his genitals and buttocks. Frozen in its hand was a lethal looking club that looked like it could do some serious damage like crush someone's skull.

"If you keep thinking like that you're not going to learn anything," Taylor replied. "Don't be so negative. You still want to be an anthropologist, don't you?"

"Of course."

"Well, one of the key qualities of an anthropologist is open-mindedness, the ability to accept different viewpoints and ideas, and also to be inquisitive and curious about the world. They're ravenous for knowledge and love learning. Most of them would be jumping up and down at a find like this."

She nodded. "You're right. I should be grateful I'm in this program considering how hard it was to get in. But what do I know? I'm just a lowly teaching assistant slash grad student."

He turned to her and smiled. "You're not *lowly* to me. C'mon, just be positive, Jan, and everything will just fall into place. You'll see. Good vibes go a long way, trust me." He turned back to the cave man. "Besides, look at this guy! He's living history! How often does a fully intact artifact like this pop up?"

"Don't forget that mammoth you and Professor Reynolds found," Jan interjected.

"Yeah, but that wasn't nearly as intact as this. Plus, this man has been preserved in ice."

Her eyes widened. "Meaning he could be resurrected?"

"I'm not saying anything just yet but I'm not discounting that theory, either. Remember, I'm an anthropologist and I have-"

"An open mind," she finished for him, grinning. She was a young, slender woman with shoulder length red hair.

He smiled. "You got an A for today's lesson." Taylor studied the cave man some more. He was a tall, lanky man in his early fifties with long dark sideburns and narrow, slanted eyes. "Several years ago a colleague of mine at Harvard returned from the Arctic, where this fellow primitive man was discovered, with seeds he had unearthed there. Interestingly, he played around with them and they grew to be a type of vegetable that's never been seen before. He figured the seeds were millions of years old."

"Wow. Is that how old this guy is?"

Taylor nodded. "Give or take hundreds, if not thousand of years." He adjusted the controls of the tank that held the block of ice.

"What are you going to do with him?" she asked curiously.

"Well, there will be the perfunctory scientific tests and analysis, and of course there's the new exhibit on prehistoric peoples.

In my opening speech I'm going to mention old Arc here," he said proudly.

"Arc?"

"That's the name I gave him." When she looked at him quizzically, he continued: "It's short for Arctic."

# # #

Over the next few days preparations continued for the gala opening of the exhibit on Saturday. Taylor, Jan, and museum employees placed the final finishing touches the day before. When the big day finally arrived Taylor stood behind a podium in front of a large audience in the campus museum's auditorium.

He smiled at the crowd. "Ladies and gentlemen, thanks very much for coming. You lucky folks will be the first to see and experience the Prehistoric Peoples exhibit. And believe me; you're in for a real treat. A lot of exhibits have focused on dinosaurs and Stone Age animals but very few concentrated exclusively on early humans. Who were these people? What were they like? What did they eat? Wear? How did they behave and think? What were their customs and traditions? What happened to them? This exhibit addresses all those questions. Later, I'll talk about my latest discovery, aptly named Arc. So now, without further ado, let me show you folks some slides." He looked at Jan, sitting in the middle aisle behind a laptop. "Jan, could you turn off the lights and begin the show? Thanks."

# # #

The security guard made his usual rounds in the anthropology building, checking to make sure all the doors were locked and all the lights were off. When he reached Professor Taylor's laboratory he saw that the door was ajar and the lights were still on inside. He went inside but didn't find anyone except a primitive looking man being held inside a tank-like container. The guard didn't see that the ice was melting, nor did he see the water leaking from the tank. He simply did his duty: turning off the lights and locking the door.

# # #

On Tuesday, Taylor returned to his lab to find the cave man gone. The tank's door was ajar and the interior was wet and smelled of mildew. He checked the tank's control panel and noticed that someone had defrosted the block of ice. *But who? And why?* He was certain that when he left here last week all the controls were normal. Frowning, he examined the laboratory's door and lock and saw scrape marks on the keyhole and the door handle. He called security. Moments later, the same guard came.

"No one broke in?" Taylor asked.

"No, sir. However, the door was open a little."

"I'm positive I locked the door when I left."

"Are you the only one that has a key?"

"Yes."

"Perhaps someone else has one, too, sir."

But who?

"Who would want to steal a cave man?" Jan asked.

Taylor wished she wasn't so naïve but she was a student, after all. "Treasure collectors, hunters, jealous professors and scientists who wished they could've discovered something like Arc, black market dealers, the list goes on." He frowned, seething inside. "Whoever did this I'm gonna bury them."

"Now, now, Professor, calm down. You don't want to do anything rash. You've got your career, your tenure ship, your lengthy body of academic journals and work, all your degrees, your wife and children."

"I'm not married and I don't have kids."

"Oh, sorry," Jan said, embarrassed. "If you need to talk to someone, you can talk to me."

He didn't look at her. "Thanks. . . I should've gone to the lab over the weekend and checked on Arc but I was swamped with the new exhibit, opening weekend and all. You know. You saw how busy I was, people were following me everywhere asking questions like they were my groupies or something."

She chuckled. "Yes, I saw that. Hey, you're an important man, an expert in the field."

He sighed. "Yeah, yeah, yeah."

"So the police already talked to you?"

"Yes."

Jan's brow furrowed in thought. "Where would you take a million year old prehistoric cave man? Or where would he escape to?"

An imaginary light bulb popped above Taylor's head. "You think Arc left the lab on his own?"

"You implied that anything's possible."

He crossed his legs, thinking a moment. "Hmmm. Well, if I was a cave man I'd go to a cave or an underground chamber, or tunnel, away from people. Seeing the mass of people on the streets would probably startle him." He grabbed his corduroy blazer.

"C'mon, let's go."

# # #

He navigated himself through the unfamiliar terrain, this new, confusing landscape that he suddenly found himself in. Waves of nausea, dizziness, headaches, and body aches rippled through his body. On top of all that there was disorientation, puzzlement, and hunger. The latter was really a problem now. He hadn't eaten in a long time. It was time to hunt and he gripped his long club tightly. He staggered his way across the campus, the lawn's soft grass under his bare feet, steering away from groups of strange looking beings. They looked like him and yet looked different, too.

He took refuge in a small creek that was under the shelter of some trees. Walking along the creek he eventually reached a wooded area on the edge of the university. He embraced the silence, the solitude. Where were his fellow clan members? He did not see them. His hike through the forest brought him to a young couple who were necking and making out under a tree, oblivious that he was observing them. He watched in fascination as the woman kept sticking her tongue into the man's eager mouth, noticing the way the guy fondled her buttocks. Amazingly, their lips never separated. He wanted to keep looking but his ravenousness prompted him to action and he stepped forward, crushing a small twig with his foot.

The couple stopped kissing, turning in his direction. The woman gasped.

"Get the hell out of here!" the young man said.

He approached the couple slowly.

"Are you deaf?" the man said. "Go away or I'll kick your ass!"

"Let's go, Ronnie," the woman said, clutching his hand tight.

"Let me take care of this, babe," Ronnie replied, pushing her behind him. Ronnie stood his ground as he got closer.

But before Ronnie could even blink Arc swung that long, lethal club at him viciously, smashing young Ronnie's skull. The peaceful tranquility of the forest was shattered by the sound of bone being crushed. The woman screamed. Ronnie collapsed on the dirt like a sack of potatoes, blood pouring from his head. His eyelids fluttered quickly and his body started convulsing. The woman tried to intervene but Arc pounded his club on his face until it was unrecognizable. The woman continued screaming. Arc simply grabbed her by the arm so hard that it popped out of its socket. She cried in agony. To silence her he knocked her on the back of the head and she went limp immediately. Then he threw her across his big shoulder like a ragged doll and disappeared into the forest.

# # #

Taylor and Jan searched around Tilden Park, the Berkeley Hills, and some wooded areas on campus but didn't find Arc. It was sunset as they trudged down a grassy hill towards the university. Taylor closed his phone.

"What did the police say?" she asked.

"They've sent out search crews but no luck yet. It's going to be dark soon."

"So he'll be returning to his cave?"

"Most likely."

"Wait, this is crazy! So we're assuming he was revived and is lurking around out there. A million year old man, and boom, he's alive."

"Stranger things have happened. Remember those seeds I told you about."

Jan nodded. "I'm trying to keep an open mind about things but this idea just seems wild. You're sure you don't have any enemies that could've stolen Arc for their own twisted fantasies?"

"I wracked my brain but couldn't think of anyone. Are you hungry? All this running around has my stomach growling."

She chuckled. "Thought you'd never ask. Let's go to Fat Apples. My treat this time."

# # #

A few days later, Taylor was sitting in his office scanning the news headlines during his lunch break. An article about the discovery of a dismembered, half-eaten corpse caught his eye. The female victim was a student of the university but not one of his. A second body, that of a young man, had also been found. No witnesses, no leads yet. What piqued Taylor's interest was the fact that the police had found bare human footprints and animal fur near each body. He immediately thought of Arc for he was barefoot and thought about the animal fur he wore. Now call it coincidence or what have you but he couldn't stop thinking about the possible connection. It was a crazy theory but he decided to go with his instincts about this. If Arc was responsible for these grisly murders he had to be stopped.

A knock on his door brought him back to the present. He went to it and opened it. Standing there was a stocky twenty something woman with dyed purple hair and numerous tattoos. "Hi, Professor Taylor."

"Hello, Kim. Still have questions about the paper?"

She beamed at him. "You got it."

"Come in."

She sat down in a chair before his desk, taking out a notebook from her backpack. "Hey, I swung by the museum yesterday. The new exhibit rocks! I love the realistic, life-like figures of the early humans. My little brother and sister went with me and they really liked the interactive features, playing with each one, pressing every button, listening to all the audio."

Taylor smiled. "It wouldn't be a real exhibit without that. Glad they enjoyed it."

"Oooooooh, tell me about this cave man you dug up in the Arctic!" Kim said enthusiastically.

"Well. . ." he replied, stalling for words. "Well. . ."

# # #

He built a small fire in the cave, sitting next to it. The flickering orange flames created eerie shadows on the walls. Among other things, there was numerous graffiti. He studied the spray paint in fascination. None of it made any sense. He liked the colors, though. Trash was scattered everywhere. He sifted through empty potato chip bags, candy bar and gum wrappers, cigarette boxes, empty beer cans, and plastic bags. All of it puzzling to him. He sniffed them, licked them, twisted them, bent them, ripped them apart, rubbed them against his skin. He was in awe, trying to absorb and learn about this new world as much as he could. Perhaps he would understand things over time.

He heard a rustling sound outside the cave and spun around quickly, staring at the entrance. Nothing. Seconds later, something shuffled around in the cave. He grabbed his club, trying to find the origin of the noise. He pounded the club in a dark corner of the place, snatching a dead mouse up by its tail. He buried the animal in the dirt, covering the mound with a rock. Then he left the cave.

He walked through the forest. Moments later, he approached a two-lane road. Parked on the side of the road was a car with three people in it. Arc watched as two men pulled a young woman out of the back seat and dragged her, kicking and screaming, into the woods. One of them gagged her. Arc followed the three as they walked down the dirt trail. His facial expression grew hostile as he saw them going towards the cave. Following the trio silently, he observed as the men yanked the woman into the cavern. He saw one of the men; a tall, heavyset man with wispy dark hair and a goatee take the woman's jacket off as the other one held her. Before the goateed man could touch her slacks Arc entered the cave, his club clutched in his hand at the ready.

The men turned towards him, surprised. The woman looked astonished, too, but more out of relief than anything.

"Who the fuck are you?" the goateed man said.

When Arc remained silent, the other gentleman, a guy with a close cropped afro and a tear drop scar on his left cheek, said in a Caribbean accent, "You heard da man. Get the fuck out of here!"

Arc stared at the men challengingly.

"Ahh, so you wanna stare fight now, huh?" Goatee asked. Arc didn't respond. "Who is this joker? Look at the way he's dressed, like some savage."

"I'll take care of him," the man with the tear drop scar said. He approached Arc. "Go! You hear me? G-"

Before he could finish the word the club had already swung as fast as a baseball bat, striking him squarely in the face. They all heard something crack, specifically bone. Tear drop's eyes were as big as saucers, his jaw dropped wide open. He didn't even know what hit him. The next blow smashed him again in the face, and so did the next one and the next one, until rivers of blood flowed down his head. He crumpled to the ground.

His buddy, Goatee, couldn't believe what had just happened. He just stared at his fallen friend, at Arc, and back to his friend again. He was hoping to get some quick pussy and leave without any problems. Boy, was he so wrong! He held the woman in front of him like a shield.

"Step aside!" Goatee ordered.

Arc merely gazed at him and the woman. She was crying, trying to free herself from Goatee's grip.

When Arc didn't budge he moved forward, pushing the woman ahead. Suddenly, he shoved her hard towards Arc and tried to make a run for the cave entrance. Before he could reach it Arc jumped him and they landed on the dirt. They wrestled on the ground. The woman bolted out of the cave. Goatee was big and strong and it looked like he could easily beat Arc but he couldn't fight him off. Goatee reached into his pocket and took out a knife, hoping to end this fast. He should've prayed, it might've helped.

Arc knocked the knife out of his hand and grabbed his club. Before Goatee could get up Arc hammered the top of his skull with a crushing blow. And again, and again, and again, and again, until his bloody head rolled loosely on his neck.

# # #

The lecture had ended and afterwards there was a question and answer period. Taylor remained on the stage. He recognized quite a number of his students in the audience, including Jan. The rest were museum patrons.

A nerdy looking man in his early twenties with big glasses raised his hand.

"Yes, Roland."

"Is it true that early humans were omnivores?"

"Yes, that's correct," Taylor replied. "They ate berries, nuts, as well as meat."

"What about human meat?"

"I have read articles supporting that theory. If food was scarce or unobtainable cannibalism was an option."

Someone in the audience snickered.

An elderly woman sitting in the front row raised her hand.

Taylor nodded at her. "Yes, ma'am."

"Could they talk?"

"The brain capacity of the Neanderthal was similar to that of modern humans and a limited range of speech was possible. Earlier humans also showed indications of intelligence by way of the tools and clothing they made, by their customs and traditions, by the fact that they buried their dead. These same peoples were capable of some speech but it was probably not as advanced as that of the Neanderthal."

"Were they violent?" the elderly woman asked.

"Well, it was a volatile time they were living in and they had to survive. The world was constantly evolving. They had to defend themselves from predatory animals, not to mention each other at times. They had to defend their homes."

Kim raised her hand and he nodded at her. "Can you talk about the recent murders on campus? Rumor has it that a primitive, savage person committed them."

Taylor cleared his throat. "Uhhh, I do

not have any information on the subject." He looked at his watch. "Well, thanks very much for attending, folks."

#

"Did you see this?" Jan asked, bursting into the empty lecture hall, waving a newspaper in her hand.

Class had just ended and Taylor gathered his papers and folders and put them in his briefcase. "What is it?"

She ran down the stairs of the amphitheater-type room to where he stood on the stage, showing him the paper. On the front page was a headline that read: **'Remains of two more bodies could be the work of "savage throwback."'**

He scanned the article. "'Bare human footprints and traces of animal furs were found at the crime scene,'" he read aloud. "'Police also uncovered a campfire in the cave and grilled meat hanging over the fire. Police said the meat was human and had come from the two victims.'" He skipped down to another sentence and read: "'Primitive cave drawings depicting humans hunting animals were on the wall.'"

Jan frowned. "What are we dealing with here, Professor?"

Taylor thought for a moment and then said, "C'mon!"

#

After Taylor explained to the homicide detective in charge of the investigation what his theory was the detective looked at him impassively. Taylor thought he might explode into laughter or something but he didn't.

"Look, Detective Kwan, I know it sounds crazy but please trust me on this one," Taylor continued. "I've studied primordial humans for a long time and know how they think, how they act. Please let me assist you with this investigation. I don't think you're looking in the right places for this man."

"Where should we be looking?"

"In caves, in tunnels, underground dwellings, away from crowded urban areas."

Detective Kwan considered this for a moment, tenting his fingers together calmly. "There's someone I'd like you to talk to. Come with me please," he said, leading Taylor and Jan to an interrogation room down the hall.

Sitting alone at a table was a young woman with bruises on her face. She looked sad and tired.

After Detective Kwan closed the door he said to the woman, "Alice, this is Professor Taylor and his assistant, Jan. Can you describe to them the individual you saw in the cave?"

The detective, Taylor, and Jan sat around the table.

Alice dried her eyes with some tissue, looking at them hesitantly. "Well, he wasn't wearing anything except for a piece of animal hide around the lower part of his body. . .he looked, looked kinda. . .kinda like one of those indigenous Indians down in the Amazon rainforest but not exactly like that. . .he, he, uhhh. . .he was more like a. . ." She trailed off, not being able to find the exact word.

"Cave man," Taylor finished for her.

Alice nodded slowly, drying her eyes. "Yeah, cave man like from the dinosaur era. . . and he had this long club. . . he bludgeoned those guys to death with it. I'm grateful to this man because he saved me."

Taylor nodded. "Did he say

anything during this incident?"

Alice shook her head.

"Is there anything else that stuck out in your mind about this man?"

She looked away, licking her bruised lips. "Can't think of anything more. . . I'm just thankful that he saved me. When you find him I want to thank him personally."

# # #

Taylor and Jan went to the cave crime scene with Detective Kwan. The Professor studied the primitive drawings on the wall. It showed humans hunting the wooly mammoth.

Jan covered her nose and mouth. "Oh, God, what's that smell?"

Taylor squatted down in front of the extinguished campfire, seeing bits and pieces of blackened meat in the pile.

"Hey, check this out," Jan said.

He walked over to where she was and saw footprints in the dirt. They appeared to be about the size of an average human foot.

"Where are you, Arc?" Taylor asked quietly.

# # #

Taylor strolled through the university museum, looking at the various artifacts on display. Even though he had seen them a lot he tried to view them with a fresh, objective eye as if he were a first time visitor. He stopped before one of the centerpiece dioramas of the exhibit, a large reconstructed cave with a family of early humans. The life-sized, life-like figures were skillfully crafted and created and appeared very realistic. The period detail had also been captured pretty well, Taylor thought, looking at the draw-ings on the cave wall as well as the clothing, the tools, and down to the condition of the family's teeth, fingernails, and toenails.

The males squatted over the bloody carcass of an animal, preparing to butcher it with some knives made of stone. The females were sitting on the ground, stretching out animal hides that would be made into clothing.

Taylor moved on to another diorama. This one had cave men figures holding spears, hunting a mammoth in the snow. He went further on, stopping in front of a complete skeleton of a Cro-Magnon man. Next to it was the skull of a homo erectus human.

Suddenly, someone tapped Taylor on the shoulder and he spun around.

Jan stood there, smiling. "Can I join you?"

"Don't do that again! You scared me. Sure, tag along. You know, I'm really amazed by our exhibit."

Seconds later, a man wearing a Cal sweatshirt approached them with a book and a pen in his hand. "Professor, could you autograph this book?"

He eyed the cave man book he wrote, grinning proudly. "Nice to know there are still copies floating around out there, Brian," he said, signing the book.

"Yeah, thanks to eBay," Brian replied.

Taylor laughed. He and Jan walked on. To their left some children were pressing buttons at an interactive booth where they could listen to Stone Age humans 'talk' and explain to them what a typical day in their life was like.

"Wow, you're famous," Jan remarked. "I'm honored to be in the presence of a celebrity."

"Oh, hush. Don't tell me you're jealous. Oh, by the way, remember the cops dusted my lab and the door? Well, turns out the only fingerprints they found were mine and some other ones they couldn't identify. I think whoever broke in used gloves."

Her brow furrowed. "Hmmm. Who could it be?"

# # #

He had to move on. His home, the cave, had been boarded up and sealed with yellow police tape. He had pounded the wooden board angrily but it wouldn't budge. So he stormed off, hiking through the woods for miles. The sunlight felt nice and warm on his face. He stopped for a moment, marveling at a large bird flying in the air. Further on, he saw a squirrel and tried to catch it but it raced up a tree.

Soon he approached the end of the forest. Strange, shiny machines cruised up and down the road before him. He looked at them curiously and when he got too close to one a loud noise emanated from it.

"Get outta the way, dipshit!" someone said from one of the machines.

He gazed at them with hostility, making a low, growling sound, raising his club. When another shiny machine came by the loud noise was repeated.

"Look out, you idiot!" a woman said.

He swung his club at the machine but missed. Another machine approached and he tried to hit it but missed again. He growled angrily, running across the road before other machines came. When he reached the other side he walked down a road with large dwellings on both side of it. Some as high as a tree. Humans standing outside these dwellings stared at him as he went by.

"Cover yourself up, mister!" an elderly man said. "There are children around."

He saw little humans throwing a round object to one another. One huddled behind his mother's skirt. Another said: "Hey, look it's a cave man!"

"Vince, get away from him!" a tall human said.

Arc kept walking, ignoring their stares. He kept going down a tree lined street that took him all the way to a busy thoroughfare with even bigger machines that were louder and faster. Humans backed away from him as he walked by. He reacted the same way, avoiding big groups of humans. He saw a sign outside an entrance, eyeing it with an innocent curiosity. What did it say? He ran down the stairs of this place. When he got to the bottom other humans were waiting on a platform as a long, large machine approached. The machine carried lots of humans, zooming off fast. Arc watched as it went away, looking at its bright lights.

He jumped down onto the tracks, walking along them towards the dark tunnel.

"Hey, you're gonna get killed, blood," a human said to him. "A train's coming."

Arc looked at him and kept going. A cool draft blew out of the tunnel, blowing his long, unkempt hair back. It felt good. The tracks were cold beneath his bare feet. Soon he was in the tunnel, his eyes adjusting to the darkness momentarily.

The nausea and body aches persisted but he kept moving forward. It would be okay. He would learn to adapt to this new world. But where was his clan? And the animals he once knew were all gone.

He hid in the cool comfort of the tunnel, away from the bizarre humans and their unusual ways.

# # #

Taylor and Jan followed Detective Kwan down into the BART station.

"We have eyewitnesses reporting that they sighted this man in the train tunnel," Kwan said. "One person claimed that the suspect tried to stop the train, standing in front of it. We followed him into the tunnel but haven't been able to locate him."

"Did he hurt anyone?" Taylor asked.

"No."

They reached the platform and saw a train departing. Mobs of people had gotten off of it and were in their face now, trying to see what was going on at the opposite track. The police had cordoned off that track and directed the rubbernecks to exit the station.

Kwan led the Professor and Jan to the edge of the platform. "I'm going to have to ask you two to wait here," he said. "It's too dangerous."

"Oh, c'mon, Detective, we've gone this far," Taylor said. "I know what we're dealing with here. I've lectured, studied, wrote books on the subject, quizzed many students on this topic. You're gonna need me in there to communicate with him."

Kwan looked straight in his eyes. "Okay."

Taylor turned to Jan. "Stay here. I–"

"No way!" she protested. "I'm not going to miss seeing possibly the greatest anthropological discovery of the century. And one that came back to life!"

"All right. Stay behind me."

The trio went into the dark tunnel with some uniformed officers who had their guns drawn. Taylor felt a cool draft blow against his face. It felt refreshing. Millions of thoughts raced through his mind, the top one being the excitement he was trying to contain. He couldn't believe he might actually encounter a live prehistoric human. The prospect was both daunting and exhilarating. For someone that had slaved behind years of academic work, teaching, doing research, writing in journals, this was a dream come true. He felt like a kid again, as corny and cliché as that sounded. Some of his fellow colleagues at Berkeley and at other universities were probably jealous of his find, though he didn't know who offhand. Whoever it was they *may* have a key to his lab and they *may* have. . .no, no, no, he didn't want to go down that path, especially since he didn't have any substantial proof to back it. *Yet it still bugs me*, he thought. His mind turned to the fame and glory he'd get from this, the money, endorsements, financial backing for more projects and excavations, book and movie options, numerous talk show interviews, he'd be in the limelight for years. Not that he cared for it. Indeed, Taylor was definitely not a self-centered ego maniac, though some of his friends probably thought otherwise. No, he'd be in control and would handle things responsibly. Or would he? *Would fame change me?*

Another cool draft blew against his face, bringing him back to the present. His eyes had adjusted to the darkness of the tunnel.

"So where did you find this man?" Kwan whispered.

"In the Arctic. I led an archeological expedition there."

"What's it like out there?"

"Well, there's still a lot we don't know about the area, like what's out there, who or what lived there in the past, what could be buried there. A lot of research is being conducted, however."

The group continued walking down the tunnel, not seeing anybody. They heard a train pulling into the station in the other tunnel, in the opposite direction. About ten minutes later, Jan whispered to Taylor and Kwan, "There's someone dead ahead, to our left."

Taylor squinted his eyes in the darkness and was able to make out the shape of a person. Their physical features were as black as ink, however. "Good eyes, Jan," he whispered.

An eerie silence filled the tunnel. The person just stared at the approaching group.

"This is the Berkeley Police Department," Kwan said. "Step forward with your hands on your head."

The dark figure didn't move from his position near the wall.

"This is the police," Kwan repeated. "Step forward with your hands on your head."

An uneasy stillness hung in the air. That's when Kwan flicked on a powerful flashlight and pointed it ahead. The person put their arms before him, shielding himself from the light. Taylor saw Arc. In Arc's right hand was the long, deadly club. There was dried blood on it.

"Drop the weapon!" Kwan ordered.

"Let me work my magic," Taylor said.

"Go for it."

Taylor approached Arc slowly and cautiously. The cave man stared at him with dark, penetrating eyes, his club raised. Taylor looked at the club, keeping a safe distance between the two of them, and kept his hands up in the air. Taylor maintained a calm, harmless demeanor and Arc acknowledged this by lowering his club. Moments later, Taylor took a step forward and Arc did the same thing. Taylor mimicked throwing a weapon down on the ground, slowly and carefully, like he was teaching a child. Arc studied him but did not part ways with his precious club. Taylor repeated the gesture. After what seemed like an eternity, however, the cave man finally released the club and it landed on the ground with a thud, echoing throughout the tunnel.

Taylor pointed towards the opposite direction, to the station. He mimicked walking towards the station. Arc watched him and after a moment followed, like a dog following his master.

When a uniformed officer bent down to retrieve the club Arc turned around quickly, glaring at the officer and baring his sharp teeth. The officer tried to grab the weapon but Arc beat him to it, wielding the club proudly once more.

When the officer aimed his gun at Arc, Taylor screamed, "No!"

Arc swung his club at the officer's face, cracking his skull open. He then tried to hit the other officers and that's when they opened fire, bringing him down in a thunder of bullets that echoed loudly throughout the tunnel. Taylor watched in horror, his eyes wide open. Jan covered her ears with her hands.

Smoke blew in their faces. Taylor ran over to Arc's bullet-riddled body, kneeling down. Arc coughed up blood and appeared to want to say something, raising his head a little. Taylor leaned in close to listen but no words escaped the cave man's mouth. Only a sad, hopeful look remained on his face as he grabbed Taylor's hand. The last thing he did was squeeze the Professor's hand gently before he took his final breath. Then it was all over.

"Sorry," Kwan muttered behind Taylor's back.

The End

Derek Muk's short stories have appeared in various small press magazines. He's had chapbooks published and recently had a collection of horror/science fiction stories published called "The Occult Files of Albert Taylor".
http://theoccultfilesofalberttaylor.word-press.com/

Missing...Verne?

By Patrick Rutigliano

Please excuse my penmanship,
My hands are quite a mess.

I pulled them from the flames you see,
My dials and readouts in distress.

Eight days I labored in the dark,
My work a force of will.

You may see my lab's remains,
The foundation smolders still.

However, this tragedy is not the point of my concern.
I post this flyer only in hopes of finding Verne.

It is not an easy task,
Even I'm not sure as to which group he belongs.

He is surely not a canid beast,
His blue tongue a foot too long.

Nor is he a felid,
Although his eyes are slits.

I taught him how to "speak" and "stay,"
But he never quite got the knack of how to "sit."

Green scales coat his body,
And a spine or three.

Yet, I'm loathe to say, "reptilian,"
Coarse fur rests in-between.

Six limbs sprouted from his trunk,
Four of them are legs.

The other two are vestigial arms,
He uses them to beg.

Tentacles dot his stubby muzzle,
Their tips and bases red.

Of his stranger traits,
Are the spores they tend to shed.

He is a friendly beast, and will likely come when called,
Yet do not tempt him with toys or treats.

Especially a ball!

Patrick Rutigliano has two works to be published in Shroud Publishing's upcoming *The Terror of Miskatonic Falls* anthology and another work to be published in the upcoming Library of the Living Dead Press anthology, *Putrefied Poetry: Rotting Rhymes for Undead Times.*

Bertha's Place

By Christine Lucas

"Sarah, faster! Chewers!"

Sarah glanced over her shoulder at Josie, clenched her teeth and pedalled faster. Her muscles ached. She hadn't ridden a bike since her teens, and that was almost a decade ago. In the fading sunlight, shadows detached from the walls of the deserted town, shadows with human form: zombies, as bright and harmless as turnips. Where were their flesh-eating cousins Josie had just warned her about? She glanced around. And where was Josie? When she turned her gaze back ahead, it was too late to avoid the chewer.

Sarah screamed and slammed the brakes, trying to evade the filthy creature. Her bike's lights hit the chewer's face and it screeched, raising an arm to cover its eyes. A *severed* arm, cut from its unfortunate victim lying in a pool of blood. Sarah lost her balance and fell sideways, face to face with the dead woman's glassy stare. The chewer turned its opaque eyes on her, a wide snarl on its twisted face—too wide to be human. It picked at its chin and peeled off a shred of brownish flesh.

Sarah froze. Her throat, burning and dry, closed on her scream. *Damned virus.*

The chewer reached out to her, its outstretched hand twisted in an odd, talon-like shape. A wedding ring dangled from one misshapen finger. As if mesmerized, her eyes followed the ring. *The poor fucker was a human once. It had a name, a family, a life. Like everyone else. Like me. One of these days, I'll end up* *chewer food ...or one of them.*

Strength returned to her limbs and she kicked the dirt, pushing herself away from the vile hand. She sprang to her feet.

"No!" The scream finally left her throat. Somewhere at her right, she heard Josie scream as well.

She put all her strength in her kick. Bones cracked under her boot, but fractures had never stopped chewers before. That one lay on its back, its limbs twisted, a horrid gurgling sound coming from its throat. Sarah looked around for Josie, her heart racing. Where was her baby sister? They had come so far. She couldn't lose her now.

Damned car. If they had found fuel, they wouldn't have to continue on bikes.

Sarah scanned the area for Josie. At the end of the block, she finally located her sister's bike, lying on the ground, the front wheel bent. But where was she?

Another scream chilled Sarah's blood. All her instincts urged her to flee.

Drawing in a sharp breath, she tiptoed closer, each step slow and careful, her boots almost noiseless on the pavement. One glance around the corner and she wished she *had* fled.

Bloodied and limping, Josie swung a broken table leg at a chewer closing in on her. Her left arm hung limp at her side and blood dripped from a wound under her left breast. And—Oh God—was that a bite mark on her forearm?

"Sarah, run!" Despite her injuries,

Josie managed a blow to the creature. It whimpered and rubbed its torn mouth. "I'll stall it as long as I can!"

"I won't leave you!"

Sarah snatched pieces of broken cement and threw them at the creature. It turned around, its pus-crusted eyes fixed on her. It snarled, and a string of greenish drool dripped on its chin.

Josie kicked it behind its knee and sent it yelping on all fours. "I've been bitten! Run!"

Sarah weighed a rock on her hand, her eyes blurry. It *was* a bite mark. She had to run.

Josie is dead — worse than dead.

Her knuckles turned white around the rock. She spun around and started running uphill, away from the streetlight, the damned chewers and her lost sister. She ran until she could no longer hear the screams and the growls, neither the hellish slurping sounds. She ran until the desolate city was far behind her, until she tripped and fell face first on the moist ground. Her jaw hit a root and the coppery taste of blood filled her mouth. Her muscles ached, her lungs burned and her head throbbed so much her vision blurred. With the remnants of her courage, she rolled onto her back and lay still.

I'm all alone now.

At least her parents had been spared this. They had died several years ago in a car accident, and Josie had been her best friend and refuge during hard times. How would she live without her? A lump in her throat choked her, but the tears wouldn't flow.

The stars twinkled through the foliage. The scent of spring filled her nostrils. Only then did Sarah notice her surroundings. As if untouched by the Apocalypse, the forest burst with life. The mixed scents of pines, thyme and wild oregano soothed her burning lungs. The breeze cooled her sweaty skin. A lone nightingale joined the choir of crickets, and their nightly gossip eased the burden on her soul. She sat up.

Then she saw it.

Further uphill, a light flickered. The breeze carried a new scent, filling her heart with yearning. *Cinnamon and apples.*

Someone lived up there.

Sarah pulled herself up and started walking.

#

If there was a path to the house, Sarah didn't find it. She made her way through the forest, stumbling often. Twigs scratched her face, thorn bushes pricked her calves through her jeans, and a jolt of pain ran from her right foot up to her lower back at every step. Still, she held her head high and her gaze fixed on the twinkling light ahead. The common zombies couldn't start a fire or turn on a generator — they had forgotten how. Chewers couldn't care less — they ate perfectly well in the dark.

Someone else was alive up there.

She'd heard from other travellers that up north there were no zombies and a survivors' colony. Rumour had it that the virus could not survive in low temperatures, so she and Josie had started their journey, wherever the road would lead them — as long as it was cold.

Josie.

Fierce pain in her gut weakened her knees. She grasped a low branch to keep herself up.

I left her there.

Her baby sister was dead. Worse than dead, if she'd become one of them. If they

73

ever met again, Josie wouldn't recognise her. Only as a snack, if she had changed to one of *those*, depending on how her immune system reacted to the virus. But chewers were rare — she'd heard than only one in ten thousand bitten got the hunger. Sarah drew sharp, quick breaths. Each time she exhaled she forced out some of the pain. The core stayed though, a burning she couldn't fight away. But right now, she didn't need this extra weight.

She started counting steps to distract her mind. Fifty paces uphill, she reached a clearing. A cobblestone path led to a cottage house. A low fence, broken in places, circled a small yard and a vegetable garden. And right in front of her, in the middle of the yard, were clotheslines with laundry hung out to dry: an apron, towels and a tattered dress with a faded floral print.

Sarah had never expected to feel such joy from someone's laundry.

Shadows moved at the edge of her vision. She moved closer to the fence and then she saw them: at least four zombies loitered close to the forest. They swayed to the night breeze, almost like thin trees themselves, their forms lean, relaxed, peaceful. The skin at the back of her neck prickled and she hurried to the front door. The smell of apples and cinnamon filled her nostrils anew. She knocked on the door.

"Hello? Someone here?"

No answer. Terror gripped her heart. Was another zombie living here, her laundry forgotten, the apples and cinnamon just scattered on the floor? She knocked harder.

"Hello? Please?"

Footsteps behind the door brought tears to her eyes. The door was unlocked and opened just a crack. A short, old woman peered outside.

"Who's there?" The woman blinked, her brown eyes still holding the remnants of deep sleep.

"Please!" Sarah moved closer. "Please, I-I need shelter."

The old lady measured her from dishevelled hair to worn boots, her eyes more focused now. "Good heavens, girl, what happened to you?" She stepped back and opened the door wide. "Come in, dear."

Sarah stepped inside the house and back in time, it seemed. Nothing inside reflected the recent Apocalypse. The house smelled of apple pie on a cold winter morning, mingled with the definite whiff of feline urine. The furniture — old-fashioned, wooden, sturdy — was clear of dust and decorated with all sorts of embroidery. Countless portraits of all shapes and sizes hung on the walls. A thick-headed tabby cat trotted down the stairs, into the hallway and rubbed his ginger fur against her calves. A sudden sense of relaxation washed over her. Her vision blurred. Sarah grasped the armoire at her right to support herself.

The old woman bolted the door and rushed to help her. "My dear girl, you're exhausted! Come, sit down, and I'll make you some tea." She led Sarah to the living room.

"Thank you," Sarah managed to mutter as soon as she collapsed in a worn but comfortable armchair.

The old woman smiled. "Call me Bertha. I'll go make tea now. And don't mind Felix. You're sitting in his chair, but he could use the exercise."

"I'm Sarah. Thank you."

She relaxed deeper in the chair while Bertha shuffled off to the kitchen. Felix jumped on the coffee table and fixed his yellow eyes at her. Steady and unblinking, his gaze seemed to measure her. Despite her weariness and the recent horrors she had faced, the cat's insolent gaze made her skin crawl.

Determined to ignore the cat's attempt to stare her down, she glanced around. The furniture was as ugly and old-fashioned as those in the hall. Yet something was different here, something unsettling she could not pinpoint. Perhaps it was the collection of ancient Egyptian miniatures on the mantle, alabaster statues of creatures with animal heads: cats, dogs, birds, even a cow. Or perhaps it was the herbs hung to dry along the walls. Or perhaps it was just the abundance of cat fur on everything around her.

Another cat napped on a worn armchair across the room, her lean black form one with the chair's back. Her whiskers twitched and her paws trembled, as though she dreamt of hunting.

Bertha returned with a tray and shooed Felix off the table. "Don't mind them. It's a long time since we've had any visitors and they have forgotten their manners. Here." She handed Sarah a cup of steaming tea and a piece of apple pie.

Warm apple pie. The inside of Sarah's cheeks tingled from the sudden influx of saliva. When had she last tasted apple pie? *In another life.* With a hurried thanking nod, she stuffed her mouth, helping the pie down with gulps of tea.

Bertha settled in an armchair across the coffee table, and the two cats rushed to join her. Felix settled on the chair's back, behind Bertha's neck, his orange body posing as an oversized boa. The black one curled up on her lap.

"Th-thank you," Sarah muttered between gulps. "It's really good."

"You're welcome." Sadness coloured her voice. "When was the last time you had a decent meal?"

Sarah shrugged, wondering if it would be rude to ask for seconds. "I don't remember. Josie and I ate anything we found in the deserted stores on our way here. Mostly junk food."

"Josie?"

The pain returned in full force. "My sister."

"Where is Josie now?"

Sarah put her cup and plate down. She didn't care for seconds any more. "Lost. Or worse."

"Ah."

Sarah settled back in her chair, avoiding eye contact. "And how long have you been here?"

Bertha put her own cup down too. "I've always been here."

Sarah looked up. "But how do you get by? With the... situation outside and all?"

"We manage. More tea?"

"No, thanks." For the first time in days, Sarah felt warm—*safe.* Her eyelids grew heavy. She pointed at the single photograph atop the mantle, among the Egyptian miniatures. "Handsome young man, that policeman. A relative?"

"My son, Pete."

Sarah curled on the chair. "Could I just sit here a while, please?"

Bertha stroked the cat on her lap. "Of course, dear."

Sarah closed her eyes. Caught between the bitterness of loss and the warm sweetness of apple pie, she fell asleep.

# # #

In the weeks that followed, Sarah almost forgot her plans to go north, helping Bertha with the chores, feeding the chickens and tending to the garden. She stayed in Pete's vacant bedroom. The old woman didn't talk much about him. Apart from his name, she didn't find out much more. She suspected he had ended like Josie.

Bertha's place was a haven during this Apocalypse, a window into a world lost for good. There were often freshly-baked pies on the table along with warm bread and lemonade. The cats were plump and cuddly, their purr more comforting to her aching soul than any shrink could ever be. The zombies never came close, and she hadn't heard the chewers' shriek since that fateful night.

And still, something bothered her. Suspicion prickled the back of her mind every time Bertha produced another delicacy in the kitchen. Where did she find all those ingredients? The flour, the marmalade, the cans of *cat food*? Once, she asked Bertha about it.

"We manage." Bertha offered her a cryptic smile and a slice of pie.

Sarah took a bit. Lemon meringue pie—Josie's favourite. She almost choked on her mouthful, her throat closing on a sob. Tears flowed uncontrollably and Bertha reached out to her.

"I miss her! I miss her so much!" *My fault. I left her there.*

Bertha stroked her hair. "I know, dear." Pain stretched her voice. Sarah had no doubt that she did.

Sarah didn't cry again—only in her sleep. Almost two weeks after her arrival, she woke up in the middle of the night drenched in sweat. She sat up, her throat burning. Another dream of Josie, her cries for help still echoed inside her head. She reached for the glass of water at her nightstand when a strange smell filled her nostrils: something burning.

She sprang to her feet and rushed barefoot to the corridor. The smell was stron-

ger there—sweeter. Sarah stopped and blinked. *Burning incense?* Then she heard the eerie sound—chanting? Mystified, she grasped the railing and tiptoed down the stairs. Halfway down, she crouched on the worn carpet and dared a peek below.

Bertha knelt behind the coffee table, a tray of incense burning before her. She waved a big white feather over it, scattering the smoke. Felix sat atop the table, watching the thin column of smoke unfold, while Bertha spoke in a slow, monotonous voice.

"...gatekeeper

Of the eternal bars, now open quickly,

O thou Key-holder, guardian, Anubis." [1]

Wait. What? Had the old woman lost it? All alone up here, with only random zombies for company, it wouldn't take long.

"Send up to me the phantoms of the dead

Forthwith for service in this very hour." [1]

That's it. I'm leaving first thing in the morning. Sarah started to crawl back up as noiselessly as possible, when someone knocked on the front door. No, not a knock, but more of a bang, as though someone was pushing the wood.

Her skin prickled. She darted up the stairs and hid in the shadows. Crouching on the floor, Sarah craned her neck to watch. She flexed her muscles, ready to flee at the first sight of danger.

Bertha rushed to the door with Felix right behind her. "Welcome home, Pete." She held the door wide open.

Sarah gasped. A zombie stood at the door, in a tattered policeman's uniform. Although pale and emaciated, with sunken eyes and bluish lips, his face had a striking resem-

76

blance to the photograph on the mantle. In his hands he held a crate filled with supplies: flour, grains, cans of cat food, among other goods.

Felix rubbed his back against the zombie's legs, purring. Bertha brushed Peter's sallow cheek with her trembling hand.

"Good to see you again." Her voice faltered. She took the crate from him. "I'll see you next week. Okay, son?"

Had Peter understood? Sarah could not tell. He just groaned and turned around. She fled back to her bedroom before Bertha closed the door. Her heart raced.

That zombie cop still wore his handgun.

# # #

Sarah monitored Bertha's movements over the following days, keeping her face blank and her smile casual. She accepted the pie Bertha offered her, guilt and uneasiness mixed up in her heart. The old woman had been nothing but kind to her, but she could not shake off the creepiness of that night. There were no more rituals until a week later. Peter returned with another crate. This time, there was another zombie with him, carrying supplies as well.

While Bertha was busy with her turnip son and his companion, Sarah tiptoed to the kitchen and the back door. Keeping to the shadows and as close to the wall as possible, she made her way around the house and hid behind a barrel. Under the sickle moon, the figures of more zombies lined the edge of the forest, swaying back and forth like reeds in the breeze. Her heart clenched. Was Josie among them?

She willed her pain back and focused on the exchange at the front door. Bertha took the crates, thanked the zombies—much difference that would do—and went back inside. Pete and his companion turned slowly around and limped through the yard, their eyes vacant, their mouths hanging open.

Sarah measured the distance and checked the window by the door. No sign of Bertha. She sprang to her feet and raced to the two zombies. So close to them, she tasted bile, but forced herself to go on. When she unholstered Pete's gun, his step faltered for a moment. Her hand froze mid-air. Had he sensed the theft? Then he went on, as if nothing had happened. Some of her burden lifted off her shoulders and she hurried back inside.

When she'd have snatched enough supplies, she'd move on. The gun added to her confidence.

If only she knew how to use it.

# # #

She decided to wait until the full moon to leave, to save her flashlight's batteries. Hoping she wouldn't accidentally shoot herself, she kept picking on the gun, trying to figure it out. There was supposed to be a safety switch, and where did new bullets go in? Perhaps Pete carried extra ammo, and she'd check him when he came back. Two days before the full moon, he returned, and Sarah waited behind the barrel, with the hand tucked in her jeans' waist—just in case. This time, there were three of them, carrying goodies. She dared a peek. It was Pete, a redhead boy, and—

Those jeans, that blue jumper... *Josie?*

She collapsed behind the barrel, her legs too week to support her. Under the matted hair, the dried blood on her arms, the festering wound on her forearm, that was her baby sister. Her throat closed on a sob, and she hid her face in her palms. Josie, who loved lilies, dream catchers, and the sound of crystal chimes in the night breeze, was now nothing more than a drooling vegetable with blank eyes. Her mind was gone. Was her soul gone too?

How could Bertha handle this? Didn't her heart bleed each time she saw Pete like that?

A shriek at the edge of the forest chilled her blood. Her head snapped up.

Chewers.

She sprang to her feet, rushed to the back door and then to the front door through the kitchen, gun in hand. Bertha, deathly pale, stood frozen, holding a crate with supplies. She knew what the shriek meant.

"Bolt the door! Now!"

"Pete... I can't leave him to them." She stood by the door, between Sarah and her son, her knuckles white around the crate.

She waved the gun at her. "Do you want to join him? Or become chewer supper? Bolt the door, now!"

Bertha's lower lip trembled. Her gaze darted from Sarah to Pete and back. "Pete..."

Sarah sighed. "Okay." She grabbed Pete's arm and tried to pull him inside.

Pete didn't move. Something snapped—had she dislocated his shoulder or elbow? She dropped his arm. Outside, the chewers shrieked again. Cowering away from the door, Felix hissed, his amber eyes fixed on the moonlit yard and the creatures slouching closer.

"Please, Bertha." Her voice was kinder now. "Think of your cats. Do you want them to become chewer food too? Your son is gone." *So is Josie. I'm abandoning her. Again.*

Bertha drew in a sharp breath and dropped the crate to a corner, cans and packs

scattering all around. She tried to close the door, but Pete stood rooted on the threshold. Sarah joined her, sometimes pushing, sometimes pulling with all her strength, sweating and swearing through clenched teeth. Pete didn't move one step—only moaned. The chewers shrieked again, and Sarah felt light-headed. Big lug of a zombie cop blocked the entrance and would get them all killed.

The time for compassion was over. She stopped pushing, stepped back, and aimed the gun at his head.

Bertha gawked at her. "What are you doing?"

"Move aside!"

Bertha slid between gun and zombie, raising her arms. "No. You won't shoot Pete."

"He's already dead!" Bertha was much shorter than her son. With a bit of luck, the bullet would miss her. Sarah drew in a sharp breath and squeezed the trigger.

Click.

Click. Click. Click.

Nothing.

Sarah blinked. *What? Why?* The gun wasn't empty. Was the safety on? She lowered her arm and glanced at the damned gun. Sweat dripped in her eyes and she wiped her face with her sleeve. Why wouldn't it shoot? Was it broken? She flicked the safety, hoping that would fix the problem. She aimed it again at Pete's head just in time to see the chewer sneaking in behind him. A second chewer grabbed the redhead zombie and pulled it down. Josie and Pete stood still, oblivious to the danger. Bertha screamed, and retreated behind Sarah.

Sarah aimed the gun at the chewer and pulled the trigger. This time it discharged. The bullet scraped Pete's forearm and hit the chewer's torso.

The head, you idiot. Hit the head!

The chewer squealed and turned its malformed face to her. Its left eye hung loose from the socket, and green pus oozed down its cheek. It snarled and sniffed the air like a jackal. Pushing Pete away, it advanced, ignoring Pete, who fell down and just sat there. Apparently, it favoured non-zombie flesh more.

Fuck.

Sarah backed away, and fired the gun a second time. She hit the chewer's gut. Behind it, she caught a glimpse of the second one munching the redhead's forearm, the bone now exposed to the moonlight. Josie would be next. She clenched her teeth and fired a second time. And a third. And a fourth. One bullet broke the one-eyed chewer's collarbone. Another scraped its throat and ended in the doorframe. The fourth missed it completely and shattered a vase at its right.

Sarah backed away, cursing herself for not checking Pete for extra ammo when she snatched the gun. Close to the staircase, she tripped on a can and fell backwards. Her head crushed against the railing, her vision blurred and the gun slipped from her grip. She blinked, struggling to focus, only to meet the hungry snarl of the one-eyed chewer a few feet away. It licked its cracked lips, then grabbed her ankle.

"No!" Sarah tried to kick it with her other leg, her fingers searching for the gun. "Bertha! Help!" Where had the old woman gone? Had she fled, leaving her to deal with the chewers? *As I left Josie?*

The one-eyed chewer pulled her closer. Behind it, the other one slouched inside, holding a severed hand. Sarah kicked harder, aiming at her captor's good eye.

"Let me go!"

Felix leapt on the one-eyed chewer, hissing and scratching its head with all four sets of claws. Shreds of greyish flesh peeled off. It let her loose. Sarah kicked her way back, and finally got hold of the gun. She aimed it at the one-eyed chewer, but Felix was still firmly attached to its head. Blasting its head meant killing the cat too. Her fingers flexed around the handle, the trigger tingling her skin.

Josie loved cats. And Felix had come to her rescue. She couldn't just shoot him.

The one-eyed chewer grabbed Felix with both hands. More shreds of flesh peeled off from its forehead and cheek, hooked on the cat's claws. It tossed Felix aside. The cat crashed against the far wall. Whimpering, Felix crawled under the armoire. The chewer turned back to Sarah.

"Die, fucker!" She pulled the trigger.

Click.

"Oh, come on!"

Click. Click. Click.

Both chewers charged. She kept retreating. Her head throbbed, her ankle itched from its fetid grip, her vision was still blurry. She tried to pull herself up, to flee. They were faster.

That's it. I'm dead.

She kicked as hard as possible. Bones cracked under her boots, but that wouldn't stop them. She might as well give up.

"Let her go!" Bertha's voice halted their attack. Confused, Sarah gawked at the old woman, who stood at the living room entrance, with injured Felix cowering behind her. She had her arms crossed over her chest, her smudge feather in her right hand. Had she lost her mind? Why was she still there? Any sane person would have fled by now.

The chewers growled, undecided which one to get first. Bertha held out her feather, aiming it at them.

"Run out, thou who comest in darkness, who enterest in stealth, his nose behind him, his face turned backward, who loses that for which he came."[2]

Bertha's rumblings seemed to affect the chewers. They released Sarah, and she crawled up a few steps. The one-eyed chewer glanced around, scratching its arm. The other one turned to the door and started that way, then stopped and glanced up, at Sarah, with a hungry growl.

"... Comest thou to kiss this child? I will not let thee kiss him."[2]

A faint glow shrouded Bertha, and Felix didn't cower any more. He stood in front of her, his head held high, his eyes glowing. Still as one of Bertha's miniature statues atop the mantle, only the twitching tip of his tail around his forepaws showed some distress.

"... Comest thou to harm him? I will not let thee harm him."[2]

The feather glowed painfully white now. The chewers shrieked, not from hunger this time but from anguish. They crawled toward the door, but the light shrouded them in its merciless grip. They clutched their chests, as though they suffered heart attacks. Curled in a foetal position, they twitched and moaned.

"... Comest thou to take him away? I will not let thee take him away from me."[2]

Her voice was thunder, her feather was lightning. A blinding flash filled the room and Sarah hid her face in her palms. When she dared a glimpse between her fingers, nothing moved.

Pete and Josie were just outside, unharmed, slightly swaying in the night breeze. The remains of the third zombie were scattered all over the yard. The chewers lay dead, their hands still clutching their chests, black blood dripping from their ears and eyes.

Only Felix moved, paw after paw, belly close to the ground, sniffing the cadavers. And Bertha...

"Oh God, Bertha!"

The old woman had collapsed, panting, leaning against the doorframe, her feather, normal now, lying by her palm. Her face had taken an ashen shade.

Sarah ran to her. "I'll get you some water. Hang on, please?" *Oh, God, don't let her die! Please, don't!*

Bertha gripped her wrist and pulled her down beside her. "Too late... the price, paid." She coughed, and rosy froth coloured the corners of her mouth. "Keep my cats safe." Her nostrils flared, as she struggled for air. "Keep my ... boy safe." Her voice faltered, and she coughed up fresh blood. Her grip tightened. "In my dresser... a blue notebook... the rituals..."

"Hush." Sarah stroked Bertha's cheek. "You'll be all right."

The grip around her wrist loosened, and Bertha's hand fell aside, her eyes fixed on the moonlit yard aside. Sarah lowered her head and wept.

# # #

Sarah burned the chewers' remains and buried Bertha in the back yard, where wild chamomile and thyme grew in abundance. The freshly-dug soil became the cats' favourite place to nap and play, and Sarah joined them often. Sometimes, she thought she saw Josie among the zombies gathering at the edge of the forest. Once she had mastered Bertha's ritual, perhaps she'd see her again.

About a month later, she found Pete dead by his mother's grave, with Felix curled atop his chest, purring peacefully. Could

Pete have known? Their minds were gone, but were their souls gone too?

Sarah finished burying Pete and wiped her palm on the seat of her jeans. She smiled. Perhaps Josie wasn't completely lost.

In Bertha's place, wondrous things happened.

The End

1. The Greek Magical Papyri in Translation, Including the Demotic Spells: Including the Demonic Spells, by Hans Dieter Betz

2. P. Berlin 3027, ca. 16th century BCE, J. H. Breasted, Development of Religion and Thought in Ancient Egypt, p.291

Christine Lucas' work has appeared in *Andromeda Spaceways Inflight Magazine, Murky Depths, Aoife's Kiss* and the *Aether Age* (forthcoming) and *Footprints* anthologies from *Hadley Rille Books*, among other magazines. Her short story "Dominion" is included in Ellen Datlow's anthology "Tails of Wonder and the Imagination".

Zombie Romance

By Selena Martens

Your blood should be savored
As a miracle, your brain so fragile, so intricate
So many twining branches of thought and memory
Your intelligence is so attractive, delicious

And your pumping heart, so red and juicy
I want to pick apart every secret lust until
My fingers are coated and sticky with blood
My teeth go snap on the valves of love

I want to tear you open and examine every part
I can't see, dig my fingers into the mire
Of your innermost being
Till the ooze of your organs sluices over me

I'll gnaw at your bones like an overenthusiastic guardian angel,
Or a parasitic worm, entangling you in loving tendrils
Glorifying my obsession of every part of you
And I'll lick my lips—no one will ever love you more than this

Selena Martens is a library technician, living and working in Parry Sound, Ontario. This is her first published work.

Seduction

By Milan Smith

It started at midnight. We were on Bourbon Street and I saw his face in the crowd, his eyes on me as he followed. As we walked, neon lights flashed and music blared from the bars and strip clubs around us. I stopped from time to time to watch women on second floor balconies throw beads to men on the street, and once someone fell against me while scrambling for a trinket. Whenever I looked back I'd see him smile, still there, still close. Sometimes someone walked between us, hiding him, and he'd be gone when the crowd moved past. Looking around I'd see him on the other side of the street, watching, and I'd walk on.

The night air was so heavy and hot that I almost stopped for a drink. But, it wouldn't be long now, and wanting it done with I went on, threading my way through the tourists that wandered up and down the street.

I'd moved to New Orleans two months before, and saw him the night I'd arrived. He was dark-haired and tall, looked 30, but I knew he was older. He'd stood on the highway just outside the city and watched me pass. I had only a glimpse of him then, but I saw him many times after. There was no pattern to it, to my seeing him. Whenever I sat in a restaurant, he'd walk past and stop and stare at me through the window, then leave before I could reach the door. Every time I went downtown I saw him in the crowd somewhere, just watching. Or he'd stare at me from the roadside in odd places, even late at night on dark corners. But, tonight he stayed in sight—except for that little game of moving from place-to-place in the crowd—and I'd expected that, since tonight it would happen, whatever was supposed to happen.

As I moved farther down the street, the crowd thinned out and the lights grew dim. I turned down a side street and left the tourists and their chatter behind. Far down the road I saw the light of a restaurant, but I stopped in the shadows where the smell of stale beer and vomit rose up from the gutter. I looked back and saw him standing 30 yards away. I looked around once more, to make sure this was the place, but it didn't matter, because now he stood only a few feet away. Startled, I stumbled back. He looked from one end of the street to the other, then nodded.

"A good place to meet," he said. "Quiet, out of sight."

"I thought it'd be best that way."

"That's considerate of you."

I said nothing; I decided to wait for him to start this. I watched him light a cigarette and blow out the smoke while he stared down the street. Then he turned to me and held out the pack. I waved it away, and said, "Vampires smoke?"

He smiled and looked towards the restaurant down the road. "Bad habit from my youth. I still can't lose it." I saw him run the tip of his tongue over his teeth, lingering over one of them, then he took another drag. "So you know who I am?"

"Yes."

"And you're not afraid?"

"Should I be?"

"Yes," he said. Then, "No. Not really, there's nothing to be afraid of. I wouldn't hurt you."

"Wouldn't hurt me? A painless death?"

"A kiss really. A prick on the skin, like a lover's touch."

My heart beat faster now.

"But you knew about me," he said, "and you knew I'd come for you."

"Yes."

"How?"

"My sister told me."

"Is she one of us?"

"No," I said, "she's a witch."

He nodded. "Does she throw spells? Read palms?"

"She can 'see' she was born with it. It's always been in our family, more or less, on the female side. More than her mother, less than her grandmother."

"And she told you I'd come?"

"Yes. She said when and what you looked like, and even your name."

"Which is?"

"Jakob."

He looked at me again, and stepped closer. "Jakob. Yes, I haven't used that name for a long time. I've often changed it—it makes it easier to disappear. But, yes, Jakob was my name given."

As he leaned towards me I stepped back, until I touched the wall behind. "What's your sister's name?" he asked. I didn't answer, and he smiled. "Don't worry, I wouldn't hurt her."

"It's not that, that doesn't matter. She's dead."

"Oh?"

"She killed herself."

He turned away again, and stared down at the road. "I'm sorry," he said.

"Thank you," I said. "I suppose I should thank you. For caring."

Jakob shook his head, but still looked away. "I'm not any different from you, Thomas; I'm more human than you think. I feel and hate and love just like you. I'm really no different at all; I simply have a sweet tooth that prefers blood sugar to table sugar."

"It's hard to see it that way."

"Even after talking to your sister?"

"Yes."

"What else did she tell you?"

"That you can't hurt me unless I want you to. Or kill me, unless I want to die."

"And you do."

"No. I don't."

"Yes. I smelled it on you. When you first came to the city, Thomas, I could smell it on you. Young healthy flesh that wanted to die, that hated the living around him. That's why I followed you. You knew I was there, didn't you?"

"Yes, I saw you. You wanted me to."

"Yes, I did." Jakob looked up into the sky and watched the stars. He pointed to them. "Do you realize that those are the same stars, more or less, that Odysseus sailed by 5,000 years ago? They're still there, and will be after we're gone, even after the next Odysseus sails to them across the heavens. After all people are gone. What is living but a chance to see the stars and then go away?"

I shook my head, I didn't understand. "What I mean," Jakob said, "is that life isn't so wonderful, we're here and then we're not, and none of it ever really matters."

"Not to you."

"Or to you. I've watched you. I've

smelled you. You live out of habit, from the thought that dying is wrong, but you don't know why. You want to die, but can't do it, can't kill yourself. You're sick of life, aren't you?"

"No." But, yes. My fiancé had killed me, had cut up my insides when she left me. Left me for my best friend since high school, the worst of all endings. She left and when she did she didn't say goodbye or even tell me why, she left a note on the table, took her things and moved away. She'd quit her job without telling me and moved away – with him – and all I had after three years was that note. And the ring, she left that.

"You stink like rotted meat," Jakob said. "You're already dead. All you have to do is say it, and it'll come."

"So kill me. If I want to die, it should be easy. I won't fight you."

Jakob shook his head. "You know I can't. You have to ask me."

"Kill me."

"You have to mean it."

"You said I wanted to die."

"But, you're holding on. Let it go, let go and I'll take care of you."

There were times I'd considered letting go. I've been letting go a little each day. Nothing mattered once she left me. My job didn't, so I lost it. Then my sister killed herself. My parents had died years before, so I had nothing left and it was then I first thought about it. That is, following them. It would have been easy, I thought, and I even planned it out. But, I couldn't do it, not quite. And so I came here, to New Orleans. But for what? I came to the city I'd loved since a child, hoping it would be better. But every day I still thought about her, my ex-fiancé, and the knife would twist. Then I'd think about how I knew nothing of what she did,

where she was, where she worked, was she happy or sad. She'd just dropped from my life, no goodbyes, no explanations, and so the knife twisted again. It didn't seem to get better, even seven months later. But, I was told that living was better than dying, and with that prejudice I've held on, even as I'd lost my job and gained weight and lost touch with my friends.

"I want to live," I said.

"Why?"

"I have something to live for."

"What?"

I didn't answer.

"It's painless," Jakob said. "You'll fall asleep and it'll be over. No messy gunshot wounds, no overdoses which usually fail. And no guilt, because I'll do the — dirty work. It's always easier if someone does it for you."

"You must like killing people," I said.

"Like it?" Jakob said. "Like it? No. No, killing gets old. So tiring. But, you get hungry and you have to find someone, someone willing, and it's not so easy. People like you aren't on a shelf somewhere."

"How many people have you killed?"

He sighed. "It's been a long time since I wondered that. A very long time. I would think 50 a year, for 130 years. You figure it out, 5000, maybe 6,000?"

"One a week?"

"Yes."

"And the others? The ones you've killed. How'd they — how was it for them?"

He looked at me. "They let it happen," he said. "Some struggled with it. With themselves, I mean, but they were all happy in the end. I like that part, that they were happy. They were unhappy before. It's not so hard."

I thought about it. Just cock my head

and feel his lips on my skin, and I'd fall asleep. It wouldn't be hard. And dying can't be so bad, my sister did it. We never knew why, she just did it, and she wouldn't have done it if it was so bad, I thought. She could see, after all, she'd know if it was bad, so why not follow her?

"I don't know," I said.

Jakob lit another cigarette and turned away from me. He stared into the sky and I watched his back. I looked around, to see if anyone saw us, but I saw no one except those on Bourbon Street, people who walked along drinks in hand, drunk and laughing and talking. Their voices carried over to us, a murmur. I noticed the heat again, and felt the sweat on my face.

"What don't you know?" Jakob said. He didn't turn around.

"I don't know anything," I said.

He stood still another moment, then said, "There's something I want you to see." He flicked away the cigarette and turned and walked towards me and reached out a hand. He moved so quick I couldn't stop him as he gripped my throat. I grabbed his forearm with both hands as his thumb and fingers dug into my neck, and I felt myself rise off the ground.

The building across the street shook and the sky dropped. Then I saw the rooftop of the building across the road. We were now on the ledge of the building I'd been leaning against. Jakob had somehow climbed a two-story brick wall while holding me with one hand.

He didn't stop, he now loped across the roof, my legs dragging as I watched the world recede before me, and he stepped on the far ledge, jumped and we floated through space, my legs drifting in the air. My insides rose inside me, and frightened I tried to scream, but his hand around my throat stopped me and all I could do was gurgle as we crossed through the air, a long strangled gurgle. Then we landed on the next building, and my feet banged on the roof, then dragged along as he ran to the far ledge.

Over and over we did this, crossing building after building in our journey over the Quarter—jump, float, land, run and jump, float, land, run—and I thinking it would never end. But at last we stopped, and his grip tightened as he leaned over a roof ledge, and as he strangled me I thought I'd die right there. I beat his arm, and he loosened his grip so I could breathe. Afraid to fight him, I lay quiet and waited, until he pulled me over and I hung in the air above the street.

This was Canal Street. It was empty but for a taxi that drove past and a few people that walked off in the distance. We moved a few feet down the face of the building, then Jakob jumped and I gurgle-screamed as the air whipped around us until we hit concrete. Then Jakob ran across the road, and I watched the Quarter disappear as my heels scraped the asphalt.

I saw a building appear on my left. It was a hotel, one of the many that choked downtown Canal Street, and I looked for a lighted window and a helpful face as we rushed by, but everything passed in a blur. Then we stopped.

Jakob turned toward the building, and I thought we were going through a door, a service entrance, but instead, I saw the ground leaving me. We were climbing again.

As we rose, I remembered that these hotels were tall, eight or 10 or 12 stories high, and with that thought I began to thrash, my legs kicked air and my hands beat his forearm. Jakob's fingers tightened around my throat, I felt his fingers and thumb dig into my neck, and I stopped. I gripped his forearm with my hands to keep from choking, but the rest of me hung limp.

Then we reached the top and Jakob pulled me over the ledge and dropped me to the roof. He now sat on the ledge, bent over, wheezing, and I lay on the concrete and felt my heart thump and my throat ache. When my heart slowed and I could breathe normally, I got to my knees, one hand on my neck, and I faced him.

"You crushed my throat," I said, rasping. "I'm lucky you didn't break my neck." Jakob looked over at me. "You said you'd never hurt me."

"Oh," Jakob said. "Well, I meant not much."

I shook my head, stood up, walked to the roof ledge and looked over and down at the road. It was dark and empty. To the left was Canal Street, and I watched a car drive along it. "I had to do it that way," Jakob said. "You might not have gone willingly, and I couldn't risk you fighting me. It was the best way."

I turned and sat on the ledge. I noticed a breeze and it felt cool in the hot and humid air. It was dark here, heavy shadows, but light from the moon and the lights of the city let me see well enough. I could see his face, at least. We sat for a long time, both of us still and silent, when I suddenly felt tired. "Why are we here?" I asked Jakob.

Jakob stepped on the ledge and looked down. Then he looked up again, at me. "Stand up here," he said. I did. Slowly. "Look down." I did. "Are you afraid?" As I peered down, I felt giddy, the sight sucked my breath away, but I wasn't as frightened as I thought I'd be. I didn't really care, actually. If I fell, then I'd be dead. A sudden gust

would solve my problems. I leaned forward, just to see.

"What are you thinking?" Jakob asked.

"I'm not afraid," I said. "Not much, anyway."

"Well."

"Well, what?"

"You're not afraid to die. So you must not care to live." I looked back down but didn't answer him.

We stood on the ledge for some time; I watched the street below, then stared across the buildings before me, a shadowy landscape that sparkled with lights.

"I so often feel like Sisyphus," Jakob said, "rolling the stone up the hill, almost reaching the top, almost, then having it roll back down and having to start over. That's what I go through every week. I usually succeed, but then I have to do it again, the stone always rolls back."

"You like your Greek myths."

"I was raised on them, all boys of my generation were. It was so driven into me that it's now second nature."

"And you're like Zeus, the all-powerful?"

"No Thomas, I'm more like Antaeus. The giant that was invincible when he touched the ground, but powerless when lifted off his feet. I have limits."

I nodded and said nothing more, and he too fell silent. As we stood, I almost forgot about Jakob, about why I was there, and my mind wandered back to my problems, my loneliness, the loss of everyone in my life. I wondered what I'd do tomorrow, what I'd think of this night, and how I could never tell anyone I'd met a vampire, and how that would make me feel more lonely than ever.

I barely noticed as Jakob lit another

cigarette, and as the red tip danced in the dark. "I wonder what your fiancé is doing now?" Jakob asked, and the knife thrust in again, cutting cutting cutting. I choked and bent over in a squat.

"How'd you know that?" I asked. "How'd you know about her?"

"The same way I knew your name. I listened. I followed you for a long time and I listened. I wonder who she's with right now. Is it still your old friend, or someone new?"

"Stop it, Jakob, stop it."

Jakob stopped. "I'm sorry, Thomas, I shouldn't have said that. I had no right to do it. This has to be your decision, whatever you do."

"Go to hell."

"Of course."

I stayed bent over for some time, ready to cry, almost ready to roll forward and to the ground below. I knew he watched me, not too closely, but I felt his eyes on me even as he stared at the road or up to the stars. I stood up, but I didn't look at him. I now hated him, hated him for doing that to me. Before he'd just offered me a way out, but now he pushed me. And he mentioned her and I hated him for that.

"Give me a cigarette," I said. He held it out and I shuffled along the ledge to take it. The breeze grew stronger and I had to lean close as he lit the cigarette, then I sucked deep and felt the smoke rush into my lungs, and I coughed.

Jakob laughed. "It's hard at first," he said, "but you get used to it."

I didn't answer; I just took another drag and another, and watched the burning end crawl towards the filter. When I finished, I threw the butt to the street and watched the red tip float down in the dark. I smiled.

I hated my ex-fiancé, I hated her for leaving me and most of all, for leaving the way she did, with no goodbye, just leaving an open wound in my chest and not caring that it'll never heal because of the way she left. And I hated Jakob for reminding me of her. And I hated my sister for killing herself and leaving me all alone in the world. And I hated myself for caring so much that it killed me, that all these people could hurt me and they did and none of them cared. "Give me another," I said. Jakob did, and we hunched close together to block the breeze.

The second cigarette didn't choke as badly, and I finished it quickly and I watched it sail into the darkness. And as I watched it fall, I decided that no one really cares about anyone else, not lovers, not family, and not this bloodsucker who pretended he wanted to help me help myself. I have no friends at all, no one does, we're all alone.

What a lonely place the world is.

Yes.

"Give me another," I said. Jakob did, and I turned to him and I watched the lighter flame up and I sucked in smoke. Then he closed the lighter with a snick, but this time I didn't turn away. Not this time.

The cigarette slipped from my fingers as I threw my arms around his waist and leaned back, which lifted him from the roof edge.

"Yes, Jakob," I said, as he grabbed my shoulders, "I want to die." And I stepped off the roof.

We dropped and tumbled and fell head first, and I felt the wind slap me as we rushed to the street. He looked down as we fell, my arms wrapped around him, and I heard his cry. A strange sound, I thought, and if my life achieved nothing else, at least I'd have heard a vampire scream. I didn't consider then how pointless that was, how little value that held, I only felt the satisfaction of knowing that he screamed because of me. Then he looked up, I saw his face, and I knew I was wrong. He didn't scream at all, he laughed. He laughed and I saw the joy in his eyes before he looked down and threw out his hands and clutched for the ground that came for us. And he laughed as we hit.

＃＃＃

We were a mess. Jakob was pulp, and died on impact. I should have died; they don't know why I didn't, although landing on Jakob possibly helped. My legs and arms and back were broken, my skull fractured, spleen ruptured, and one of his ribs snapped and drove itself into my lung. They had a hard time separating us.

The physical therapy has been intense. It's taken me months to get one arm working well enough to write this. I'll never be what I was before, but they say I'll be able to walk again and get around, although I may have a limp, and probably will have arthritis in a few years. But I did survive, I will not die, and I will walk out of here.

I've had months to think through everything—there was little else I could do anyway—and whatever else has happened to me in the past is now in the past. I don't know what's in my future, but I no longer want to die. I think Jakob wanted to die more than I did, and he succeeded. But for me, whatever desire I had was lost in the fall, it slipped away like old memories, barely missed and almost forgotten. I died in the fall and was reborn. And that, I suppose, I owe to Jakob.

The End

Milan Smith has published 35 short stories in various magazines, including *Horror House, Niteblade, Midnight Times,* and *Crimson Highway.* After he got his B.S. degree in Business from the University of Florida, he worked in the business world for two years and hated it. Then he got job as a reporter for a year and hated that. Finally, he decided to try writing and now works part-time at night and writes during the mornings and he loves it.

Wimpire

By Patricia La Barbera

I close my eyes tightly
when I bite someone's neck.
I find blood unsightly,
even a speck.

Other vampires grin
at my sad affliction.
I stay in my coffin
and rue my addiction.

Someday they'll acquit
when I win the bet
to gulp from a goblet
but just not yet.

Patricia La Barbera's publishing credits for poetry include *Fear and Trembling, House of Horror, SNM Horror Magazine, Flutter, Emerald Tales, BluePrint Review, Big Pulp, Everyday Weirdness,* and *Short, Fast, and Deadly*. She is the first place winner in the 2010 Connecticut Poetry Society competition.

Her publishing credits for prose include *Flash Me Magazine, With Painted Words,* and *69 Flavors of Paranoia*. Upcoming publishing credits include *Punkin House Digest* and two short stories in anthologies by *Static Movement*.

www.patricialabarbera.com

The Rock House

By Alice Kemp

"Do you think it's much further?" Sarah asked as she cast an anxious glance at the westering sun. She was beginning to think this whole camping trip was a bad idea.

"You worry too much," Jim answered. They had been married for less than 24 hours and already he was getting exasperated by her whining.

"Well I don't think it's a good idea to be caught out in these woods at night. And the sun's going down awfully fast."

He didn't bother to answer, just increased his pace a bit. She did have a point.

"Slow down! My legs aren't as long as yours."

Instead of slowing down, Jim came to a complete stop. "Well what do you want? You want to be out hiking in the dark or sitting by a nice warm campfire?"

"Well, sitting by a campfire, of course. What kind of a stupid question is that, anyway?"

"Then we're gonna have to speed up. So quit your whining and pick up the pace." He followed his own suggestion by setting out even faster than before. Right now he didn't care if he did leave her behind. The honeymoon was over before it had really started. The blonde-haired, blue-eyed couple that everyone thought went so well together were off to a rocky start.

While trying to keep up with her husband, Sarah's thoughts turned with increasing frequency to that nice Native American man she had met at the same party where she had met Jim. Only now she was beginning to think she had married the wrong man. Jim had been quite attentive to her, and the stories he related of his camping trips had sounded pretty romantic, at least while sitting on a sofa sipping a glass of wine.

But there was something in the depths of the young Indian's eyes that kept drawing her back to him. At least until he went off with another woman, one of Sarah's friends. That friend later told her what a wonderful lover he was. But Sarah was already engaged to Jim.

They trekked up another hill when Jim came to a stop again. "There, look there. That's the sign showing the way to the rock house."

"Thank God! I was really getting worried." She followed him up the little side trail. In another minute they reached their goal: a large rock house, or shallow cave, carved into the side of the cliff by erosion. It was easy to see that they weren't the first to use it for a campsite, by the looks of the old campfire rings already there.

The young woman's imagination easily pictured the way it might have been in the distant past: a young warrior with his new wife, cooking the rabbits he had shot with his bow and arrows while she seasoned the stew with fresh herbs she had picked nearby. But her reverie was unpleasantly interrupted by the sight of the graffiti that more recent campers had left on the cave walls.

Unburdened by imagination, Jim unstrapped his backpack and let it fall to the ground. He glanced around at his wife who seemed to be having trouble with hers. They were on this week-long camping trip at his insistence. Sarah had never shown much enthusiasm for outdoor activities, especially hiking and camping.

"Jim, can't you help me with this, please?"

"Christ, can't you even take off your backpack by yourself?" But he did go over to help her, since that was better than listening to her complaining about it. Then he glanced around at their site, noting with satisfaction the pile of dry wood and kindling already laid up for the next campers, namely them.

"Here, help me set up camp. I'll start a fire so you can cook up some supper. You do know how to cook, don't you?"

"Of course I can cook. I just never cooked over a fire before."

"You'll get the hang of it. Just don't burn my meal. I'll set the rest of our stuff out."

As they worked at their respective tasks, Sarah heard her husband chuckling to himself.

"What's so funny?"

"Oh, I was just thinking about that old man we met at the outdoor outfitters. Remember how he warned us against sleeping in this cave? Said a bad spirit named Okeena lived here and would cause trouble for us. I think the old man had a bad spirit in him, called Alzheimer's." He laughed out loud at his own joke.

"I don't know, Jim. He was a Native American and they know things we don't.

Besides you didn't have to be so rude to him."

"The only thing they know that I've seen is how to ruin a good camping trip." He looked up from where he was rolling out their sleeping bags and shouted up to the roof of their shelter. "You hear me, Okeena or whatever your name is? I ain't afraid of you or any other spirits. So come on and do your worst."

"Oh, you shouldn't have done that. What if the spirit heard you? It might make him mad. Oh, I don't think I'll be able to sleep tonight."

"That's okay, Sarah. We'll give that old spirit an eyeful tonight," he said while casting a lustful look in her direction.

His wife turned red but didn't say anything, busying herself with the meal instead. Finally it was ready and they sat on a handy log to eat. An owl hooted nearby, causing Sarah to press tightly against her husband.

"Now don't tell me you're afraid of a little owl? Stop being such a scaredy cat. Umm, you did pretty good for someone who never cooked over a fire before."

Sarah brightened up at that unexpected compliment. "I just had to keep a closer eye on the cooking than normal. Otherwise it wasn't that hard." She was grateful that there was something she could contribute. She wondered if Okeena had had a wife and if she cooked for him here. The old man had said that Okeena had been a lusty warrior and his spirit was said to seduce any women that slept in this cave. She wondered how the old man could know that. The thought of being seduced by a Native American spirit kind of excited her.

After cleaning up from the meal, they sat and stared into the flames for a while, not saying much, just letting themselves get hypnotized by the fire. Suddenly Sarah jerked upright.

"Did you hear that?"

"Now what? Are you gonna be scared by every little noise around here? Come on, I'm gettin' sleepy anyway, let's go to bed." He leered at her as he said it.

"I don't know if I can sleep."

"That's okay. I wasn't thinking of sleep just yet anyway. Come on, let me help you get undressed."

"Are you sure there's no one else around? I feel awfully exposed here."

"Don't worry, there's no one around but us." He fumbled at her shirt, tearing it in the process.

"Now just wait. I can get undressed by myself." Finally the two climbed naked into the combined sleeping bags. The thought of making love in a somewhat exposed rock house like this just aroused Jim that much more, while it had the opposite effect on Sarah who contributed little to their lovemaking. Jim didn't seem to care, or even notice as he finally finished and rolled off her. Curling up on his side, he quickly fell asleep.

Sleep did not come so easily to Sarah. She lay awake for a long time, trying to find a comfortable position on the hard ground while thinking back to the day that Jim had first suggested doing a camping trip for their honeymoon. It had sounded like fun at first, but the reality of the physical exertion involved and the flies that wouldn't leave her alone, combined with the lack of creature comforts she was used made her physically miserable. Now the discovery that her new husband was a lousy lover totally uninterested in satisfying her made her feel miserable emotionally and left her

wishing she hadn't agreed to this. And this was only the first day. There were six more to go. She didn't think she could take even one more day like this.

At last though, Sarah finally drifted off into an uneasy sleep. Strange creatures and Indian medicine men danced through her dreams. At some point she dreamed of seeing a misty figure just outside the range of light cast by the dying fire. Curiously she felt no fear, only curiosity. Somehow she didn't feel menaced by this strange apparition.

It had a vaguely human form which floated just off the ground. It seemed to beckon to her, so she crawled out of her bag, still naked without realizing it, and padded over to where the misty figure waited at the far end of the rock house. She noticed primitive paintings on the wall that she hadn't seen there earlier. The symbols drawn there were highly erotic. She felt lust rising within her, unbidden but not unwelcome.

As she got closer to the mist, she could see that it was really a young man, also naked except for a loincloth and beads. He was definitely a Native American who was quite handsome with his flashing eyes and well-developed form. It was obvious he has a rather large erection beneath his loincloth which further stirred the flames of her own lust.

The mist had completely dissipated now. The young Indian held his arms out to her and she gladly went to him. The thought of being unfaithful to her husband never even entered her dreaming mind. She felt as though she were under a spell, but a wonderful one. As she lay with her dream lover, she was overjoyed to discover how sensitive he was to her needs. He brought her to climax again and again, until she lay spent and panting on the ground beside him.

But he wasn't quite finished with her. Raising her up, he led her to a feast spread out on the ground. That hadn't been there before either, but Sarah didn't stop to question it. The food looked delicious and her lover, who had never uttered a sound, now urged her to partake of it. He chose a succulent-looking haunch of pig for her and placed it up to her mouth. Sarah bit into it and was amazed at how tender and juicy it was. She couldn't seem to get enough of it, as the juices ran down her chin and dripped on the ground.

At last Sarah could eat and drink no more. Sadly she watched her Indian lover dissolve again into mist and disappear into the night. This was truly the most vivid dream she'd ever had, and certainly the most erotic.

The sound of birds woke her. She lay there for a few minutes, savoring the peaceful morning air. Jim lay quietly beside her, so she gently climbed out of the bag to get washed up before he woke. Grabbing her bath things and some clothes, Sarah walked down to a nearby stream and managed to clean up thoroughly despite the iciness of the water. It was invigorating though and she felt refreshed and ready to face the new day. Sarah could still vividly remember the dream of her Indian lover and wondered if she would dream about him again. She fervently hoped so.

Walking back up to their campsite, she noticed her husband still lying in his sleeping bag, so she nudged him with her foot.

"Get up sleepyhead. I saved some soap for you." When he didn't respond, she reached down to shake him awake. His body flopped onto its back, revealing a sight that made her scream and scream again.

A small group of hikers getting an early start found her at the entrance to the rock house, squatting on the ground with a vacant look on her face. When she didn't respond to them, they went over to the campsite. What they discovered made one of them run the three miles to the nearest ranger station to get help.

Jim was still lying in his sleeping bag. His throat had been torn out and he had been partially eaten. A later examination at the local morgue showed the bite marks to be human.

Sarah was committed to a psychiatric hospital. Nine months later she gave birth to a black haired, dark eyed boy with a distinct Native American look. When his baby teeth came in, they were unusually sharp. After he reached the age of ten, he ran away from his foster family. Stories eventually trickled in of a feral boy running around naked in the area of Okeena's cave, biting campers in their sleep.

The End

Alice Kemp has been reading horror stories for a long time and decided to try her hand at crafting them. This is her first published work.

www.aakemp.com

94

Flesh Consumerism

By Kim Keith

Lifeblood is a battery
for re-animation; a tendon snapping
is nothing personal, just a craving
for what lies beyond fungus fingers
and hallowed ground beneath the nails.

BTU's spreading, from host
to the graven cold tongue
slathering a dilated eye
like a peeled grape, tender
yet firm enough to offer resistance
against incisors slicing the surface.
The after-death is a callous place:
feed or return to maggot food,

much like rungs clasped
by pink-skinned hands
that make for good leftovers,
microwaved or not.

Kim Keith's work has appeared or is forthcoming in *The Houston Literary Review, Barrier Islands Review, Mad Swirl, LUX Creative Review, The Shine Journal,* and *Short, Fast, and Deadly.*

Breathe In, Breathe Out

By M.J. Nicholls

Glasford wheezed into another summer; its inhabitants breathless in their dread. As the smog increased its density, the government cut inhalers for the 'useless' elements of society – those contributing little to the fight for preservation, using up valuable oxygen.

In a tenement in the Viscous Quarter, where the smog was dense in soot, one man opens his letter from the council. His inhalers are to be stopped, effective immediately.

Mimus put the inhaler to his ear. A sparse puff of gas settled inside the canister. There was still, at best, a good ten hours' air in there. He pressed his lips to the mouthpiece, savouring its cool salve. A quick prayer never hurt. *Come on God, pull yer finger out.* He pressed down on the canister, sucking the last half-lungful into his throat.

The oxygen tingled in his lungs, its menthol hum bringing instant relief. It broke through the build-up of soot, clearing fresh holes for easier respiration. He lay back on his bed in despair and delight, knowing this was his last puff, savouring the choke of freshness. All over the country, he pictured men like him who had fallen on hard times, struggling for air in their stuffy dens. Is that what the council wanted? To scare them into suffocation?

He couldn't afford to expend energy on bitterness. He was alone now, cast from the republic. So be it. Survival was the aim. The republic had freed him from their grasp, vetoing his death. He owed them nothing.

In ten hours' time he would be too weak to walk, so he hit the streets. Donning his time-worn breathing mask, he stepped into the smog.

The sun's heat collected in the cloud, the atmosphere like a furnace. Too hot to think, too hot to die. Shafts of sunlight poked through the clouds, dancing in fiery red crackles. The cloud levels were at stage five, meaning a person could spend up to an hour outside before needing a hit of their inhaler. Mimus had less time than he thought.

Tracing the street by the outline of the pavement, he headed to Merideth's. She had been his wife before the need for self-preservation had outgrown the need for love, and a mutual dependence living arrangement was no longer viable. She had shimmied up the social ladder to an apartment in the purified quadrant, where the smog clouds had been diluted. He knew the visit would be futile, but he might find an inhaler lying around somewhere. Or better still – he could steal her allotted inhaler. She probably had insurance, being rich. She'd get a replacement, maybe. What did it matter?

He fought through the stoory nimbuses, vanishing into the afternoon gloom. Cutting a swathe through a line of critical cases, queuing outside the pharmacy to renew their inhalers, he wondered if he could sneak inside or take someone's place. Two men lay slumped in the doorway, their coats ribboned with drool, taking pretend puffs from empty canisters. Another was on his knees attempting to siphon air from a crack in the door. One man in a haggard coat had carved a slit in his hand and tried sucking in air from under his skin. Their eyes were fierce, alert. They watched every move he made.

Fearing confrontation, he lost himself in the smog, creeping with stealth into the purified quadrant. Often he pretended to be a secret agent, weightless and soundless, passing through the soft fabric of space and time. Soon the clouds broke into smaller clumps and a gap opened between their hazy outlines. Buildings and lampposts began to take shape – their silhouettes opaque smudges in a black and white photograph.

Across a stretch of large apartment complexes, one or two windows had been washed from the inside. Their panes had already begun to cloud over, a light frosting of soot settling like stains on inside curtains. The high street came into focus. Mimus stood watching the shoppers scuttling in and out of boutiques for gas masks, overalls or lunch, bumping and snarfling past each other. They were too wretched to be insects.

Merideth's apartment complex loomed into view. Situated between the clear district, where three mountainous fans directed the smog down into the poor areas, the building's façade was as black as his own. Its only differences were the occasional clear windows, the chimney convertor (changing carbon to nitrogen) and the slightly wider apartments. Mimus feared that she was as poor as he was, that there would be nothing to steal.

The doorman seemed to have fallen asleep under his mask, so Mimus slipped past him and headed upstairs to Flat 14. The lifts required key code authorisation and he wasn't skilled enough to override their circuit boards. Pausing on the top step, he realised the doorman was a tramp – the stench from his coat too noxious to come from a civilian. He wondered whether it was worth searching his pockets, but didn't want to risk wasting oxygen on a brawl. One punch to the ribs was all it would take.

He ascended the stairs with slow steps, stopping at each floor to check his breathing. On the ninth floor, he felt his heart rate increase and took a longer break. He noticed the stairs were coated in dust – deadly to inhale. Keeping his head bent upwards, putting a crick in his neck, he arrived at last on the fifteenth floor. He pressed the buzzer to Merideth's flat. Catching her off guard, she opened the door without peeping first. He had planned nothing beforehand, so thinking quick, he lunged at her.

They fell with an exertive swoop to the floor. Mimus took in a great heave of smog air and released Merideth when the door swung shut. As she staggered to her feet, her breath intense, he removed his mask and called her name. She stopped en route to the telephone, keeping her back turned to him.

"Mimus. I told you not to come around here." She stopped to control her lungs, putting a hand to her chest and assessing her level of wheeziness. "I told you very clearly that you are a leech to me," she said. Mimus copied Merideth, taking in a reluctant breath. The fresh oxygen had worn off and the smog carbons were sealing his throat again.

"They've stopped my inhalers," he rasped.

"So what. None of my business. Get out before I call the police."

"I think it is your business. It's society's business."

"I'm calling the police."

Mimus found his feet and followed Merideth to the front room. He kicked the telephone from her hand. She shrieked, leaping back from the phone. Her heart rate rocketed.

"Mimus . . . don't do . . . anything violent. You know . . . we don't . . . have the oxygen for that," she said, shaken. He watched her chest heaving in rapid waves. It pleased him to see her suffer – watching the tightness build in her throat, her eyes searching the room for her inhaler.

"Do you still keep it in the toilet cistern?" he asked.

"No, don't you dare, you –"

He stomped into the bathroom (her flat was the same design as his own) and wrenched up the panel over the cistern. He retrieved her inhaler from its waterproof pouch while Merideth stood in horror at the door. She was no longer defiant – clasping the hem of her blouse and focusing on her breath. Trying to resist was too much of a risk. The wheeze was strengthening. Merideth was borderline asthmatic: more susceptible to suffocation and permitted a larger dose of oxygen.

"You know, I always envied your extra five puffs," Mimus said. "You fooled those clowns in the pharmacy, that's for sure."

"Please, Mimus, don't –"

She couldn't bear to say it, to even *think* that her last few precious puffs might be lost. She had three left. After this incident she would need to use one, maybe even two.

Mimus thought about the ensuing tussle if he tried to walk out with her inhaler. She would paw his face, grab his legs, pin him to the floor, and when they were down, she would call the police, who would give *her* an emergency hit, but leave him for dead. No. It wasn't worth the risk.

He pressed the inhaler into her trembling hand, noting the look of intractable hatred on her face. He almost missed it.

"You are an ugly cunt," he said. He slunk out the apartment. Merideth allowed herself a sigh of relief.

# # #

Slowly, with the slightest sense of urgency he was permitted, he walked to the business district. His daughter Sky, whom he hadn't spoken to since he punched her fiancé during the vows, was his last resort. She worked as a decision-maker for the republic, sealing fates like envelopes. If he scoured his recall, he could just about remember having the tiniest fondness for her, though nothing quite as impractical as love.

Sky was a child during the smog's formation, one of the first babies sealed in a ventilator until toddlerhood. Mimus remembered nights when he'd come back from the pub, wheezy and boozy, and suck with abandon from her oxygen pipe. It was bliss. Careless, sure – but bliss all the same. Often Merideth would rush her to the hospital in the middle of the night, her life hanging in the balance. That wasn't bliss. That was careless.

As a consequence of Mimus's air theft, she had grown up with a permanent rasp – the throaty husk of a lifelong smoker. Mimus knew his parenting skills had been weak, but what was he supposed to do? Few people stayed sane as the clouds blackened the sky, grounding life in darkness. It felt like the end, like doomsday stretched out over decades. An unending preview of the inevitable finale. No one expected to survive the natural duration of their lives, and most were disappointed when they did.

It wasn't an ideal time to drop in on Sky – the sting of the punch still felt between them – but she was often compassionate, albeit when backed into a corner. As the smog thickened, it was time for people to make decisions. This included dropping relatives or friends who might interfere with personal air provisions, as Merideth had done to Mimus. Sky knew early on Mimus was a drain on her air, and fled home at fifteen.

After a brisk hour's walk, he arrived at Sky's office block. It was only a few streets away, but he'd expended more energy than he realised tussling with Merideth. Smog enhaloed the grim peak of the structure, where two ornamental gargoyles gazed down over the city with knowing doom. This was the building where the decisions were made, where bastards in suits had voted to cut his inhalers in air-conditioned rooms.

Peering in through the Perspex window, he looked for a way in without being spotted by the receptionist or security guard. This was impossible, so he fixed his gaze on the fire alarm and strode inside. Tossing the fluff in his pocket onto the floor, he chased it along to the wall, where he stopped beneath the alarm. The guard and the receptionist were both staring at him, so he had to just go for it: he punched the glass with his fist.

The guard strode towards him, not wanting to waste oxygen on security protocol, and escorted him outside. As the workers evacuated into the car park, Mimus searched the masked faces for his daughter. Pushing through clumps of faceless bureaucrats, he located Sky amid a group of men with slicked-back hair. He opened his mouth to speak but nothing came out.

Eventually, Sky turned to meet her father. She stared at him, her expression unreadable beneath the mask. She wondered whether to blank him or acknowledge his existence. It was unlikely he would go away, so she excused herself from the huddle of colleagues and walked into a quiet corner. He trailed behind her, wiping the sweat from his brow.

"What are you doing here, Mimus?" she asked.

"Dropped the 'dad,' have we?"

"What the fuck do you want?"

"Look, you have to make a decision. They cut my inhalers. Your people cut 'em. If I don't get a hit in the next ten hours, I'm dead meat," he said.

"So? What do you want me to do about it?"

"Don't you care, Sky? I'll be *dead meat!*"

Sky stared at a squirrel inching up a tree. She was outraged that her father thought his paternal connection entitled him to instant compassion. The squirrel struggled up the bark, reluctant to increase its speed. It had to make a decision: to risk food over oxygen.

"Mimus . . . I know your inhalers were cut," she said.

"What?" Mimus stared at his daughter's lips. He was listening for the words he wanted to hear.

"I said, I know your inhalers were cut. I authorised their cessation."

"You what?"

"Mimus, you know you have nothing to contribute to the republic. You are, and have always been, a waste of oxygen."

"You mean . . . you'd leave me to *die,* you'd do that to your own father?"

"Mimus, you were never really a father, were you? You have always been a leech, to yourself and to everyone around you."

Mimus bristled with shame and rage, his left fist shaking. He wanted to punch her, but he couldn't waste the energy. He opened his mouth again to insult her, to leave as he had with Merideth a violent parting shot, but his mind was a drought of spite. Instead he let his arms hang limp, like a sullen child, then took leave of his broken daughter, the daughter he had broken. Were it not for the shared bloodline, they would be strangers.

# # #

He returned to the streets, inhaling an heroic gasp of smog. He was an outcast, a roach, a *leech*. Crouching down between two dustbins, he felt the tight rasp in his throat. The need to breathe was an overwhelming burden. He had to make a decision. If he could surrender his life, he would. The time had come. But he was too afraid of that final breath – his lungs sealing up at last, death moving in. If there was an easier way . . .

Drifting past shop fronts, he scrambled his mind for potential solutions. *Suck exhaust pipes. Tunnel underground. Steal air from a stranger's throat.* He stopped outside a retirement home. The structure had fallen into disrepair, its windows boarded and its walls graffitied. Inside, a spotty youth sat behind a counter reading escapist literature. An idea slithered into Mimus's mind.

He was forty-seven and he was dying. They were over seventy and they were dying. They had inhaled twenty-three years more oxygen than he had, so what right did they have to leech upon *his* rightful share? Creeping into the home's dim orange vestibule, he slid past the youth unseen and made his way along a damp corridor, surrounded by brown doors. He tried each knob in turn; all locked until he found the last door wide open.

Inside, an old man was asleep in an oversize rocking chair. On his bedside table,

illumined by an overhead light, was an inhaler. Mimus tip-toed into the room, taking each step in tandem with the man's strained breaths. His wheeze was strong and Mimus knew he would need a puff when he woke up. He thought of the old man reaching for his inhaler, the onslaught of terror when he saw it missing. Then . . . the slow encroachment of death. The old man would know how it felt to be a useless member of the republic, to have his lifeline snipped by a self-serving stranger. *Fuck 'im.*

Pocketing the inhaler – only three puffs left – he crept out the retirement home, sucking oxygen in the safety of the street. The air was euphoric, but it would only see him through the night. How could he expect to survive in the long-term if this was the best he could do? Maybe Merideth or Sky would take pity on him. *Not bloody likely.*

He returned to the retirement home the next day, having used up the last three puffs. Outside, he saw a body in a bag being placed into an ambulance with no sense of urgency. So . . . the first casualty. What did he care? He had given the old man freedom. He only wished he had the strength to check into the afterlife, to meet someone with the courtesy to put him out of his own misery. *Ta for the puffs, you old bugger.*

The front entrance was blocked by paramedics, those enviable bastards who had *permanent* access to inhalers, so he would have to find another way in. The dead man's room was vacant, so he wrenched the wooden panel and climbed in through the window. Checking first for any extra inhalers, he crept into the corridor, chancing upon another open door. The commotion of loss having distracted the old people, he nipped into as many rooms as he could, pocketing seven inhalers until a nurse came stalking down the corridor.

When she slipped into one of the rooms, he made his exit out the open window. His pockets were stuffed with unused inhalers, fat inhalers, extra-thick inhalers and standard inhalers. The loot would last him another month, tops. And it had been so easy. Could he spend his time simply stealing inhalers from the soon-to-die to prolong his own life?

You bet I can, heh-heh.

# # #

As he went about his life, conserving his oxygen, news circulated about the stealings. Five elderly people had perished as a result of his light fingers. He concealed the inhalers in the skirting beneath his bed, covering the hole with a papier-mâché mould. The skirting looked complete to the casual observer, though he wouldn't survive an apartment raid. Still, no one had seen him, his prints were undetectable – he had made it.

One night, a week after the theft, he thought he saw one of the elderly people sitting at the foot of his bed. He dismissed the sighting as Dickensian crap, but their shapes became more vivid, more real. In his dreams, he watched the elderly wake from their sleep, turn to take their inhalers, then panic . . . he saw their eyes frantic with despair as they struggled in the dark to breathe, to take in that precious oxygen, then . . .

In a world of perpetual night, when the smog rarely permitted even a sliver of sunlight, the visions had space to roam, far from the cavern of his dreams. Alone in his hideout, safe from the police, the republic, the *leeches*, his conscience became a reposi-

tory for the horrors of the dead.

Spectres rose from the foot of his bed, their faces knotted in anguish. Slowly, taking great care not to strain their backs, they fell to their knees and lurched under the mattress. Mimus covered his eyes. In the darkness of denial he heard them clawing at the skirting – the grisly scrape of nail on plaster. Soon, their sandpaper rasps filled the room – low moans caged in airless lungs. Weary, they emerged from the struggle, their hands clasped to their throats . . .

Please, one more puff, let us breathe, let us breathe

The torment was unending. He couldn't bear their rasps, their scrapes, their corpses piled up on the floor . . . eyes rolled loose; mouths hung open . . . the absent ghost of oxygen. He moved his bed from the skirting to the corner of the room, where he sat watching dozens of bodies fighting for inhalers. Limp in silence, a spectator to suffering. Soon, the void of their eyes turned to him, as though he had something to offer, as though . . .

The inhaler

They knew. They knew he was their murderer. Mimus sucked in a lungful of smog. He choked, spluttered, moaned. The spectres advanced. He clasped the inhaler to his chest. He wouldn't let them have it. Never. But they were closer now, he saw his soul mirrored in the transparent shimmer of their bodies, and it was sick, it was broken, it was black. They stretched out their arms to him. He flung the inhaler onto the floor.

I can't breathe

He backed into the corner, taking in rasps of smog. His throat tightened. He felt their cold hatred on his skin, their death in his bones. He saw the end coming. It was too dark to face. The spectres swooped around his inhaler, failing in their attempts to lift it to their mouths. They beat the ground in defeat – soft, incessant thumps – their lungs locked in a mocking rattle.

I can't breathe

His throat was sealing up. He couldn't move. The spectres were moaning louder, taunting him with their pathetic death ritual. Bodies were piled up around the skirting. Their hate formed an impenetrable force field. If he didn't get a puff in the next two minutes . . .

I can't breathe

He clutched his neck. Someone was strangling him from inside. Rolling onto the floor, he crawled to the inhaler. The spectres waved him away with their fists, their bodies melting to bone.

I can't breathe

He reached out to the inhaler. Spectres came from behind, pressing their fingers to his throat. This is what it felt like to be a useless member of the republic. This is what it felt like to die.

I can't . . .

The End

M.J. Nicholls is a bediveled imp clacking out experimental fiction in Edinburgh, Scotland. He is currently undergoing creative irrigation. His works have been published in *Gold Dust Magazine, the Delinquent* (UK) and *Piker Press* and *New Paradigm* (US).

My Autobiography
By John Grey

when I see
a discarded umbrella,
torn panels
flapping in brute wind,
broken spokes
taking root
in muddy banks,
am I the only one
who imagines
Mary Poppins's
rotting corpse
floating in the Thames

John Grey has been published recently in the *Georgetown Review, The Pinch, South Carolina Review* and *The Pedestal*. with work upcoming in *Alimentum* and *Big Muddy*.

What Happened To Johnny
By Chaz Matthews

There used to be a cemetery out by the edge of the lake. Funny place to put a cemetery. Not so much funny ha-ha, but funny strange. The ground is so wet there, on account of the lake. Not good digging, even in dry weather.

I was only around sixteen years old the year that Johnny Pulhaus went missing. Disappeared, more like it. Not that anyone much cared to define his fate or seek out his whereabouts. Johnny was Wolf Lakes' town hoodlum, and most people were glad to find him no longer within town lines.

Let's see...if I was fifteen or sixteen that autumn, that would make it 1956 or 1957. In the late fifties, especially in the small towns, people didn't take kindly to having a greasy haired, hot rod driving, tattooed rock n' roller type in their neighborhood. That was Johnny Pulhaus.

Not that Johnny was a bad guy. Although I never spoke to him while he lived here, I used to see him a lot. I was an inquisitive, lonely kid, and as such I used to frequently sneak down to the cemetery by the lake, because it was only a few yards away from Johnny's trailer. I would lean against an old gravestone in my stiff new denim jacket and starch collared Arrow shirt and huddle there against the wind, in the strange stop-motion of the falling dead leaves, and listen to Johnny play guitar. He would sit by his bedroom window and play for hours, and I would listen the whole time.

The notes he played were lonesome, solemn, yet stirring and driving. They rang with a bluesy clangor against the ancient stone monuments of that graveyard. The songs he played sailed out on the ghostly, crisp October air and seemed to be playing with the movements of the twilight clouds and stars.

It sounded like the gunfire of ghostly cowboys and the tribal war cries of the American Indian braves. It sounded like neon and concrete and convertibles, and highway speed and twisted metal and blood and shattered bones. It sounded like factories and airplanes and railroads and beer bottles clanking on tables, and men telling tall tales and money and sex and death. Like a wolf cub searching for its mother in the dark. It sounded like America.

Sometimes as it got nearer to nightfall in that cemetery, the dark strains of Johnny's music seemed to make the very limbs of the twisted black trees dance and sway in their ageless rhythms. The tones were lilting and eerie. Sad and sinister. I never left until he put the guitar down and turned off the light. I loved more than anything to hear Johnny play.

Well, pretty soon my mother put an end to my cemetery trips, saying it was unhealthy and morbid. Instead I would stay in my room reading comic books at night, still humming Johnny's melodies in my head.

A few weeks after my last night in the cemetery, I heard some kids talking at the bus stop. They said that Johnny hadn't showed up for work at the mechanics' shop. He had disappeared. Even his latest girlfriend didn't know where he was.

This news threw a panic into my teenage heart. The thought that I'd never hear that guitar again nearly drove me to tears.

That day, as I sat through the endless tedious hours of school, the mystery began to thump inside me like the rock n roll beat of my heart. I had to be the one to find him, I had to know what happened to Johnny.

You see, I was a lonely kid, as I believe I told you already. Not popular with girls. I had no close friends to speak of. I didn't run with any of the gangs or "clicks".

I spent most of my time reading comics or watching the black and white horror shows at the theaters or on the television. I obsessed over the latest rock n roll records and the old blues and cowboy songs. I loved to hear those droning, electrified voodoo rhythms and their tales of whiskey, women and the devil.

Maybe that's why I identified with Johnny so much. He was alone too. Sure, he had a different girlfriend every week, but at the end of the night, as only he and I knew, it was always just that big Orange guitar, and Johnny Pulhaus.

That's why I had to find him.

My first step in solving the mystery was going to be talking to Johnny's last girlfriend, Sandra. She was older than me, and she drank and smoked and swore, and did bad things in the back of convertibles. But she was also very beautiful, and I wasn't used to talking to girls.

So it was with major butterflies in my stomach that I rode my bike all over town, looking for signs of her. Wolf Lake was a small town, and it didn't take long.

I found her at the soda shop, smoking and sipping a chocolate coke.

She was with another boy, who had styled himself in imitation of either Elvis Presley, or Johnny Pulhaus. But he was greasy, loud and nervous, while Johnny had been cool and quiet.

"Can I talk to you?" I asked her, sitting beside her at the Soda Shop counter.

"It's a free country, worm," she said, and the bad Elvis clone laughed loudly.

"Well," I said, "I'm wondering if you knew where Johnny Pulhaus is.."

"Stop right there," she said. "I already told the cops I didn't know where he went. He was acting strange, talking bullshit, and I dumped him. That's all."

"Acting strange?" I said.

"You a parrot or something?" she snapped.

"Buzz the fuck outta here, bug." Said the bad Elvis clone.

"Sorry. How was he acting strange?" I said, my courage really flowing now. I had to know!

"Talking about his guitar, and the cemetery. Shit, I dunno." she said, and sighed.

"Look, the cops think he was involved in all the grave robberies that happened a few nights ago, right before he disappeared. You don't seem like a bad kid. Stay away from this, it's not......" she frowned, looked uncertain.

"It's just not right," she said.

I thanked her and left. The bad Elvis clone-boy said something to Sandra and they laughed, as I walked out the door. I'm sure he was mocking me, but I didn't care. I was on fire with new information...grave robberies? That wasn't even in the papers!

The next step was clear.

The cemetery.

The cemetery was a place I used to love. I found it calming, even at night when Johnny's guitar was sounding particularly eerie and I was huddled among the tombstones listening, half in fear, half in awe of the music.

But that autumn night in 1957 as I approached the old cemetery, the familiar smells of the nearby lake mingling with the scent of dead leaves and the crisp October air, my heart was pounding.

I began walking through the haphazard rows of scattered and shattered tombs as I always did, but it was only seconds before I realized there was something wrong. Most of the graves, both centuries old and fairly new, had been re-dug. The earth was freshly disturbed and the grass was patchy and dying under the thin layer of dead leaves that covered the area.

Was this the aftermath of the grave robberies that Sandra talked about?

I continued walking towards the fence that separated Johnny's property from the cemetery. A sense of foreboding crept over me like nothing I have ever experienced before, and certainly not since. Nonetheless I needed to know what had happened to Johnny. I kept walking until I reached the old rusty chain link fence.

I began to climb it, snagging my jeans and sleeves several times on the sharp crumbling metal edges of the fence as I ascended. I had never done this before, never crossed the line into Johnny's backyard. Spying on him had been one thing...trespassing on his turf could have meant trouble. Perhaps it still would.

I dropped silently into Johnny's back-yard. I noticed the familiar artifacts; the pink lawn flamingo half buried in muddy dirt, the unused kiddy pool left from the properties' previous owner, and the dozens of car engines and a myriad of broken or derelict car parts, strewn in various stages of rust, all over the back yard.

I crossed in the moonlight to Johnny's bedroom window and peered in. There was no one in there. I could see his bed, and the outline of his guitar case. "Gretsch", it read, and his amplifier; it was a tan color and said "Fender" on it.

I crossed the patio to the back door of the trailer and pushed softly. It opened without much effort. I stepped inside. The smell was awful. It was if ten dozen rats had crawled into the trailer and died. I covered my nose and mouth and continued into the small, moonlit kitchen. There were broken phonograph records and torn books everywhere.

It was then I heard the noise, and froze in my tracks. There was a scratching sound, like the scrape of a boot, or a hoarse intake of breath. It was over too soon to be sure. I walked towards it, and heard it again. It was coming from the closet in the living room. I crossed the room slowly and carefully and closed my hand around the closet door knob. I counted to three and opened the door.

It was Johnny. Or what was left of him. Curled into a fetal position with one arm extended. He had open, horrible wounds and scratches all over his arms and face, his eyes were blackened and his clothes were torn. He looked barely conscious and he was still scratching lightly on the door with his fingers, as if he hadn't realized I'd opened it.

"Johnny!" I shouted. "What's going on, what happened to you?"

He looked up at me then, and I saw

that one of his eye sockets was completely empty. What the hell had torn out Johnny's eye?

" Quick..." he said. "They're coming."

"What? Who??" I said, then I heard the pounding. It was the sound of a march, of hundreds of feet walking on towards a destination, the steps getting louder and more sure. Something WAS coming. Then as suddenly as I heard the sound, I knew.

It was the dead. Johnny hadn't stolen the bodies. They had come for him. They had come for the music of Johnny's guitar. They wanted to hear it even worse than I had.

"I had...I had to keep playing, every night..." Johnny croaked, "or I knew they'd come. First it was one dead body tapping... tapping on my window, then it was two. Then one night..." he coughed, and a thick spurt of blood flew from his lips.

"One night it was all of them. All...of... them."

Johnny began to cry. I kneeled down and awkwardly put my arm around him. I could see he didn't have long to live. "The only thing that makes them go away is the guitar?"

"They can't rest in peace...." he sobbed. "But the music...they need the music...I told them I couldn't do it anymore, I had a life to live...I tried to leave, to run away. They brought me back."

Then Johnny pitched forward onto the carpet at my feet, and with a long sigh, was dead.

I knew what I had to do. I ran into Johnny's bedroom and opened the guitar case. I'd never learned how to play guitar, though I'd sure wanted to, but right now, that night, I was going to play as if my life depended on it. Because it did.

As I plugged the guitar into the am-plifier, I heard the front door of the trailer burst open, and then came the murmuring. I can't describe it any other way, it was the voices of a hundred or more, whispering in a monotone mixture of sadness and fury. They could not quiet, they could not rest, not after the lives they'd lived and the places they'd seen. Only the music, only that sound could soothe them. They would have it, always and forever. They would have it or else.

I heard them coming towards the bedroom door as I strapped on the guitar. As soon as my fingers touched the strings, I could no longer control them. The music poured out of me, and I had never played any instrument before. It was Johnny's music, lonesome and angry, like the dead that now smashed through the trailer on their way to me. I was playing it! Somehow, it was coming out of me! My fingers flew across the fret board. Delta Blues moan mixed with western swing twang, and the alien music of other worlds.

I was doing it. Somehow, I was doing it.

And the dead paused at the door. I could see some of them, their shattered faces and bloated gaseous bodies shining greenly in the moonlight. Their lipless smiles and limbless grace. Their patchy tufts of hair and their tattered burial suits and dresses. Their cancers and their broken necks. They stopped, and they swayed in time to Johnny's music. MY music now. As I played, more came and pressed their faces and fingers to the window. One dead woman caressed my face as I played, and I could smell the sick scent of bile and rot and death all over her. She was wearing a tattered hospital gown. I played on, closing my eyes and gritting my teeth as dead children danced a slow swaying dance in Johnny's tiny bedroom and dead men held their dead women and sobbed.

In the morning, they were gone. My song slowed and halted. My fingers ached and burned. The dead had shuffled off with the sun and into their graves again. But they would be back. And they have been, every night for almost fifty years, their numbers only growing as the news of Johnny's old Gretsch guitar spreads through their dead underground somehow.

There are more here every night to hear the music. But I'm old now, and getting ready to die myself. The sooner the better. I have served them as long and as faithfully as I could. Soon, I will join them on the other side of this world.

And someone else has to play this guitar. Maybe someone like you?

The End

Chaz Matthews was born in 1970 in the wilds of western Michigan. Born into a large working class family, he became exposed via his parents to the sounds of classic country music, rockabilly and especially, Elvis Presley and Hank Williams.

Chaz moved to Boston in 1992, joining a collection of ill-starred bands which went nowhere, but led to the formation of The Dimestore Haloes in 1995. The Haloes became underground punk darlings, recording several singles and four full length CDs with various labels and being featured in virtually every punk fanzine of the day. Riotous opening slots for The Unseen, Dropkick Murphys, Ducky Boys, Groovie Ghoulies, The Casualties, The US Bombs, and Nashville Pussy solidified their fan base and made them a legendary band in underground punk circles.

The Haloes became notorious for bad behavior and were often seen as controversial within the strict politically correct realms of the '90s punk elite.

The Boston Phoenix said the Haloes "Should have been huge", and this is a sentiment expressed frequently by fans and observers of the band in their shambolic glory days.

Chaz became obsessed with literature at this point as well. Always a fan of Horror fiction, EC Comics, Stephen King, Clive Barker and the like, his reading habits now stretched to include Cormac McCarthy, Jack Kerouac, Charles Bukowski, Poe, Jim Thompson, Raymond Chandler, Raymond Carver, Richard Matheson, Billy Childish, Baudelaire, Dostoyevsky, Chuck Palahniuk, Steinbeck, Henry Miller, Nelson Algren and more.

Chaz wrote for several fanzines during the Haloes years, such as "Anorexic Teenage Sexgods", "Flipside", "Maximum RockN-Roll", and "Now Wave", and was a regular columnist in the legendary "Hit List" Magazine.

In 2003, The Dimestore Haloes broke up. Chaz released his first solo disc, "Amazing Graceless" on the Chicago based "Full Breach Kicks" label in 2005. In 2006, the tragic suicide of original Haloes drummer Jimmy Reject nixed the idea of any Haloes re-union.

Around this time, Chaz wrote extensively for Texas-based Rockabilly magazine "Rockabilly Monthly" (now called simply "Rockabilly" Magazine), and self- published his first novella, "Lost In The Supermarket", which is now out of print.

Since then, Chaz's music has been down-loaded via his internet websites, and his Blog read by hundreds of weekly viewers. He plans new book and CD releases for future years, as well as possible live shows (he has an unreasonable fear of playing live these days) and plenty of online downloadables.

He lives with his wife and cats in Boston. He spends all his money on cheap guitars and obscure books. He is still lost in the super-market.

Note from Editor: Whew! Dude's a little wordy...

Morning
By Lyn C. A. Gardner

Each morning I wake and stare
at the ceiling, our painted spaceship
floating in a sea of stars that dim with dawn.
I'm afraid to look anywhere else.
I fix myself up there, fighting to forget
what makes my heart beat so hard
just to find myself breathing. I can't turn off
the heavy smell—blood and dead meat—but memory, at least,
fails before the sticky mass that damps my sheets,
the source of the tackiness that coats my hands.
I turn my head, then stop at the feel of
short tufts of tawny fur that tickle my arms and cheeks,
hair that's fallen out to coat my pillow like down,
cut off from me as I eased into slumber,
back into the old me. The window's open.
I don't want to know whose knee
I'm clutching like a grisly teddy bear.
The aftertaste of blood is sharp and sweet.
My human self seeks quick similes:
the tang's like orange, some citrus-flavored meat.
I need these lies to hide the deep delight
that causes me to lick my lips,
to pat my matted head, pulling out shreds of heart
still clinging to my regrown human hair—
stuck firmly as lost love. I wish that I were dead.
I lie still, while the blood sings through my limbs
against my will. I don't dare rise.
Each morning I lie still for an hour at least,
fighting the world I wake to, hating
the dawn that brings the room to life.
I can't bring myself to swing my legs and stand.
Already with wakefulness this heavy weight
crushes my chest—the burden of *his* body, limp with death,
the one memory I cannot escape.
I try to hold it in, not to breathe—not to cry.

But he's everywhere, my absent husband,
marked out by the space he left behind—
this cold sheet, this bunched pillow where I bury my nose
for his full-bodied scent—drawing him in so close, so real—
I fling the bedclothes back, run down the hall—
stop, panting, hand pressing my heart
as I see they're safe, two miniature heads intact,
two small bodies shivering with breath.
I take a step toward them, and there he is!
Shining athwart the threshold, my husband's ghost
stands sentinel, his eyes imploring, loving—
warden with a wicked wound clawed out of his chest.
The blood dissipates like smoke when it strikes the floor.
He opens his arms to me, just like that night he saved me.
I couldn't see for hunger. I howled until he opened the door,
then asked him just to check, please check—
said I heard the children crying. When he left to look,
I chewed through the straps.
He blocked the way—one last embrace—
Now I stand watching, tears upon my face,
as his ghost smiles that everything's all right—
once more, our daughters made it through the night.

Catalog librarian by day, Lyn C. A. Gardner coedits the journal *Virginia Libraries*. She's
had over two hundred poems, stories, and articles published in *Strange Horizons*, the Green
Knight Press anthologies *Legends of the Pendragon* and *The Doom of Camelot*, *Challenging
Destiny*, *New Myths*, *Talebones*, *The Leading Edge*, and more. Two stories and a poem earned
honorable mention in *The Year's Best Fantasy and Horror* (Ellen Datlow & Terri Windling);
three poems were nominated for the Rhysling Award (SFPA). Gardner is an associate
member of SFWA and MWA and a graduate of the Clarion West Writers Workshop.

The Churchyard Incident
By Chad Strong

Mist gathered in the fields as Freddie stepped off the paved road onto the long gravel drive. Loose stones crunched and rolled under his sneakers. Warm yellow light invited him through the dusk to the farmhouse ahead, but the narrow driveway was fringed with shadowed scrub and ancient oaks that reached for him with gnarled, bare autumn branches.

A breeze brushed his left shoulder, then dropped to worry dry leaves along the ground. Something rustled in the brush and Freddie skipped aside, his eyes fixed on the darkest shadow they found.

'A rabbit,' he thought. `A rabbit.' The rustling ceased. He carried on, hating the noisy gravel—he'd never hear anything coming over his own footsteps. Reaching the front porch, he knocked, and glanced around. Thick mist appeared caught in the woods beyond the house. It tore away, reaching for the house—and him—like fingers of rent vaporous wool. A moth fluttered against the porch light. Freddie heard someone running thump-thump-thump across the hardwood floors inside the house. The runner's feet skidded to a halt and their owner flung open the door.

"Freddie!"

Freddie's apprehensions vanished the second he saw Rand, who grabbed his thin arm and yanked him inside. Freddie giggled.

"Man, Freddie," Rand said, "You gotta do somethin' about that hair of yours."

Freddie's eyes followed Rand's gaze to the hall mirror where, by some queer trick of reflection, the porch light behind him seemed to set Freddie's red hair into a halo of fire.

Rand slammed the door. "Come on—Chris's already here."

"Who's—?"

Rand pulled him into the living room without giving him a chance to take off his shoes. "Freddie's here!"

Heat burned Freddie's cheeks as he stood before his friend's parents, both seated in cozy armchairs. On the pine table between them, two cups of tea steamed on a white doily.

"Hello, Freddie," said Rand's mom, setting her crocheting on her lap. "Nice to see you again."

Rand's dad shook his paper and peered over it. "Hello, son."

"H-hello—." Freddie's eyes skipped across the strange boy sitting silently in the wooden chair in the corner.

"That's Chris." Rand leaned his forearm on Freddie's narrow shoulder. "This is my best buddy, Freddie."

A smile erupted from Freddie's face. He was Rand's best buddy.

Rand's mom remarked: "You boys must have seen each other on the road and not known you were both headed here. Chris arrived only a few moments before you."

Chris rose and approached Rand and

Freddie. His mouth quirked in what might have been a smile. A lock of his straight black hair fell over his round black eyes. He flicked it back with a jerk of his head.

"Hey, kid."

"H-hi."

"Listen to Chris's deep voice!" said Rand's mom. "He sounds so much older than the other two."

Rand's dad grunted agreeably.

Rand shook Freddie's shoulders. "Come on—we're outta here." He steered Freddie toward the back door. "Remember, Mom!" he called over his shoulder. "No coming out to check up on us!"

"Yes, dear."

The back porch was buried under a pile of camping gear. They all grabbed some and hauled it to the center of the big back yard. They worked quickly in the fading light, setting up the tent, unrolling sleeping bags. When Freddie fumbled with one of the hooks, Rand took it from him and snapped it deftly into place. Shrugging, Freddie smiled. "Thanks." Then he blushed as he realized Chris was watching.

At last, they stood back and observed their encampment. Rand had stripped down to his white T-shirt, having worked up a sweat pumping up the air mattresses. Glowing like the rising three-quarter moon, he stepped forward with a kingly bearing and shouted for the stars to hear:

"I declare this a good camp!" Freddie sucked air through his mouth and tried to think of something to add. Rand's bright grin interrupted him. "I gotta take a leak." He pivoted and trotted off toward the back fence. Freddie raised a hand to point at the back door of the house.

Chris crossed his arms in front of his chest. "You don't go in to use the toilet when you're camping, Carrot-Top."

Cold hurt stiffened Freddie's heart at even so old and empty an insult. He turned away from Chris and followed the path Rand had pressed in the damp grass. He didn't have to go, but he had to get away from Chris.

"Hey, man," Rand greeted him over his shoulder.

"Hey."

"What's with you, man? Did you get bad news from the doc this afternoon?"

"No." He turned and glanced at the boy near the tent. "I—I guess I kind of figured it would just be you and me for camping." He brushed his foot through the grass.

"Oh. Well, it was gonna be, but then they brought this new kid in after you left, and I figured he was okay, so I invited him to come along. The more the merrier, right?"

"I—I guess."

"So come on—loosen up. It's gonna be great!" With that, Rand howled at the moon and sprang off racing in circles around the yard.

Freddie watched him, wishing he could be inside Rand's skin, feel that life energy rushing and sparking. Already handsome at fourteen, perfectly proportioned in muscle and bone, Rand had never had an awkward stage and probably never would. The girls at school already whispered and giggled over him—a very different kind of giggling than when they saw Freddie.

"Come on, Freddie!" Rand yelled, waving.

Freddie scuffed through the damp grass and crawled into the tent after Rand and Chris. A propane lamp glared a harsh white light from the center of the tent. It

113

swung a bit as he fidgeted to get comfortable on his air mattress.

"So, whadayou guys wanna do?" asked Rand, pulling on his plaid flannel shirt. "Wanna tell ghost stories?"

"Yeah," Chris agreed. He shook his dark hair out of his eyes and looked at Freddie.

"That all right with you, kid?"

"'Course it's all right," Freddie said, trying to answer the way he figured Rand would. Halloween wasn't really until next Thursday, but their parents wouldn't let them camp out on a school night so they were having their last camping night of the year tonight, the Saturday before Halloween.

"Freddie's no weenie," Rand declared, smacking the redhead's knee. "He's just been sick a lot. It ain't his fault."

Freddie's cheeks heated and his normally almost translucent skin glowed to rival his freckles. He ducked his head after a grateful glance at his friend.

"If you say so," Chris said. "But I bet he was thinking that it's not Halloween yet—as if that's a good enough excuse not to tell ghost stories." He stared at Freddie, his dark eyes glittering with smug shrewdness.

A tremor rippled in Freddie's belly. He crossed his arms in front of himself and broke the gaze with Chris. He flushed again. How had Chris known that?

Suddenly Freddie recoiled as Chris lunged toward him. Chris's hand clamped on his shoulder and Freddie wished he could dissolve through the nylon membrane of the tent and run away.

"It never has to be Halloween for ghost stories," Chris said, his face too close to Freddie's. "Any time of the year will do. It's just that at this time of the year, those who know say that the veil between the worlds grows thin, and it's easier for spirits to cross back and forth."

"Yeah," Rand chimed in. "It only gots to be dark and spooky. Like tonight."

"Well, it makes for a nice touch," Chris agreed, amusement quirking the corner of his mouth. "Evil lurks at every moment. It can manifest any time, anywhere, any way. And you'll never know just how—at least not until it's too late." He paused, then began to chant: "Evil comes in many guises; different shapes and different sizes."

Rand caught on immediately and chanted in time with Chris: "Evil comes in many guises; different shapes and different sizes. Evil comes in many guises; different shapes and different sizes!"

They sprang at Freddie and grabbed him. Freddie shrieked, half from fright, half from Chris's painful grip. Chris's fingers were like sharp sticks, poking into his flesh. Freddie barely noticed Rand was tickling him and laughing.

"Ow! Let go!"

Chris and Rand reared back and raised their arms above their heads like monster claws.

"We're gonna get you!"

"No!" Freddie shrank back against the tent wall.

They began the chant again, over and over until Freddie was cringing in the corner, his palms pressed tight over his ears. "Stop it! Don't say that!" A sob escaped his tight throat.

"Aw, give it up," Chris said, dropping back on his own sleeping bag. "Before he pees himself and brings the whole tent down on us. What a wimp."

Rand kneeled next to Freddie.

"They're just words, Fred. They don't mean nothin'."

"Yes, they do," Freddie blubbered. "They're evil words. They mean—."

Chris guffawed. "What do they mean, kid? They mean the boogieman's gonna get you?"

Freddie choked, trying to sit up and recover himself, explain what he felt about the words. But he didn't know if it was the words themselves or Chris's voice, which seemed so much older than his and Rand's, so much older than anything. Freddie heard something in those words, in that voice. Usually he could make a picture in his head that helped him explain strange things to himself, but he couldn't see anything that made any sense this time. "Maybe. I don't know. But—."

"But, schmut. And you're right—you don't know. So quit being such a wimp."

Rand lightly punched Freddie's shoulder. "You okay now, Fred?" Freddie nodded and sniffled. He hoped he hadn't embarrassed Rand by being such a baby in front of his new friend. He rubbed his neck where Chris had dug his fingers in deep. He cast a glance and saw Chris watching him.

Rand flipped onto his back and hollered, pumping his arms and legs in the air as if he were running. "Hey, look, Freddie! I'm goin' nowhere fast!"

They all laughed. Freddie wiped his eyes on his sleeve.

"You plan to win that race on Monday?" Chris asked Rand.

"You bet!"

"You're the best runner on the team." Rand grinned.

"I'm coming to watch!" Freddie promised. "I'll cheer and everything!"

"Cool."

Chris drew up his knees, draping his forearms over them. "You're a real pal, aren't you, Carrot-Top?"

Crimson burned Freddie's ears. Rand quit his mock running and let his feet drop to the mattress with twin thumps. "Don't call him that. He hates it."

"Sorry, Ran-man." Chris looked around the tent like he was bored. Then he said, "Come on—let's do the ghost stories. Did you hear the one about the Specter Axe Man?"

"Yep."

"What about the Hounds from Hell?"

"A gazillion times."

Sighing heavily, Chris appeared to think a moment. Freddie hoped he wouldn't come up with anything.

"What about the one with the kid who disappears in the churchyard?"

"Uh, nope," answered Rand. "You hear that one, Fred?"

Freddie shook his head.

"Okay, then, this is it," Chris declared. He wriggled on his mattress, getting comfortable. "It happens in a little town like this one. There's this old church on the edge of town, where nobody goes anymore."

"Is there a graveyard?" asked Rand, leaning toward him.

"Yeah. All old and busted headstones and stuff."

"Cool!"

His voice thin and tentative, Freddie asked, "What kinda church is it?"

Chris scowled at him. "Whadaya mean, what kinda church is it? It's just a church."

"It might be important."

"It's not. Any stupid old church'll do."

"Think of the old Crossroads Church, on the way to the gravel pits," Rand suggested.

"Anyway," Chris continued, a wicked gleam glazing his dark eyes. "One day, outa nowhere, comes this old man. He's really, really old with pure white hair. He doesn't talk much to adults—only to kids. The kids really like him. He's always got great stories for them. One kid especially, Timmy, hangs out with him a lot."

"What do they do?" Freddie asked, getting curious.

"Just take walks in the forest and talk about stuff. The old guy tells Timmy lots of stories. One day he tells him about the time he was the caretaker of the church in his hometown, and one night he was out there late and he saw this kid running around the church backwards. He said the kid ran around three times and then right before his eyes—just vanished."

Rand straightened up. "Get outa here!"

"True story. And then Timmy wanted to find out if it was true or not, so he ran around the church three times backwards and he disappeared, too."

"No way!"

"True story," Chris repeated, nodding.

Freddie cleared his throat timidly. "Where did they disappear to?"

"The Other Side."

"Of the church?"

"No. Of the spirit world. Where demons rule."

Dark things sprinted behind Freddie's mind's eye and he shuddered. "Did—did they die?"

"No. They'll never die. They're still alive, being tormented by the demons."

"What do the d-demons do to them?"

"Terrible things. Awful things. Dark things. You couldn't take it, Freddie."

"Can they ever get out and come back?"

"No. Never."

"But they were good kids, weren't they? Why did they have to end up there?"

"It doesn't matter if they're good. It's their destiny." Chris turned a cock-eyed grin on him. "But they take bad people, too, to work for them and catch the good ones for the demons to play with. In exchange, the demons won't torture them. Unless they screw up."

Freddie wrapped his thin arms around his knees and pulled them into his chest, trying to fend off a chill colder than the damp night air that was seeping into his flesh, poking his insides, seeking his bones. The three of them sat in death-like silence. Then Rand began to chuckle and finally burst out laughing.

"Freddie—you should see yourself! You're whiter than usual!"

Freddie flushed, crimson staining his pale cheeks, creeping into his scalp, and blending with his flaming hair under the glare of the propane lamp.

Chris appeared to be looking right through the roof of the blue nylon tent. "The moon's rising."

Rand sucked in a deep breath and howled like a forlorn wolf.

Freddie curled into his knees, his forearms pressing over his ears. "Don't, Rand, please!"

"Aw, you ain't scared again are you?"

Freddie lifted his head tentatively. "A—a little."

"It's just a stupid story."

"I—I know. I mean I don't know."

"Well, know."

"Why don't you go try it," Chris suggested. "Then if you disappear you'll know for sure." He chuckled derisively.

"No way!"

"Sure, Freddie," Rand said. "I'll even do it with you."

Freddie shook his head emphatically. "Uh-uh."

"Come on—it'll be a blast!"

"No! I don't wanna disappear and get tortured by demons!" He grabbed the edges of his sleeping bag and wrapped them around himself.

Chris muttered some curse out the side of his mouth. He shook his head at Rand. "How did you ever pick this weenie for a best friend?"

"Shut up." Rand cocked his head and studied Freddie's face.

Freddie was afraid and he knew he couldn't hide it from Rand.

"Well, Freddie, there's only one way to fix this." Rand crawled the foot or so to the doorway and unzipped the tent flap. "Let's go."

Freddie blinked at him. "Go where?"

"To the old church. I'll run around it backwards and you can see it's just a story and you won't have to be scared anymore."

Cold fire seared through Freddie's chest. "No! You don't have to. I'm not going!"

"Then stay here and Chris'll come with me to prove I did it." He waved his arm and Chris crawled in front of Freddie and followed Rand out into the night.

"Wait! Don't! What if it's for real? Rand!" He heard their footsteps receding through the grass, their voices drifting away. "Wait! Don't leave me here alone!"

"Then come on!"

Freddie hesitated a moment longer. The glare of the propane lamp was no comfort when even his shadow was alone on the blue tent lining. Suddenly realizing he could no longer hear the other boys; he gathered his sleeping bag securely around his shoulders and plunged through the sliver of an opening into the blackness of the world outside.

Momentarily blind, he stumbled in a circle before finding his bearings in the feeble light of the low moon. He set off after them, but paused at the house and gazed up at the warm yellow light in the windows.

"Shouldn't we tell—?"

He left off, knowing they were too far away to hear him. He hustled out to the end of the driveway, hating every noisy, crunchy step. He peered down the black top, but they were already out of sight. The damp road was a silvery incision between the forest and the fields. He looked again, both ways, hoping he'd just missed their silhouettes in the mist.

Maybe they were hiding. "Come out, you guys!" Holding his breath, he listened. Nothing but the flutter of tiny creatures hiding in the brush. Nothing human. Not even a giggle. "Where are you?"

An urgent autumn breeze pressed at his back and he started walking. The old church was just over a mile away, around the corner. They couldn't be that far yet. He ran a few yards, then, out of breath, fell back. He'd never catch up.

Then he remembered the trail that cut through the woods and came out at the church's back yard. That would save him time! He hurried forward again, only to come up short when he found the path. The old boards across the ditch were gone. It was nearly two yards across. There was cold, dark water in the ditch. The path was a black hole in the trees on the other side.

"Afraid of the dark, Carrot-Top?"

Freddie spun around to face Chris, his heart leaping into his throat, thumping painfully. His eyes searched the darkness. "Where's Rand?"

"Halfway to his destiny."

"What do you mean?"

"We all reach our destiny, some sooner, some later. Some even share a common one. All are inescapable. Perhaps yours is to save Rand from the one I have chosen for him. Perhaps not." Chris grinned.

In all his life of being teased and taunted, Freddie had never seen a grin drip with so much malice. He looked around again for Rand. Chris chuckled, then laughed, then vanished.

Freddie gasped, stepped back. Chris was gone! And Chris was...He didn't know what Chris was, but whatever he was, he was evil. A sudden weakness quivered in Freddie's stomach and knees. He tottered on the pavement, rocked by the sudden birth of his unexplainable fears into reality.

He had to get to Rand. Stop him from doing whatever it was Chris wanted him to do. Somewhere in the distance the wind gathered and with a strange, un-wind like roar rushed toward him, ripping at the trees and tearing at the sleeping bag around his shoulders. He clutched the bag tightly, refusing to let go though it whipped and flapped about him, one corner stinging him in the eye. He leaned into the wind, his eyes squinted nearly shut, tears streaming from them. He took one step, then another. The seconds he balanced on one foot seemed eons while the other made its gambit for the next piece of earth. He wasn't even sure he

was headed for the ditch anymore.

Then suddenly the wind stopped. Freddie could not breathe in the vacuum that encapsulated him. His heart pounded madly in his chest until at last his lungs drew air. Panting, bent over his knees, he focused on the trail once again. Chris was new in town—he couldn't know about the path.

Freddie wished he had a flashlight. He judged the distance across the ditch, backed up, and took a run at it. He leapt and landed hard on the other side, his hands grabbing for any purchase on the earth, his feet slipping and splashing into the cold muck of the ditch. His soaked sleeping bag seemed to suck him back deeper into the mire. Slithering out from under it, he scrambled up the bank.

He'd never taken the path in the dark before, nor ever taken it alone. Rand had always been with him. The soft dirt was dampened by the autumn rains but not yet saturated into mud. Some portions were slick with old fallen leaves, while in the more sheltered spots the leaves were still crunchy beneath his feet.

A searching breeze rustled the few remaining leaves overhead. The thin bare branches scratched and scraped against each other like dried-up finger bones. Freddie moved on.

The path became darker and darker as he moved deeper into the forest. He stepped cautiously, his hands spread before him in the black void. He stumbled over a root and fell, the earth an invisible barrier that stopped his fall into nothing. He wondered if the wind would descend upon him now and finish him off.

Suddenly he thought he heard voices. Pushing himself to his feet, he trekked forward, more careful of roots and rocks now. Moments later, he emerged at the edge of the church's back yard. He scanned the clearing between himself and the white-washed church, but saw no one.

The small clapboard church seemed incandescent in the wan light of the mist and moon. An historical landmark, the church had stood on this spot for a hundred and forty years. It appeared sturdy, but hadn't been structurally sound for years.

Freddie's eyes searched the church-yard, examining the precise black shadows of the pine trees dotting the unkempt lawn and the headstones crouching just beyond them.

"We gotta wait for Freddie, so he can see." Rand's voice carried across the empty air.

Freddie saw them now, silhouetted against the pale gravel driveway.

"Hey, Freddie!" called Rand, waving. Freddie waved back, his voice squeezed silent though he wanted to call out so desperately in relief.

Then he felt Chris's eyes on him and the breeze became wind as it skimmed low through the mist, across the grass, and shoved his feet out from under him.

He landed hard in the turf, losing the air in his lungs with a grunt. The ground was wet and cold and quickly soaked his clothes. The need to get to Rand overcame the chill that already stiffened his flesh. He reclaimed his breath, regained his feet, and trudged the rest of the way to the other boys.

"Where ya been?" asked Rand.

"I—."

"We thought maybe you went home or somethin'."

Freddie shook his head. "I couldn't

see..." He looked from Rand to Chris.

"Well, at least you made it." Rand clapped Freddie's shoulder with an open palm. "Now you can watch, too."

Freddie's heart twisted in his chest. He started to speak but Chris cut him off.

"Let's get started."

Rand asked: "So, what do I gotta do, again?"

Chris pointed at the church. "Just run around that counter-clockwise. Three times. Backwards."

"I'm cold," Freddie asserted, trembling, his arms clutched about his thin frame. "Let's go home."

"In a minute, Freddie." Rand moved off to the southeast corner of the church.

"Don't do it!" Freddie screamed, the hysteria in his voice shocking even himself.

Chris grabbed his arm before he could run toward Rand. "You're really getting annoying, you know that?" His voice was the warning hiss of an asp and his dark eyes threatened Freddie with unveiled hostility. "Stop interfering."

Freddie shrank from Chris. "Let go!" he cried, yanking his arm free.

Chris yelled to Rand. "Go on! Get started!"

"Yeah, yeah!"

"Stop pushing him!" Freddie demanded. "You're making him do it! I know! Leave him alone!"

"You know nothing," Chris hissed back.

Neither one noticed Rand come halfway back to them. "Geez, will you guys chill out?"

Freddie spun to him, tripping over tufts of saturated grass as he tried to get to him. "Please don't do it, Rand. Chris is evil. He wants to hurt you."

Rand chuckled, his hands on his hips. "Come on, Freddie."

Freddie heard Chris coming up behind him. He was running out of time and everything he said just made both Chris and Rand more determined to take this right to the end.

"So, are we doing this?" Chris asked.

"Yeah, for sure."

"Carrot-Top whining again?" With one hand, Chris shoved Freddie so hard he stumbled backwards and nearly fell.

"Hey, take it easy!" Rand warned him. "So he's scared—in a minute I'll show him there's nothin' to be scared of." He turned and walked back toward the church.

"Rand!"

"Relax, Fred!"

"Yeah, shut up already, Carrot-Top. Or I'll hit you so hard Rand will see you cry."

Freddie wrapped his arms even more tightly around himself. The menace in Chris's voice hung in the air, writhing like a palpable, though ethereal snake.

Chris called out: "Make sure you start where I put that stick! And don't stop until you cross it after the third lap!"

"You got it!" Rand waved at them before stripping off his flannel shirt. He was easy to see now. Like the church, his white T-shirt reflected the light of the risen three-quarter moon.

Freddie focused on something mutely glowing at Rand's feet. It was Chris's marker, a broken branch long since stripped of its bark and bleached white like a bone.

"You stand here," Chris commanded Freddie. "And I'll stand on the other side to make sure he doesn't try to hide in the bushes and fool us." Chris walked away and disappeared around the far side of the church.

Freddie stood there, silent and stymied. How could he make Rand see Chris for what he was?

Warming up with jumping jacks, Rand called out: "You guys ready?"

Chris answered, "Yep!"

Freddie swallowed, trying to pop his ears. Some weird sort of pressure change had overtaken the churchyard. He suddenly felt light-headed and woozy. The earth and the air shimmered, and the night seemed somehow darker, the hovering mist more dense, yet he could still see Rand beneath the moon.

The moment Rand began to run, Freddie's eyes attached themselves to him with an umbilical-like fastness. As Rand rounded the corner to Chris's side, a sudden sweat broke out all over Freddie's body. His trembling erupted into spasms of violent shaking which he tried to contain by squeezing himself even more tightly within his own arms. When Rand came into view again, Freddie tried to cry out to him, but all that escaped was a thin, raspy nothing of sound.

Rand began his second lap. He stumbled a couple of times over uneven turf, but even backwards, he jogged with a rhythm he looked like he could maintain forever.

Freddie's pounding heart hurt more than he'd ever imagined it could. He forced himself to breathe in and out as Rand again disappeared behind the little church. He clutched his fists against his chest. The seconds crawled by, sluggishly indifferent to Freddie's dread. At last Rand appeared, swinging around the southwest corner. But there was still one more lap.

'Always the jock,' Freddie thought, knowing Rand would never go any less than all the way. He forced out a sigh, freeing the stale air trapped in his lungs. Then he sucked a deep breath through his mouth. The cold air smarted against his teeth. As Rand rounded the last corner to complete his third lap, Freddie started toward him.

He watched for Chris. Sure enough, Chris came around the corner to observe Rand's finish. Freddie felt instant repulsion, but he fought the urge to run. Instead, he jumped up and down and waved at Rand. Rand waved back.

"Don't distract him!"

Freddie's eyes darted to Chris, who was striding straight toward him through the mist. Except the mist was coming before him, swirling and reaching as though propelled by an unearthly wind. Freddie stood transfixed as the first chill fingers of it reached him and coiled around him.

Suddenly Chris was in Freddie's face and Freddie couldn't block the blow to his sternum that left him on his knees in the wet grass, gasping, barely able to hear the words Chris hissed in his ear.

"I'd send you, too, just to get rid of you, if you weren't so weak! But your flimsy soul would implode and die too quickly. Rand's tough. He'll survive a long time. Maybe even forever."

Freddie's voice came out raspy. "And—and you'll hurt him forever...?"

"Not me, but the others, yes."

"I said leave him alone!"

Both Freddie and Chris looked up, startled, into Rand's furious face. Rand jabbed a finger into Chris's chest.

"I'm tellin' you for the last time to leave him alone! Stop pickin' on my buddy!"

Chris tore his eyes from Rand's to stare toward the church. "You didn't finish. You didn't cross over the stick..."

"So what? I ain't lettin' you hurt Freddie! And I ain't playin' your stupid game anymore. So just get lost!"

Chris's lip twitched and curled into a snarl. He stared hard into Rand's eyes, then into Freddie's. Freddie smiled stiffly back. Chris tensed, as though ready to strike, then pivoted and walked away.

Freddie stared after him, momentarily numb in the silence. Briefly, a cold breeze swirled around them, then was gone. Dry leaves quaked on nearby trees as Chris disappeared into the forest and the mist.

"Come on," Rand said, helping Freddie up. "Let's go home."

The End

Chad Strong's work has been published in *Tyro Magazine, Horse Illutstrated,* and *The Selkirk Journal.* He was the 3rd place winner in *The Hamilton Spectator*'s Summer Fiction Contest, July 2001, and this story won 2nd place in *Anthology Magazine*'s final fiction contest before that magazine's temporary closure (circa 2003 -2004).

Razors Edge
By Douglas Pugh

ball and fist
may carry it
for a while

words spat
invective flung
regrets echoing afterwards

maybe

kicks and blows
animate, inanimate
target's of misfortune

or the slow seethe
indignant stew
hidden simmers bubbled long
seasoned but indigestible

indignation, shame
frustrations whet
honing the blade
within

but there is no sheath
no vessel, not this human frame

we leak through the threads
of reality, life
porous

red mist
in our veins

slashed wrists

of futility dribbling
past the band aid smiles

and we feel like we've been dying
forever

and maybe
we have

Doulas Pugh has had poetry published at *The Smoking Poet, Leaf Garden Press, Mnemosyne Journal, Short Story Library, ditch magazine, Bewilderingstories.com, The Fib Review, Shot Glass Journal* and *Every Day Poetry*.

Mercy
By Kate Larkindale

It's no fun being immortal. Take it from me. When I saw in the year 2000, I welcomed my ninth century. That's not to say that I am nine hundred years old, but at my age, a few years here and there make little difference. I still look like an eighteen year-old woman, but I just don't believe any living thing—except perhaps a tree—is supposed to live nine hundred years. The human brain, even a preternatural one like mine, is not designed for that much living.

After only eighty years or so, sometimes less, you humans start getting foggy. Alzheimer's disease you call it, or senile dementia. But whatever the name, it is the brain becoming over-full, unable to store any more information, like a computer when its memory is used up. Or something like that.

For me, it takes much longer than eighty years, but the effect is the same. I find myself forgetting things. It usually starts with language, which can be embarrassing in company.

"Ma cherie." The young man bowed and pressed his lips to my hand as he led me toward the expanse of floor where dancers spun in artful circles. His hand on my back was warm as he guided me through the complex series of steps. I smiled at him, enjoying the hard muscles of his chest against mine, the way his knee pressed against me through the sheer layers of apricot silk I wore.

"You're beautiful," he whispered, leaning so close that I could see his pulse throbbing in his throat.

"You are too," I murmured, pulling him closer and breathing in the hot, musky scent that emanated from him. "Come..." I gestured toward the doors that opened out to the grounds. He pulled away, brows knitted in a mixture of confusion and disgust.

"What did you say?" he demanded. I stepped backward, tripping on the long train that swept behind me. What had I said? The word rang in my ears and I realized I had spoken not in French, but in some other long forgotten language, and the word I had uttered sounded like one never used in this echelon of French society.

"Je m'excuse..." I stammered, then became stuck once more, unable to dredge the correct word from my addled skull.

"You are not the woman I thought you were. I bid you adieu." The young man bowed stiffly then turned, heading across the room more swiftly that I would have thought possible.

I fled through the open doors. Had I been able to, I would have blushed, but blood can only rise to my face when I've fed, and I'd thwarted myself in that tonight. It happens every two hundred years or so. I find myself struggling to find the right words. I never lose my native tongue, the language I spoke in my human years, but the languages I have learned since. English, French, German, Russian, all become confused until I speak a muddled combination of them all, mixed in with the Arab of my youth. Then I go to ground.

Going to ground is a restorative process. I choose an isolated place, usually a desert because I hate the damp, and bury myself as deeply underground as I can. And there I stay. Sometimes ten years is enough; other times half a century is needed. Then I can drag myself back to the world and begin a new life. I have entombed myself four times since I was granted immortality, each time wishing I were able to remain there for eternity. Yet always I wake, always I rise again. I surfaced just before the turn of the century and for the first time arose with a sense of purpose.

The manor house was derelict and crumbling, almost unrecognizable when I stumbled upon it while walking down the narrow country lane. A soon as I wrenched open the rusted wrought iron gates I knew the place. Perhaps not this exact manor, but ones like this. For several centuries, houses like this one were my playgrounds. The sound of music played in my ears, and my mouth watered at a remembered taste.

"A ball," I whispered, recalling the candlelit room, the tapping sound of shoes on an expanse of parquet floor. I made my way up the uneven flagstone steps and found the doors hanging from their rusted hinges. Even before I stepped inside, the idea was brewing, my mind superimposing the image of the home in its full glory over what stood before me.

"Yes," I murmured as I wandered through the moldering rooms. "This will be perfect."

Three nights later, I had the papers. One good thing about these modern times is that lawyers work such long hours. John, my lawyer, has never asked why we must conduct our business after nightfall. To him, I am just another wealthy eccentric, one of his more colorful clients. It has always amazed me that money can be an answer to so many questions. It is not difficult for an immortal to gain wealth, and believe me, I have gathered, and lost, innumerable fortunes over the years.

"Here they are," said John. "Although I have no idea what you want with that place. It is secluded, yes, but there are other houses in secluded locations that aren't falling to bits. You'll spend a fortune if you plan to fix it up."

"Ah, John." I looked up from where I was signing my name. "You know I have more than one fortune to spend. Indulge me. When it is done, that manor house will be an important place."

"How so?" He took the papers I handed to him with his head cocked. I walked to the window and stared down at the street, clucking my tongue.

"Now, John," I purred. "You know better than to question me about my business."

He flushed, bowing his head. One of the conditions I laid down when I retained him was that he would never question me. I watched his reflection in the glass.

"You're right, Ma'am. I shall be going now." Tucking the papers into the pocket of his suit jacket, he hurriedly left the room. I watched until I saw him dash out the door and scurry down the street. The streetlights played on his face, creating eerie shadows, yet I could see his fear.

"And quite rightly so," I whispered. "Although you know not what it is you fear."

In years gone by, I might have gone after him. I might have drawn him into an alleyway, toyed with him a while before leaving him, drained and empty upon the cold cobblestones. In this modern day and age, it is much harder to survive as a vampire. We live on the fringes, in the shadows. Electric light makes a mockery of night and unexplained deaths are always investigated. Not like the old days where there was always an outbreak of some deadly disease to blame death upon. Because yes, the great curse of the immortal is that we must drink blood. We can survive for a short while on the blood of animals, but it is human blood that sustains us: sweet, succulent human blood. The guilt is torture. I have yet to meet a vampire who is not haunted by the lives she has taken.

Which is not to say I have met many other vampires; I haven't. We are territorial creatures, and do not gather. I've read in novels of vampire covens, and groups living together as family, but that is not my experience. That's just another fabrication made truth by fiction, like the idea that the bite of a vampire is enough to create a new one. I laugh at that. The ritual involved in making a new vampire is long and elaborate, not to mention painful. If not, the world would be swarming with bloodsuckers. I will not go into it here, but rest assured, when we bite, we bite to feed on your life. To create new vampiric lives, we must feed you.

You humans have romanticized the vampire. I have read widely, devouring each and every book about my kind that has been published. I love that you think us so sexy, so beautiful and compelling – and we are. The transformation makes us beautiful, any flaws or deformities smoothed out by whatever magic makes us live this never-ending succession of nights. Just don't forget the danger. We are fierce predators after all. I read in one book that we read minds and can therefore chose our victims, taking only those who are evil-doers. Don't believe it. I know of no vampire who can read minds, and I certainly cannot. All living, human blood is delectable, whether it is from a priest or a prisoner, a virgin or a violent criminal. It is all different too. What we live off is not the blood per se, but the life force in the blood, what the Chinese know as chi, and every life has its own unique flavor.

I waited until he had disappeared around the corner, out of sight, before dropping without a sound from the window and losing myself among the throngs of people who seethed in and out of the bars and strip clubs that lined the street. It had rained earlier and neon flashed multi-colored hues across the narrow lanes and alleys. An air of danger permeates this part of London, and I thrived on its pulse. My shoes made an elegant tock-tock as I strode down the street, passing through the crowds with ease.

"Whoo! What a fox!" I heard someone exclaim. I turned and dropped a wink at the man who lounged against the wall of a pub, his face red, eyes unfocused. I added an extra swing to my hips as I walked away, knowing how my ass looked in the tight leather pants. He would have done, but I was looking for a tastier dish.

I found her by the river. She stood alone, staring out over the filthy water. In the light that pooled under the single working streetlight at that end of the bridge, I saw tears coursing down her cheeks. The warm summer breeze swirled her skirt around her legs. She could not have been more than eighteen.

I sidled up, leaning on the bridge railing next to her. "Don't you know it's not safe to be out here alone at night?"

"I'm not alone!" She had a ghastly accent. "My boyfriend's just over there." She gestured to an alleyway a little way from the end of the bridge. If she did have a boyfriend down there, he would be no good to her by the time he came out of that particular alley.

I brushed a tear away with the side of my hand. "What did he do to you?" I leaned closer, hanging over the edge of the bridge as I studied her face. She wore too much eye make-up and it ran in streaks down her face, making her look like she was behind bars.

"He did nothing!" She wrenched away and marched off the bridge, moving unsteadily across the cobbles in her too-high heels.

It was over in seconds. I let her go, not calling out to her, not following. When she had been all but swallowed by the shadows at the mouth of the alley, I pounced. No one could have seen me move, I travelled so fast. Before she could even gasp, I had her. My teeth sank into the soft flesh of her neck and my mouth filled with the taste of her: hot and spicy, with just a faint earthy undertone.

Far too soon it was over. I dropped her empty body over the embankment, drawing a knife across her throat before I let the corpse tumble into the sloppy mud that lined the river. With her life thrumming through my veins, I turned and headed back toward the noise and lights, wanting to immerse myself in the sordid crowd of humanity. She was nobody, unimportant, yet her death filled me with remorse. She fought, the way they all do, struggling to live.

Three weeks later, the deed tucked into the pocket of my coat, I returned to the manor. By candlelight I walked through the many rooms, examining them closely.

"This shall be my office," I decided, surveying the large corner room with its wide glass-less windows overlooking the tangled weeds of the grounds. In months they would be cleared, I could picture the garden now,

paths gleaming in the moonlight as they crisscrossed the wide lawns edged with rose bushes. I breathed deeply, almost tasting the scent of lavender and honeysuckle.

"It will be beautiful," I whispered as I turned away from the view.

And so it is. See it? A palatial house with two wings coming off the central hall-way, fourteen guest rooms and quarters for myself and my staff. I spent a fortune restoring the place, crumbling and decrepit as it was, but now it is luxurious. Nobody notices that the silk-covered bed in my room is unslept-in. At dawn I slip away into the dungeons beneath the manor. There, behind several heavy doors with even heavier locks, I rest. The entrance is concealed so that even the kitchen staff who run up and down the stairs many times a day cannot see it. I hear their footsteps in my dreams sometimes, smell the heady scent of their blood pulsing life through their veins. But they are safe. No one need fear me anymore. I have found my reason for being, my purpose on this earth, and it fills me with happiness.

The wide paths are brightly lit. It is early yet, the last traces of sunset still linger-ing in the sky. I sit on a bench and watch the last fingers of red, pink and gold disappear across the horizon. I love this time. When I was younger I never dared come out until every trace of daylight was gone, but aging strengthens us, and I enjoy my glimpses of the sunset without discomfort. The scents I imagined when the manor stood in ruins are real now; lavender and honeysuckle blend with the glorious tea-roses that line the path. I watch an ancient gentleman limping toward me, leaning heavily on his cane. Every step is an achievement, an exercise in overcoming pain. I pity the frailty of these people. After everything they have done in their lives, that they become trapped in these infirm bodies seems intolerable to me. It almost makes me grateful for my immortality.

Almost.

Daily pain, forgetting, incontinence and an overwhelming sense of helplessness and fear are only some of the indignities that face my clients. Most are alone, having lost husbands, wives, life-partners in preceding years. The sadness in these people is palpable, as is their anger. Why shouldn't they be angry? Their very biology has failed them. So they come to me for help.

"Mr. Phelps!" I call when he is near enough to hear me. "Good to see you enjoying such a beautiful evening."

"Thank you." He limps to the bench and lowers himself carefully onto it. "I love the dusk. Always have." His words are mushy, almost unrecognizable, but I understand.

"Me too." We watch the colors fade from the horizon together, faces turned toward the west. He is so frail. His breath wheezes in and out of his chest. Unable to sit upright, he is hunched over, his back bent.

"Did you see Dr. Price?" I ask as the lamps that line the pathways flicker into life.

"Yes, thank you." Mr. Phelps smiles. He's forgotten his teeth and it is a grotesque, gummy smile. "What a nice gentleman."

"He is, isn't he?" I smile back, rising from the bench to return to the manor. My work awaits me. Dr. Price awaits me, along with his partner, Dr. Singleton. "I shall see you tomorrow evening, then."

"I'm looking forward to it." His eyes do not leave my breasts as I walk away. Even at the tail-end of their lives, the men still appreciate a fine female form.

As I stride along the softly lit path, I hum a tune. I see other guests here and there, enjoying the balmy summer evening. Some raise hand to me in greeting and I respond. None of them see me for what I am. I am, to them, a beautiful woman, an administrator, nothing more. Most are so addled they do not notice I am never at my desk before sunset, and to those that do, it is easy enough to explain about my weak eyes, or a tropical fever that leaves me vulnerable to headaches. They are paid well enough that any questions they might have remain unasked.

"Never underestimate the power of money," I murmur to myself, fingering a gold coin I keep in my pocket, just in case. "Or knowledge." The light is brighter here, in front of the main entrance, and I pause for a moment to admire the stately building, now even more elegant than it was when first built.

Tongue in cheek, I have called the place Hotel California after the song. You know how it goes: you can check in but you can never leave? It seems appropriate. My manor is a last stopping point for my guests. They are predominantly elderly, but not exclusively. AIDS has been good for my business and there are almost always a few younger people here, but stooped and frail as the oldies. They stay for a week at the most. The fee includes meals in the fine-dining restaurant, and I have an excellent cellar. There are spa facilities, beautiful gardens, games rooms and more. Full time nurses care for those who can no longer care for themselves. For the ones who have been living in nursing homes, Hotel California must feel like paradise.

The two doctors await me in the hallway by my office.

"I'm sorry I'm late," I murmur as I turn the key in the lock. A lamp burns on the desk, its fuchsia shade casting a rosy glow over the room. "What do we have?"

"Mrs. Ambruzzo will be coming through after dinner," Dr. Singleton says. His hands shake a little and sweat stands out in beads on his forehead. "And Mr. Lucas should be ready tomorrow." His eyes dart toward the locked drawer in the desk.

"And Mr. Phelps?" I reach for a pen, fumbling through the papers on my desk. Do you think he will be ready tomorrow too?"

"The next day." Dr. Price glances at the door that links this room to my bedroom, his eyes bright. "He hasn't spoken with Dr. Singleton yet."

"Good." I nod as I mark down the different names on my calendar, ensuring I will not have AIDS patients two days running. Their blood tastes marvelous, but leaves me with something resembling a hangover.

"Can I..." Dr. Singleton stares at the brass lock on the drawer as if he could force it open with his eyes.

"Very well." I pull the tiny key from my pocket and unlock the drawer. I take my time opening it, enjoying the waves of desperation seething from my employee. I can smell his sweat. "Do you want yours too?" I turn to Dr. Price who has his ear cocked toward the closed door.

"Please..."

Dr. Singleton sees the patients first. Then, should they decide to stay, they see Dr. Price. Each guest must speak to both, if they intend to continue. If they cannot speak due to illness or dementia, the doctors speak to their legal representative, usually a son or daughter. It is imperative that the guest, or their mouthpiece, is fully aware of what it is we do here. They must sign documents stating this. The laws today are so much stricter than they used to be. So many people fail to understand that what I do is a service and a much needed one.=

Some people call it euthanasia, others murder. I call it mercy.

And lunch.

The End

Kate Larkindale is a currently Wellington based writer, cinema manager, film reviewer and mother to two boys. She is constantly amazed that she has any time for writing, but doesn't sleep much.

She's had work published in *HER Magazine*, *Viola Beadleton's Compendium*, *Residential Aliens*, *All Things Girls*, *A Fly in Amber*, and *Halfway Down The Stairs*.

Dismembered Heads
By Jim Davis

People like dismembered heads,
mostly because they're fun to draw:
a dumbfounded expression, drowsy eyelids,
a numb bottom lip welling with saliva and spilling over,
a thin ribbon cascading down the contour lines
of a slack jaw, dripping from a cleft chin,
the artist always catching
one drop as it splashes below, another mid-fall.
And, depending on the method of dismemberment,
a ragged or clean cut edge, where the neck
is skewered on a spear, or, perhaps,
hanging like a ripe apple, held by the hair,
or suctioned to the gritty sidewalk,
sitting languid
in a slowly expanding pool of red ink.

Jim Davis is a teacher by trade, and poetry has developed into one of his greatest passions. His first collection will be going to print this fall with Mi-te Press. The first selections from his next work in progress, tentatively titled, *Grind*, have appeared or are forthcoming in *The Penwood Review*, *Town Creek Poetry*, *Caper Literary Journal*, *The Orange Room Review*, *Disingenuous Twaddle*, and *Smash Cake Magazine*, among many others.

He has a B.A. in Studio Art from Knox College and he is currently studying poetry through Yale University. In addition to the arts, he is also an All-American football player who has traveled from Ireland to Rome, Spain to Switzerland in athletic and artistic pursuits — a unique combination of interests that fuels much of his work.

Biscuithead
By C. Dennis Moore

Cody sat for a second and stared at the hood of his car. Then he backed up a few feet, put the car in Drive, and slammed on the gas, peeling away toward home and away from here. He drove just fast enough to get there, but not so fast as to be noticed. He didn't swerve, or change lanes. He obeyed every red light and stop sign. He pulled onto his street, parked in front of his house, and got out. He rolled up the window, locked the door, went up the front walk, and inside.

With the front door closed and locked behind him, Cody collapsed onto the floor, shaking uncontrollably and crying.

He couldn't leave the car parked there, anyone who saw it in the light of morning would know. Surely there was a dent, and he knew there had to be blood. But he couldn't go out and clean it tonight, what could look more suspicious? What else could he do with it, though? He had no driveway, no garage, and no back alley.

He'd just have to get back in the car and drive, somewhere he wouldn't be seen, and, as soon as he could do it without drawing attention to himself, get the car washed. The dent he would figure out an explanation for, but the blood, he had to get that taken care of right away.

But there was another problem. Gas. The needle had been just above the E, and he wondered if he'd be able to pull into a gas station without being noticed. Even if no one else was there, don't they have those places monitored by cameras? But there was no way he could go anywhere until he stopped for gas. So it looked like his perfect plan wasn't so perfect, and he didn't think he'd be able to do it after all.

Cody was tempted to rush out and give the hood a once over, just enough to make it passable in the light of day, but again there was that nagging doubt; if even one person happened to glance out their window and catch him, what could look more suspicious than a man washing the hood of his car in the middle of the night? But who's up in the middle of the night? Who knows? That's the problem.

He stopped shaking and wiped the tears from his face. He sat on the couch with his head in his hands and his eyes closed, trying to visualize his plan more fully. He kept coming back to the idea of taking the car somewhere it wouldn't be found, but then something else came to him. If the car was out front all night, he had his alibi. If he took it somewhere else and anyone asked around, he couldn't say he'd been home all night.

Jamie's. His mind seized on the thought.

He could take the car to Jamie's. He had at least enough gas to get there, Jamie had a driveway and Cody could pull the car right up close to the house. And Jamie would understand even if no one else did that what he'd done had been an accident. He trusted Jamie with his life, and if he said he'd been at Jamie's all night, who would doubt him? So they'd gone out, got a little too drunk, and he'd passed out there. Perfect. He'd just call him to make sure he was home, then he'd be on his way.

First thing's first, though. Cody had to take a piss.

He listened to the stream hit the back of the bowl. His eyes were closed, but he kept seeing the impact flash before him and it only took a second before he opened them and stared ahead.

Then something shoved him face first into the wall.

He caught himself, splashed piss on his shoe, then zipped his pants and turned around. He was alone.

"I lost my balance, that's all," he said. "Have to call Jamie now."

He stepped toward the door, out into the hall, and tripped over something. This time he wasn't quick enough and he went down, smashing his cheek into the hardwood floor.

"Christ!" he yelled. "What is wrong with me?"

Cody got to his knees and shook his head. His cheek stung. It would swell and bruise. Nothing like a black eye because you're too damn stupid to walk on your own, he thought.

He stood up and headed for the phone. He was three steps in before a sudden, intense pain shot through his leg like a knife on fire. Cody yelped and collapsed again, clutching his calf where the pain was strongest. His leg was wet. He looked at his hand and saw there was blood on his palm. "What the fuck?" he asked.

Did he do that in the car? Did he just not feel it because he'd been in shock when he got home?

He turned his leg around to inspect it. The jeans were torn through and something had pierced his calf. But what? It was just a dent in his hood, what could have done this if he'd been inside the car?

This didn't make sense. He'd have to look in the car to figure this out. Maybe when he slammed on the brake something under his seat flew forward and jabbed him? He couldn't say. Hurt like a bastard though, now that he wasn't on the floor shaking anymore.

He hopped over to the counter where he picked up the phone and dialed Jamie's number. He put the phone to his ear and waited, but nothing happened. There was no ring, no dial tone, and no Jamie.

He clicked the phone off, then tried again, but with the same results. He thought maybe the battery was dead, but he'd picked it up off the base, so it should be charged. He followed the electric cord and saw it was still plugged in. Then he followed the phone cord and saw his problem. The cord was chewed in half.

"Rats?" he asked.

Then something hit him in the back of the head and Cody looked up in time to see the metal pot skid across the kitchen floor. He looked further and saw something on the counter. That first look and Cody knew he was hallucinating. Standing on his kitchen counter, holding a skillet above its head was . . . something, he wasn't sure what. It was about the size of a baby, but skinny. It was grey and naked, hairless. Its head was fat, round, flat. When it saw Cody was looking at it, it snarled and showed its teeth. There was blood on them. From across the room, Cody could see it had yellow eyes. It made a noise somewhere between a growl and a hiss and hurled the skillet at Cody's head.

"Shit!" he said and ducked just in time. The skillet bounced off the wall and clattered across the floor making a horrible racket and coming to a halt under the kitchen table.

Cody backed away, but didn't take his eyes off the creature. How could he? A second ago he'd been sure he was hallucinating, but that didn't stop him from ducking. And that had sure *sounded* real enough.

The thing grabbed a ceramic plate from the sink, dried spaghetti sauce and tiny bits of pasta stuck to it, and flung it across the room. It hit Cody dead center in the throat and he went down, gasping and clutching himself, trying to breathe.

That was no hallucination. Still trying to catch his breath, and feeling like there was something blocking his airway, he got on his knees and crawled down the hall, away from this. He got to his bedroom and slammed the door behind him, then braced it with his body.

He felt like his throat had been caved in. He fought the urge to vomit. Tears stood out in his eyes from the pain in his throat, and his nose was running. He wiped his face with his shirttail and sat up straighter. He still couldn't breathe right, but it was getting better.

What the hell was that thing? Some deformed midget? What was that disease that makes children look like old men? Something that started with a P. Didn't matter. Who or what ever it was, from the racket out there, it sounded like it was tearing up Cody's house.

One crash was the lamp beside the couch. One was a picture on the wall by the front door. Another, a very loud one this time, followed by a pop and a sizzle, was the television screen. He knew his house well enough to know the sounds.

"Shit," he said. His voice was hoarse, barely audible. "I have to stop this."

But what could he do? His calf was bleeding, his throat collapsed. He wondered if it had been responsible for his leg and when he recalled the blood on its teeth, he was sure it had been. It may be a fraction of his size, but it had had no problem taking him down.

Cody had a baseball bat in his closet; that ought to take care of it. But his bedroom door had no lock and if he moved and then couldn't find the bat, that would give the creature plenty of time to get in here and attack him.

Still, he had to try.

He limped to his closet. The whole time his hands rummaged inside, Cody's eyes were glued to the door. His fingers wrapped around the bat, and he pulled it out. Before going on the attack, he swallowed and felt the lump in his throat beginning to dissolve. He wondered for a second if there was some internal injury.

He took a breath, opened the door, and stepped into the hall.

Something flew past his head and shattered behind him. An ashtray. His nephew had given him that last year when Cody visited them in North Carolina. He didn't smoke, but he loved his nephew. Cody looked at the creature and saw it standing on the back of his couch, more ammunition ready, this time a marble bookend shaped like a horse's head, a refugee from the 70s decor of his parents' house.

That's gonna hurt, he thought. If it hits me.

After all, he was holding a bat.

They stared at each other a second and Cody took a step forward. Then the creature caught him off guard by charging. It leapt off the back of the couch, to the chair against the wall, flew into the air, and flung the bookend at him. It grabbed the doorway to the kitchen, swung itself around, and disappeared into the other room. The bookend went wild, careened off the wall, and thudded into Cody's chest, knocking him back a few steps, but not much else. He'd have another bruise there to go along with the one on his cheek, but he'd be alright. He brought the bat up again and continued down the hall, stopping before the kitchen door and listening. More pots and pans, he wondered?

There was no sign of the creature, though. He stepped into the kitchen with the bat held ready. He didn't see it anywhere. He scanned the counter, the top of the refrigerator, under the table, anywhere it might hide, but he couldn't find it.

Maybe it's vanished, he wondered. Left the way it came in? How was that? Now there was a question to which he would love to find the answer.

Something creaked behind him, but before he could turn the thing flew out from the cabinet and landed on Cody's head, wrapped its arms around his face and tried to take a bite out of his skull. Cody screamed, dropped the bat, and threw himself into the wall, hoping to squash the fucker into letting go, but no matter how hard he battered it, it held on tight, all the time trying to eat its way into the top of his head.

He reached up and tried to wrench it off, but it was stuck. Through the tangle of its limbs across his face, he saw the front door and headed for it. He opened it, stuck the creature into the space between the door and the jam, and started slamming the door on it. It finally stopped biting his head, let out a screech, and fell backward off his shoulders. It scampered to the back of the couch again and grabbed an empty beer bottle.

Cody turned toward it. It was ready for another attack, but he'd dropped his bat.

He glanced around quickly. The only thing within reach was a heavy bag of grass seed he'd been meaning to scatter in the front yard. He grabbed it and threw the big bag, which surely weighed twice what that thing did, straight at it.

He missed. The bag hit the back of the couch and fell flat on the cushions. The beer bottle flew at him and Cody dodged it. Then the thing grabbed the bag of seeds and held it over its head. Its claws dug into the plastic and seeds began to rain down around it. It looked at them first in confusion, and then in dismay. It tossed the punctured bag aside, got on its knees, and . . . began to count the seeds.

Cody couldn't believe what he was seeing, but there it was. The thing had gone from killer to obsessive-compulsive in a second. It collected them in its palm as it counted, slowly, meticulously. Cody stood there bewildered by what he was seeing. He took a step toward it, but the thing paid him no mind as it deposited seeds, one at a time, into its palm.

Cody inched closer, keeping his eyes on it and his hands ready, just in case. His foot nudged the busted seed bag and he pulled it toward him, then very slowly stooped to pick it up. More seeds spilled from the holes the creature's claws had made and Cody dug his fingers into them and ripped open the bag even further. The seeds came in a flood, then, all over the floor. The creature saw this, threw up its hands in disgust, and hissed, "You're a very bad boy!" Its voice was broken glass and jagged soup cans. It then went back to the task of cleaning the seeds, one by one.

Cody moved away, grabbed the bat from the kitchen floor, and stood staring at it.

And then, like a trigger, he heard his mother's voice.

"You're a very bad boy, Cody. Do you know what happened to bad boys in the old country?"

He was five and he'd just nailed one of the neighborhood kids in the head with a rock. He wasn't trying to, wasn't even aiming for the kid, but the boy had walked right into the path of Cody's throw. The kid's head bled a little, but he needed no stitches and it hadn't even left a scar. But his mother had not been so quick to forgive the accident. "The goblins punish them. Is that what you want to happen to you? Is it?"

No, it wasn't what he wanted to happen to him, and his mother had been able to get away with that story until Cody was eight and stopped believing in goblins, as well as all the other childhood myths.

And what did it mean, he'd been a very bad boy? His wreck? It wasn't like that was the first thing Cody'd ever done wrong. Did the thing make distinctions like that, big bad and little bad? Was it only here because he'd most likely left someone to die in the middle of the street? But it just didn't make any sense, and Cody could stand here all night trying to figure it out when the fact remained he had a fucking goblin on his couch, counting grass seeds!

Its palm was full so it grabbed the empty bag--Cody flinched when it reached in his direction--and stuffed the seeds back into the bag. Then it started on its second handful.

"Forget this shit," Cody said, and he bolted for the door. He jumped in his car and headed for Jamie's house. And if Jamie wasn't home, he'd just sit outside until he was. An alibi was now the last thing on his mind. If it came down to it and he was asked,

fine, he'd admit it; right now he just wanted away from that thing.

Jamie only lived a few blocks away and Cody was there in seconds. He banged on the door for almost five minutes before the porch light flashed on and Jamie opened the door yelling, "I hear you, man, quiet down, there's people in here, shit!"

Cody pushed his way in and said, "Shit, man, you gotta help me, you gotta help me get rid of it."

"What are you talkin' about? It's two in the morning, what are you doing?"

Cody sat on the couch, took a deep breath, and tried to calm himself. "Just give me a second. You ain't gonna believe this shit."

He told him everything that had happened, the accident, his fleeing panic. He told him his original plan to park his car here until morning.

"Holy shit. What are you gonna do? Did you call the police?"

"That's not all of it. There's something in my house."

"What do you mean?"

He told him the rest and Jamie stood and listened and at the end he just stared at him.

"You don't believe me," Cody said.

"Who would? I think you're drunk. You can sleep it off here, but you're wasted."

Cody looked at him and for a second he wondered if Jamie was right. Maybe he was just so drunk he was hallucinating. Maybe somebody'd slipped something into his beer?

Then the pain in his calf flared and he asked Jamie, "How do you explain this, then?"

Jamie looked at it, considered for a

second, then said, "You could have done this anytime tonight and not even noticed it. Just lay down, I'll bring in the trash in case you puke, but I'm going back to sleep."

No, something was wrong here, Cody thought. He couldn't just let it go. Maybe he'd imagined the whole thing; maybe he was so drunk his conscience was creating goblins. But if Jamie went back to bed just like that . . . what would he do if he went home tomorrow and the thing was still there? He had to know. He couldn't lie here all night wondering.

He got up and said, "Yeah, maybe you're right. Shit, I think I left my front door open, though."

"Lay down, I'll get it. Tomorrow you need to get that cut looked at."

Jamie went into his bedroom and came back a second later with a pair of jeans over his shorts, slipped into his shoes and grabbed his keys and jacket, then was out the door.

When he was gone, Cody lay back on the couch and stared at the ceiling. The house was quiet. His breathing sounded louder than usual, heavier. He tried to slow it. His foot tapped the arm of the couch. He tried counting seconds, thinking that would keep him occupied until Jamie came back. He got as far as forty when his mother's voice came again.

"You're a very bad boy, Cody! Goblins in the old country punish bad boys. They come out at night and break all your favorite toys, they pinch you when you're trying to sleep, they trip you so you fall down the stairs. You don't be a bad boy. You go right over to that boy's house and you tell him you're sorry, this minute!"

But the more he thought about it, the more Jamie's words made sense. And he'd stopped believing fairy tales how long ago? If

that thing had been real, why didn't it come to him in high school when he'd jumped Ben Tozier? After all, Ben had done nothing more than give him what Cody'd thought was a dirty look in the hall. Cody found out later Ben had been looking at the guy behind Cody that day, and he'd been kidding around because the guy had been a friend of Ben's. Cody apologized and they'd even been friends for a year or two after. But if the thing in Cody's house was real, it would have come to him then, wouldn't it?

Or in middle school when he'd embarked on a short career as a shoplifter. Until he got caught. But it never came to him then, either.

Jamie was right. Cody was wasted; he'd imagined it. That had to be it.

He'd try to sleep. And in the morning, he'd clean his car, get the dent fixed, and pray to God he could get on with his life.

A minute later, he heard Jamie's truck pulling up to the house, and he realized something he hadn't before. He was drunk, on his back, staring up, but the house was still. Nothing was spinning, and he didn't have that constant lurch in his stomach that said he could throw up any second. Maybe he wasn't as drunk as he'd thought. But if that were the case, maybe he'd been sober when the thing attacked him, maybe it had been real the whole time.

Jamie was back, he'd tell him. It was the first thing Cody asked when Jamie walked in, "Did you see it? Is it still there?"

"You're still up? I figured you'd be passed out by now. No, you're plenty drunk, believe it. Your house is fine," Jamie said.

"But how? That thing was tearing it up."

Jamie kicked his shoes off and tossed his jacket over the side of a chair and, as he headed down the hall to bed, said, "Your place is fine. Your lamp's busted, you must have knocked it over, and you smashed in your TV screen, but other than that . . . Sleep it off. In the morning we'll figure out what to do about your car."

Jamie disappeared into his bedroom, shut the door, and Cody didn't hear from him again until morning. He lay there on the couch, watching the ceiling and wondering. No pots and pans scattered across the kitchen floor? What about the grass seed? Could it have cleaned it all up before Jamie got there? He didn't know. Maybe his guilt *had* created it. He'd figure it out in the morning. He was suddenly exhausted and sleep overcame him in minutes.

When he woke up, Jamie was already up, sitting in the kitchen eating a bacon and egg sandwich and drinking coffee. Cody climbed off the couch, shambled into the bathroom to piss, then shambled back and sunk into the chair across from his best friend. His leg was throbbing. He'd taken a few aspirin in the bathroom.

"I'm never doing that again. I'm never going out again, I'm never drinking again, I'm never doing nothing again but sitting on my ass at home."

"Sure thing," Jamie said. "You hungry?"

"You kidding? Not even close."

"I looked at your car this morning. I don't know what you did, but that shit's fucked up. We gotta get that thing cleaned up now. I pulled it into my garage already. I'm gonna finish this coffee, then we're going out there."

"You got it. And thanks man, I didn't know where else to go. It was an accident,"

"I know. We'll fix it and forget it, you got it?"

They took three hours scrubbing every inch of Cody's car. They had to make sure every drop of blood, every strand of hair was gone before taking the car in to get the dent fixed. They would leave it here, in Jamie's garage for the next week, and then Cody would take it in. It was Jamie who told him not to take it in the day after the police find a body lying in the street. Maybe he'd even run it into a tree just to make sure his story matched the evidence on the car.

When they were sure they'd done everything they could to erase what Cody'd done, they got into Jamie's truck and headed for Cody's house.

"Do you remember where it happened?" Jamie asked. "What street?"

"I think it was on Lafayette," Cody said. "I was in shock, though, pretty much from the time it happened until I got home."

"Well, don't drive down Lafayette ever again, you take Olive. It's only a block away and it'll take you to all the same places."

"Yeah. I hope whoever it was didn't suffer too much. I mean . . . what if I just left 'em lying there with their lungs filling up with blood, drowning in it?"

"Don't think about it," Jamie said. "Just try to forget it ever happened. Got it? It was an accident, it should never have happened, and it won't ever happen again because from today on you don't go out drinking anymore."

"Yeah, man, I got it," Cody said. "I think my neighbors might notice my car being gone so long, though."

"You're gonna call and have your house fumigated. You'll stay at my place while they do it that should take a few days at least. After that we'll think of something else."

It sounded like Jamie had just about everything covered, Cody thought. He knew there was no way he could ever repay him for what he was doing. But he was going to spend the rest of his life trying.

They were coming up on the stoplight before the turn onto Cody's street. As it turned yellow, Jamie tapped the brake, but the truck wasn't slowing down.

"What the fuck?" he asked. He kept pressing the brake, over and over, and the light turned red, but Jamie ran it and he and Cody looked at each other with frightened eyes. "My brakes are out, man."

"You've both been very bad boys," a voice hissed. They turned and saw the creature at Cody's window.

They screamed and the thing leapt across the cab of the truck, dove to the floor and shoved the gas pedal down as far as it would go. The truck gained speed while the two inside tried to fight the thing off the accelerator, but it held tight, forcing them faster and faster and snapping at them with its teeth when they got too close. Cody reached for the door handle to hop out, but the street was lined with cars and there was no room. Jamie steered the best he could, dodged a few cars, but the faster the truck went, the harder it was down a residential street. He looked at the speedometer; they were passing eighty.

"Shit, no," Cody said from the passenger seat.

Jamie looked over at his friend, then looked forward to see what Cody was seeing. They were headed for a city bus. It had just dropped off its passengers and was pulling away from the curb. They hit it broadside, and plowed a hole almost halfway through it. Both were thrown through the windshield and their bodies torn to shreds on the broken glass and sheered metal.

In the mess and confusion, no one saw the tiny creature with the flat, round head scamper away from the wreckage.

The End

C. Dennis Moore has been writing just about 10 years with over 60 short stories and novellas in print, most recently in the *Absent Willow Review's Best of 2009* anthology, as well as the *Vile Things* anthology from *Comet Press*. By day he's an inventory control clerk, and his website is at www.cdennismoore.com.

Spectrum Crossing
By Marina Lee Sable

The rooms of your house
are distorted beyond recognition.
Stained and mildewed walls, inverted
stairs of a nightmare helter skelter,
warped doors and crooked floors.

You can never go home again.
They will be waiting for you
in the walls, in the chimney,
on the curve of stair.

So you are here
in the City of the Haunted,
lost in the patched blackness
where you walk the streets alone
terrified they might detect
the blood thud of your heart.

Lamps hiss, spitting sparks
that burn and smoke your flesh.
The sudden violet twist of street
where violet light jams your eyes
and alien voices trespass your mind.

A blue-grey ionization of air
as you accidentally step into that other realm
and the awful clutch of doom
when inchoate shapes press toward you.

Marina Lee Sable's poems have appeared or are forthcoming in *The Pedestal Magazine*, *Strange Horizons, Dreams of Decadence, Paper Crow, OG's Speculative Fiction, Cover of Darkness, Illumen, Shelter of Daylight, Basement Stories,* and *Strong Verse*.

The Blues
By Matthew Howe

A ratty guitar hung around his neck on tied-together shoelaces. The old man had staked his turf on a crumbling section of sidewalk out front of an abandoned tenement. It was a weird place to panhandle, Josh thought, not much traffic coming this way, especially at 3am.

The man's head drooped, and Josh could not see his face, only a curly shock of white hair. For all Josh knew, the guy might be asleep on his feet.

But as Josh passed by, the man spoke, his voice deep and powerful, as if it emanated from the bowels of the Earth, and not from a pair of aging lungs.

"Buck or the blues," the old man rumbled.

"Excuse me?" Josh asked. He hadn't meant to say anything, had planned to walk on by, but the force of the man's voice stopped him cold.

The man lifted his head, revealing a lined and weathered face—driftwood scorched by the sun. In this ruined landscape, a pair of shocking cobalt eyes blazed. "Buck or the blues," the man said again. This time there was a note of cold mirth in his voice.

"Wait a sec," Josh said. "I pay you, *or* you play?"

"Buck or the blues," the old man cackled - the funniest joke in the world that Josh was too stupid to get.

"Interesting," Josh said to no one in particular. He studied the old man a moment. The guy was obviously working some kind of street-busker reverse-psychology scam. Pay him not to play. It made no sense.

"Buck or the blues," the man said again, and now there was a creepy menace to his voice that Josh recoiled against. He'd spent the last 14 hours locked in an edit suite with a gaggle of dim-bulb producers ordering him to nudge that shot, trim this cut, change a dissolve to a wipe, then back to a dissolve, no a wipe, wait, a dissolve.

He was done being pushed around for the night.

Josh shrugged, spread his hands. "Ain't got a buck, dude, sorry."

"It's the blues, then," the man replied.

Josh nodded. "Awesome. You have fun with that."

He turned and walked away. His steps rang on the sidewalk in a way he hadn't noticed before, as if the sidewalk was slapping them back at him. Josh felt the hairs on his arms rise up as one. He felt an electric tingle gather as if something heavy and cold was about to fall from the sky on him.

The first note stuck him like a pistol shot in the back. A loud, steel twang. Josh froze in place, flinching.

"*I got me a woman...*" the man's voice was loud and strong. The world shook with it. "*But that woman ain't no good.*" The guitar thudded out the rhythm, low and mean, all bass strings. "*I said I got me a woman, but that woman ain't no good.*"

Josh turned as the man ran his fingers

up the neck, played a riff high and hard. It socked him in the gut.

"*That woman I been courting, man, she went and wrecked me good.*"

Josh walked back, toward the man, caught in his ominous gravity as he moved into the second verse.

"*I loved that girl so deeply. Yeah, I sure loved her so.*"

Josh paused before the man, his foot tapping the filthy sidewalk with the rhythm of the song.

"*You know I loved that gal so deeply, yeah I sure loved her so. But when I asked that girl to marry, that evil gal said no.*"

Josh's tapping foot froze. His heart stuttered as it all came rushing back.

Two years ago he'd asked his girlfriend, Noreen, to marry him. She'd refused. Not only that, she'd revealed she'd been having an affair with someone at work, and moved out of the apartment they shared. It had been the worst thing that had ever happened to him. He'd been knocked low, thrown into a black depression he thought he'd never climb out of.

Only he had climbed out of it, inch by inch. He'd healed, pushed her from his mind, gotten over it.

Or he thought he'd gotten over it. Deep down, he hadn't, and now this old bastard's song had dredged it all up again.

"Okay, stop," Josh said, as loud as he could manage.

The man turned his gaze on John, and further protest shriveled on his lips. The guitar screamed as the old man finished a solo and returned to where he'd left off. "*Yeah I asked that girl to marry me, but that evil gal said no.*"

Josh felt suddenly sick. He wanted to grab the fucking guitar from the old guy's hands and smash it on the sidewalk, but he was paralyzed.

The old man's craggy visage split into a wide smile, as if appreciating Josh's impotence. His eyes sparkled brighter, drilling into Josh's as he sang: "*Noreen, Noreen, why you gone and done me wrong.*"

Josh gaped.

"*I said Noreen, Noreen, why you gone and done me wrong?*"

Josh stumbled back a step. The old man was singing about Noreen. He knew. The old fuck *knew* and was singing about the girl who had nearly destroyed him.

Josh felt his heart melting. He knew that was sappy, maybe kind of a stupid thing to think, but there was no other way to express it. His heart had turned to a lump of chocolate left out in the sun too long and if someone tried to pick it up, they were going to get a sticky mess all over their hands.

The man played on, eyes screwed shut now, fingers burning up the fret board, deep voice hammering. "*Noreen, my love was true, baby, but your love it was a lie. I say Noreen, my love was true, but your love it was a lie. When I found that other man, all I wanted was to die.*"

Another solo came now, but it faded to insignificance in Josh's mind. Noreen's face had risen from the depths of memory to shove everything else aside.

A profound emptiness suddenly filled the void where Josh's heart once had been. A black void, no, a blue void - the blue of the sky half an hour before dawn, that deep, somber blue that always made him sad.

He reached for his wallet. He had fifty bucks in it. He dropped the money at the man's feet; the bills fluttered from his fingers. The man stopped playing, smiled at Josh. "Thank you, sir. You have a good night now."

Josh said nothing. Noreen was all he could think about now. She's been the most beautiful woman in the world. He'd given himself to her, body and soul, and she'd obliterated him.

He turned and trudged for his apartment, ignoring the sound of the old man picking up and pocketing his money. Every step was agony, every sound, from the titters of the first birds getting ready to greet the dawn to the distant hum of cars on the BQE reminded him of her.

They'd spent, what was it, six amazing years together? He wondered what he'd done wrong. Why he hadn't been man enough to keep her satisfied? What he could have done differently?

Josh reached his apartment, trudged up the stairs to the fifth floor - another thing to be depressed about.

He entered through the kitchen. From behind his roommate's door he heard giggling. Sam was in there with a girl. Sam was always in there with a girl. Rarely was it the same girl. Sam didn't have a job, lived off some kind of trust fund, did nothing but smoke dope, screw girls, and occasionally snap a few mediocre photographs that his dad's connections got into galleries. Never had to work for a living, never had to worry, never got involved with someone long enough to give her a hold on his heart.

Josh looked around the kitchen with new eyes, eyes given to him by the old man's song. When he'd moved in, he'd thought the apartment hip and cool. Now all he saw was the stains on the countertops, the dirt on the floor, the way that chips in the paint on the windowsills had been covered with a new coat, leaving uneven patched like old scabs.

It was the most depressing place he could imagine.

A swell of pain rolled through him. Noreen. Why had Noreen left him? He hadn't realized how much she'd hurt him, but now, in this crappy apartment, with his ultimate slacker roommate getting laid in the in the next room, with nothing to look forward to but more abuse from assholes at his crappy job, he understood that without her, there was nothing holding him to this earth.

The old man's song echoed through his mind. Each chord, each note, stabbed at him.

The blues. The old man had given him the blues all right. He now realized that was the deal. Pay the man or he'd play, because when he played, bad things happened.

Noreen. Noreen. Why had she done him wrong?

He shuffled to the kitchen window, disgusted by how grimy and fly-specked it was. He unlatched it, hauled on it, forcing the stubborn frame up with a dull squeak.

He looked down at the street sixty feet below, expecting to see the old man grinning up at him. But the old man was nowhere in sight. He didn't have to be in sight. His song was inside Josh's head, wrecking the place.

Josh bent, pushed his upper body through the window. The cool air felt clean. He threw a leg over the sill, straddled it, one foot planted on the kitchen's dirty linoleum, one hanging in space. He closed his eyes. Without Noreen, he was nothing.

He heard Sam's door open, his roommate's stoner voice broke the quiet. "Josh, hey man." The voice sharpened. "Josh? Hey, Josh, what the fuck? What the fuck, dude?"

Josh closed his eyes, leaned right, and the whole world was rushing air against his skin. The sound grew louder, the shrieking notes and chords of his fall building to crescendo, and then he met the sidewalk with a terrible thud and a bass roll of thunder. He felt his skull crack with a thousand snare hits, each accompanied by a flash of light. He heard the dull splat his body made, felt something split and tear, felt his organs slam against each other, ripped from their moorings.

The world went dark and dreamy. He felt a terrible dull nausea spread sticky fingers through him. He was lying on his side, could dimly see the sidewalk, an expanding puddle of blood rolling away from him like a tide.

Footsteps, a door bursting open. Sam yelling: "Josh, Josh, fuck. What the fuck?"

Then Sam leaning over him, slapping a hand to his shoulder, turning Josh's body to lie flat, incredible pain, but oddly irrelevant at the same time.

Sam's face came into focus. More faces behind him, people drawn by his fall, by Sam's shouts. Josh's field of view narrowed, like a camera trick in an old movie. "Call 911," Sam was screaming but Josh could barely hear. "Call fucking 911."

Then Sam was close, his eyes wide and haunted. "Josh, why, man?"

"Noreen," Josh whispered. "Can't live without Noreen."

Sam stared at him. "Who's Noreen?"

Another man's voice as the world dimmed. "Noreen? What'd she do to him?"

Sam answering, "I've been living with him for five years. Don't know what the fuck he's talking about."

Then they were gone, a soft blue black taking him, accompanied by the distant jangle of guitar strings.

The End

Matthew Howe's short stories have been published in *Electric Spec, Darkfire, Crossroads, Hadrosaur tales,* and *Cthulhu Sex.* His book, *Film is Hell* was published by Laurelton Media.

Gingerbread Lady

By Michael Lee Johnson

Gingerbread lady,
no sugar or cinnamon spice;
years ago arthritis and senility took their toll.
Crippled mind moves in then out, like an old sexual adventure
blurred in an imagination of fingertip thoughts.
Who remembers the characters?
There was George, her lover, near the bridge at the Chicago River:
she missed his funeral; her friends were there.
She always made feather-light of people dwelling on death,
but black and white she remembers well.
The past is the present; the present is forgotten.
Who remembers Gingerbread Lady?
Sometimes lazy-time tea with a twist of lime,
sometimes drunken-time screwdriver twist with clarity.
She walks in scandals.
Her live-in maid smirked as Gingerbread Lady gummed her food,
false teeth forgotten in a custom-imprinted cup
with water, vinegar, and ginger.
Years ago, arthritis and senility took their toll.
Ginger forgot to rise out of bed;
no sugar, or cinnamon toast.

Michael Lee Johnson is a poet and freelance writer from Itasca, Illinois. He is heavy influenced by: Carl Sandburg, Robert Frost, William Carlos Williams, Irving Layton, Leonard Cohen, and Allen Ginsberg. His new poetry chapbook with pictures, titled *From Which Place the Morning Rises,* and his new photo version of *The Lost American: from Exile to Freedom* are available at: http://stores.lulu.com/promomanusa. The original version of *The Lost American: from Exile to Freedom,* can be found at: http://www.iuniverse.com/book-store/book_detail.asp?isbn=0-595-46091-7.   He also has 2 previous chapbooks available at: http://stores.lulu.com/poetryboy.

Night Hag

By Charles Kyffhausen

All right, Brian thought knowingly when he saw what floated above him. The black skull had even blacker pits for its eyes and mouth, and its shapeless limbs gripped his body while it muttered incomprehensible words. Brian knew he was dreaming while partially conscious, and all he had to do to get rid of the Night Hag was to awaken completely.

Then he realized what had roused him in the first place. His two Irish Wolfhounds were whimpering and snarling at the apparition, and someone was probing and scratching at the deadbolt lock on his front door. Now he knew exactly how his friends had died, and he was next on the list.

#

"Smith!" Lieutenant General Donald Markham had called at the previous day's meeting. The general's audience consisted of two dozen people, and the setting was a room that didn't officially exist. The Instrumentality of Freedom's mission was to protect the United States from threats that most people could barely imagine, and it told Congress what Congress needed to know through the CIA and NSA.

"I answer for him!" Homicide Detective Mike Martelli replied on behalf of the Special Operations officer.

"Jackson!"

"I answer for him!" Brian Graham replied firmly. He and Mike had worked together, and each man knew that he could count on the other.

"Absent friends!" the general continued, and everybody drank the group's toast to the men and women who could never again answer the IOF's roll call on their own behalf.

Not everyone in the room was a soldier or adventurer. Valerie Holland was an archaeologist like Brian, and she had like Brian earned a full professorship at an age when most academicians could only dream of that first tenured step, Associate. Her specialty, however, consisted of ancient lore as opposed to the fisticuffs and marksmanship in which Brian was highly proficient. The redhead was terrified, and she couldn't hide it.

"Brian and I will handle this, Val," the heiress of the Morgan Armory, the world's biggest defense contractor, reassured her. Reconstructive surgery had only partly removed the scar that Diana Morgan had gotten at the Battle of Kafiristan under circumstances that would have qualified any member of the Armed Forces for the Medal of Honor. "Whatever got our friends will have to go through me to get to you," she continued, but Brian saw from Valerie's expression that this promise was less than reassuring.

"If the bad guys like to play with sharp metal —" a menacing voice began. It belonged to Nick Sykes, the IOF's close combat weapon instructor whose fighting knives had sent dozens of his country's enemies to their final

"Jackson and Smith were too good to be murdered in their beds, Nick," General Markham interjected. "You don't break into a former Navy SEAL's or Green Beret's home, much less even try to kill him with a knife, and walk out alive."

"It's as if someone injected them with curare or pancuronium bromide," Mike explained. "Either drug would have paralyzed them while the perpetrator did his work. He may have used a knife to let us know that the victims were helpless but still able to feel pain. The autopsies, however, found no drugs in either body."

"I'm terrified, and I'm afraid it shows," Valerie said while she brushed her auburn hair nervously.

"You helped kill that Serpent Demon even though you were scared out of your mind," Brian reminded her.

"Thanks, Brian. Anyone with good sense would fear the supernatural entities that a sorcerer can send, like an extension of his own body, to do his bidding. The sender can see through the entity's eyes and sometimes speak through its mouth even though he is hundreds of miles away."

"Anything that is solid enough to hurt us is solid enough to feel hot lead, cold steel, or directed energy," Diana interjected confidently. Her lips peeled back to bare her teeth while she continued, "If I use an electromagnetic rail gun on it, we will need a squeegee mop and a pail to collect the remains. If I use the Tesla Ray, any leftovers will fit in a plastic sandwich bag: the small size."

"All right, Ms. 'I don't believe in curses,' don't you remember what happened the last time you and Brian didn't listen to me?" Diana turned slightly red while Valerie continued, "You like weapons that draw enough

power to run small cities, but these situations call for books instead of blasters. Ancient lore, and not your father's lasers, took down the Serpent Demon."

"She's right, Diana," Brian said while he admitted ruefully to himself that even his 220 pounds of bone and muscle didn't make him a better man than the two who had just died. Anything that could kill a SEAL and a Green Beret could probably take him, Nick, and Diana too, and Val knew this despite their best efforts to pretend otherwise. "Valerie, how can we protect ourselves against these entities?"

"I don't know what is hunting us, but iron is the mortal enemy of many forms of sorcery. A steel jacketed bullet doesn't contain enough to destroy the entities in question. A large mass of iron can however harm not only the entity but also its controller."

"Maybe I had better send my wife somewhere for a while, and the witness protection program can help with that," Mike said. "She doesn't need to know about the IOF but I can tell her that a violent thug I once sent to jail called and said he knows where we live. I'm also going to pick up a steel pipe at the hardware store."

"Keep that pipe with you at all times, Mike," Valerie said almost desperately. "Your life could depend on it."

"Valerie, you had better stay with Diana and Mr. Morgan," General Markham suggested. The latter was a M1913 Patton Saber that had, through virtual reality biofeedback, been precision-balanced for Diana's hand, fencing style, and almost superhuman reflexes. "The Morgan estate is like a fortress because her great grandfather built it to keep out Nazi and Soviet agents. What are the rest of you doing for security?" The other agents told him, and he nodded with satisfaction.

#

Brian had relied on his home's security system, his dogs, and himself for protection, and all had failed. Now he struggled to free himself from the horrific black shape that paralyzed his muscles and pinned him to his bed. The Night Hag's task was obviously to stop him from defending himself against the killer who was breaking into his house, and he wanted nothing more than to turn the tables on these cowardly assassins. Anger and rage weren't enough to break the Night Hag's hold on him, though, and neither was his natural instinct for self-preservation. Jackson and Smith also had been strong men who wanted to live.

The burglar alarm went off the moment the front door opened to the intruder, but Brian knew that the police couldn't arrive in time to intervene. No one would know what had gotten him, just as no one knew what had gotten the others. The Night Hag would attack the next night, and then the next, and good men and women who had pledged their lives to the defense of Civilization would perish.

The apparition, or whoever was controlling it, confirmed his worst fears while the intruder headed for his stairwell. *You do not seem to be afraid for yourself,* it whispered cruelly. *I wonder how that redhead will die when her turn comes, though. She will want to scream, but she won't even be able to moan. That detective will solve this case by dying in the same manner, and we will slaughter that general in his bed like a pig. You and Diana Morgan cost us two hundred men and a flag at Kafiristan, and you can die with the knowledge that she will share the agonies you suffer —*

"You just made a big mistake," Brian said, and he realized that he had spoken aloud despite his total paralysis. The apparition had reminded him that he had to both live and win to save his friends as well as himself, and now he found himself with a force of will that he never knew that anyone could possess. It was no longer his will alone, but that of friends and comrades who would willingly die for their country and each other, that forced his right arm to move.

"All for one," Brian snarled while his hand gripped the hilt of the Scottish broadsword that had served his ancestors at Waterloo and Balaclava, and the blade cleared its sheath an instant later. "*And one for all!*" Flesh and bone seemed to yield to the weapon's edge despite the apparition's lack of substance, and then the Night Hag crumpled, fell, and vanished.

#

No problem, the assassin meanwhile thought when the two wolfhounds came at him. He pressed a button on the weapon in his left hand, and the terrific blast of ultrasound stopped both dogs in their tracks. Now he could murder his paralyzed victim, just as he had done to the other two men.

He burst into Brian's bedroom only to find an empty bed, and then he turned to look straight into the bore of a twelve-gauge shotgun. His senses didn't even have time to process the muzzle flash or the earsplitting blast.

#

"Tell Jackson and Smith that the IOF sends its regards," Brian told his prospective assassin's body. Then he made his smoking weapon safe, and his first phone call told the police that they were no longer responding

147

to a "hot" home invasion. Then he picked up a secure phone and called General Markham, and the two men called the rest of the IOF. Their message was simple: "Don't go to sleep again tonight, or you might never wake up. We'll decide what to do tomorrow, but right now caffeine is your best friend."

The decision was to sleep in shifts for mutual protection, and the resulting exhaustion began to take its toll. "I hate the defensive," Brian said two weeks later while he stifled an enormous yawn, and his fellow agents looked equally hagridden. Then Mike Martelli walked in with a big smile on his otherwise weary face.

"It's over!" the detective shouted triumphantly. "The Philadelphia police will have to live with the perfect locked room murder mystery because they don't need to know about the IOF but they closed our case for us." He went on to describe how a foul odor had led the authorities to a corpse inside an abandoned building. They had also found a book whose pages were human skin, along with a suitcase full of money.

"The FBI is tracing the money, and it thinks the trail will lead to an international terrorist organization," Mike continued. "I signed the book out of the evidence room for Brian and Valerie to examine, and I'm sure they will find a ritual for summoning the entity that got our friends."

"You sound pretty sure, Mike," Brian said.

"The room in which they found the corpse was padlocked from the inside, and there is absolutely no way that a killer could have relocked that door after he left. If the decedent managed to dispose of something like a Scottish broadsword after he split himself to the chest with it, though, it's the most impressive suicide I ever saw. Didn't Valerie say that a large mass of iron or steel can harm a supernatural apparition's controller?"

"She played as big a role in winning this fight as anyone here," Brian acknowledged, "and we will keep on winning."

"I wish I could be as sure as you," Valerie said. "How do you know we will always win?"

"I know because we all care far more about each other than ourselves, and also because we simply have to."

The End

Charles Kyffhausen is the SF/Fantasy pen name of the author of:

"Gordon's Last Miracle" (*Full Armor Magazine*, TBD)

"Best Served Cold" (*Fear and Trembling*, April 2010)

"Snuff Film" (*Fear and Trembling*, January 2010)

"No Earthly Power" (*Zombology III*, TBD)

"The Book of Osiris" (*Scroll of Anubis*, TBD)

"The Eye of Balor" (*Lorelei Signal*, April 2009)

"Cycle of Justice" (*Strange, Weird, and Wonderful*, April 2009)

"Too Many Mummies" (*Fear and Trembling*, June 2008)

"The Wings of the White Eagle" (*Nowa Fantastyka*, March 2007)

"The Good Servants" (*The Sword Review*, Issue 22, 2007)

"The Pact" (*The Deepening*, September 2006)

"On Camlann Field" (*Dawn Sky*, July 2005, and *Time in a Bottle*, TBD).

Zombie Heartbreak

By Lauren Hudgins

When you're undead,
your heart has ceased passionate beating.
It is beyond broken,
festering and liquefying in your chest cavity.
With deteriorated lungs,
you cannot sigh with longing or regret.
You do not moan with pleasure.
You expel gases of decay
through pale lips,
expressing nothing
but your undying need for sustenance.

Love and comfort-
abstract concepts for warm-bodied creatures.
Your locked limbs will hold no one.
You stiffen your rigor mortis
a little more,
and shamble onward, onward.
You cannot stop for death.
Death sped off without you,
kicking up dust to dust in your face.

Against your former free will,
you will consume
the hearts, flesh, and brains of others,
making them just like you.
Their screams for mercy fall upon putrefying cartilage,
dead ears.

Lauren Hudgins' poetry has previously been published in *Writer's Eye, Third Wednesday* and *Neuropsychatric Poems*.

The Beast of Harris Lake

By Adam P. Lewis

Looking down from the cliff edge at the river below, Darren made a snap decision to jump. Not knowing if the stream below was deep or shallow and bedded with rock he did not care. The only thing he cared about was escaping from the beast. Just behind him, he could hear the snapping of branches as the beast charged through the brush. Darren sprang from the rocky ledge and pin dropped into the stream below. As he sank to the bottom, he felt his feet touch rock. The stream was just deep enough to slow and cushion his plunge. His feet planted on the bottom and he sprang up through the water like a rocket. Upon surfacing he inhaled deep and waded his head above water. Looking up at the cliff he saw the beast standing erect like a man but hunched over at the mid of its back. Its nose was stuck in the air trying to find Darren's scent. With the slightest redirection of breeze, the beast's head jerked about sniffing the air for signs of his prey's whereabouts. Darren however, was below letting the current take him downstream away from the beast.

The night before, Darren was dry, safe and laughing around a campfire with two of his fishing buddies, Carl and Mick. They shared tall tales of their biggest catches which were exaggerated more from the cheap beer they drank than trying to outdo each other's stories.

Darren bit off the end of a Churchill, spit it out, leaned into the fire, and lit up. After a few drags to keep the cigar lit, he held it between his teeth and held his hands apart about four feet. "I'm telling you the truth that son-of-a-bitching catfish had to be this long. The head on that sucker was bigger than my wife's boobs!"

Carl laughed. "Then the fish's body must have been the size of your fist. Your wife's rack underneath her bra is nothing short of powder puffs!"

"You didn't let me finish, bigger than my wife's butt!"

Mick laughed and stood up. "I'm going to take a leak."

"You have our permission!" Carl joked.

"Boy, you sure are full of comedy tonight."

"Do you need one of us to hold it for or are you going to be a big boy and do it all by yourself this time?" Carl joked again.

"Maybe I'll just wizz on you instead of the trees."

Later that night the men bunkered down in their sleeping bags, talked a bit more about woman, cigars, and NASCAR before falling asleep. The night was cool, overcast and a slight mist formed over Harris Lake.

Startled from what he thought was a cry for help; Carl woke and lifted his head. A hunting guide by trade gave him a keen sense of his surroundings. He could follow a moose for miles just by looking at broken tree branches. Any slight noise drew his attention, such as this case. "Did you guys hear that?"

Mick grumbled incoherently and started snoring. He wasn't much of a woodsman as Carl; he just liked getting away from his wife and two daughters every so often. Fishing trips were his favorite escape. Neither his wife nor kids cared much for fishing and never bothered to ask to tag along. Just the thought of hooking squirming worms made the three most important women in his life gag and shiver.

"I thought I heard something," Darren responded. "I think it was an owl or a hawk."

"No, that was no owl. It sounded more like someone calling out for help."

Just then, off in the distance a howl echoed from across the lake. "What the hell was that, a coyote?"

Carl shook his head. "NO, there aren't any coyotes in this area of the Adirondacks. That was more wolf than coyote. And from the other sounds, it appears to have attacked something putting up a fight. Those cries sound like a distress call. I cannot imagine a wolf attacking something big enough to cry out like that alone. I've never heard or seen such a thing. Wolves hunt in packs during this time of year so early after winter."

Yawning and laying his head back on the pillow Darren said, "Well if it is a wolf it's eating now, we won't be attacked."

Carl laid his head down as well. "They'll only attack us if desperate or threatened, they'll run from us before we even see them."

Before the sun fully rose, the men were already fishing. Carl and Darren were up to their waists in the water kept dry by chest-high stocking foot waders. Mick was about fifty yards offshore in a rowboat just visible through the misty water top.

"Any luck yet?" Darren yelled to Mick.

"A few nibbles, no takers though."

"If I didn't know any better I would say all the fish grew legs last night and walked ashore in some Darwinian experiment," grumbled Carl, "I haven't had a single nibble."

Darren slowly reeled in his line. "Me either, I'm going to move down the lake a bit. You coming?"

"I think I'm going to stay here, Mick is directly in front of me and has gotten a few hits. The fish may be moving this way."

As Darren walked the shoreline, Mick drifted towards the opposite side of the Harris Lake. A few times, he stood up, pissed over the side of the boat, and eventually felt the urge to shit. He rowed ashore, pulled the boat onto land and walked about twenty feet into the woods. There he dropped his pants as well as last night's dinner onto the ground. After he finished, he swore in annoyance. Back across the lake was the toilet paper. Still squatting he searched about the brush for leaves large enough to wipe when he suddenly jumped in fear. Like a scared rabbit running out from under a bush he fled the woods with his pants only halfway pulled up to his waist. Tripping over himself a few times he ran awkwardly as if his legs where conjoined like a mermaid. Before he even had his pants up, he was a good ten to fifteen feet from shore rowing the boat quick as if in some kind of Ivy League school boat race. By then the mist had lifted just enough for Carl to see everything that was happening across the lake. Not knowing what exactly was going on with his friend he laughed.

"Jesus, Jesus, Christ Jesus, Jesus..." Mick repeated, as he rowed full steam across the lake.

When Mick was about thirty yards

from Carl, it was clear that something was wrong. The look on Mick's face was that of terror. Tears streamed down his chalky face, his knuckles turned white from tightly gripping the oars as they shook within his trembling hands.

"What happened to you?"

Mick stood and pulled his pants up, jumped out of the boat and yanked it ashore. Ignoring his friend, he ran to the campsite and started packing his camping and fishing gear. By this time, Darren had seen what was going on and ran back from where he set up his new fishing spot.

"What's wrong with him?" Darren asked, pointing his fishing rod at Mick.

"I asked him about five times already and the only thing he keeps saying is we have to get the hell out of here now."

Darren grabbed Mick by the arm and spun him around. "Let me go, before I end up like that guy across the lake!"

"What guy across the lake? What are you talking about?"

Carl grabbed Mick's arms and asked, "What did you see across the lake?"

Mick ripped free his arm and continued to pack his gear in a hurry as if he were saving precious items from a house fire. "Across the lake there is a man, or what I think is a man. His body is ripped, head bashed, guts all over, claw marks and chewed up... Jesus... just don't stand there and stare at me we've got to get out of here!"

Trying to grasp what their friend said Carl and Darren looked at each other thinking Mick turned crazy on them overnight. "I think he saw a dead deer or something like that," Darren said.

"I know a deer when I see one and that mess across the lake was no deer. It was human."

Carl looked back across the lake and said, "The only way to find out or not is to row across the lake look."

"I'm not going back," Mick said, shaking even harder in fear thinking about going back across the lake. "If you two want to die like that guy you go, I'm staying on this side of the lake."

"If what you saw was a human, then we have to find out for sure," said Carl.

"He's right Mick," added Darren, "we just can't let a dead body rot out here in the woods we had to at least find it and get help if not bring it back with us."

Mick froze and looked at his friends, "Something over there ripped that guy apart and it could still be there waiting to get us next."

"Then that something could have swam or walked around the lake and gotten us by now. Or maybe it's waiting in the woods behind us and get us at the right moment," Carl said.

"You're going to freak him out worse, knock it off," Darren said, nudging Carl in the back.

However, Carl continued knowing that if he frightened Mick just enough then he would join them instead of staying alone at camp. "So you stay if you want to and fight off the creature or creatures that got the guy across the lake." Darren knew at that moment Carl was using reverse psychology on Mick. "Come on Darren; help me get the boat in the water."

The two men pushed the boat into the water and started to row across the lake. Within ten feet, Mick darted from the camp, high stepped through the water and jumped into the boat.

On the way across Mick mumbled to himself. Only a few words could be comprehended such as *doomed, all gonna die, end up mutilated and damn*. The jokester around the fire last night, Carl, cracked a few jokes as he rowed but soon shut up knowing there was no way he could lighten the mood.

As the boat reached shore, Carl and Darren got out and pulled the boat onto land. At this point Mick was shaking in fear so much ripples from under the boat scattered about the water's surface.

"Where did you say the body was?" asked Darren. Mick raised his shaky hand and pointed to the right of where he had stopped to relieve himself.

"Are you going to sit in that boat or are you going to help us find it?" Carl asked.

Mick nodded his head. "Yup, I'm staying right here."

"The way he is acting, I think there may just be a body in there," Carl said to Darren.

As they approached the tree line, a smell that resembled puke and crap filled the air. At first, they thought that is exactly what Mick had done while he was here a short time ago. Puked and crapped. Hopefully they both agreed, that was what he mistook for a body. Even they knew however, Mick wasn't that stupid to confuse a body with his own bodily excrement. Searching about the area, they couldn't find any sign of a body, not even a trace of blood. Fifteen minutes went by and all they found was where Mick dropped his pants and went. Carl however did find a few broken twigs and patted down moss suggesting something big did in fact make its way through this area not too long ago. The ground however was covered with too much brush to determine what animal species left the impressions.

"What do you think?" asked Darren.

"I don't think he saw anything, maybe a light trick of some sort. It was foggy this morning."

The two reemerged from the woods, grabbed the end of the boat, and pushed it into the water and climbed in. "Did you see it?" Mick asked.

"We didn't find anything except where you crapped," said Darren as he started to row.

"And by the looks of it," added Carl, "looks like you crapped out a dead body. So that must be what you saw."

Darren laughed as Mick barked in anger. "Shut up, I know what I saw and it wasn't my own shit."

Carl joked, "We saw there wasn't any toilet paper used so you didn't wipe. How about you save your dirty underwear and we take it to the police and use it as a sketch so they know what they will be looking for after you file a report!"

The remaining boat ride across the lake was more teasing at the expense of Mick. Instead of defending himself, he sat motionless and stewed. Whatever he saw was real to him and he wouldn't confuse anything of that sort for a gutted body.

By the time they arrived back ashore near camp, Mick no longer gave his friends the cold shoulder. Instead he was scolding his friends like a father about how teasing could hurt a person's feelings. During the lecture, all three pulled the boat from the water and carried it back towards camp. Within fifteen feet from where they set up their tent and supplies, they suddenly dropped the boat to the ground and quickly sprinted to the campsite. Their eyes darted back and forth like surprised children scanning presents on Christmas morning. The camp was ravaged. Everything they owned was in ruins. Sleeping bags torn to shreds, tent sliced up like cold cuts, coolers crushed in on itself, and even their carbon fiber fishing poles snapped in pieces like twigs.

"What in the name? Why would someone do this?" Darren asked, rhetorically aloud.

Mick picked up a pair of his torn apart pants that was somewhat wearable. Rather than stand around in soiled pants he changed into the torn pair. "Dang kids," he said as he changed, "I bet it was those teenagers we past about half a mile down river when we drove up here the other night. They didn't look of age to be drinking. I bet they got drunk and trashed the place looking for beer."

"If it was those teenagers then they would've stolen the beer rather than crush the cans without opening and drinking them first." Darren said, holding up a crush can dirtied from a muddy beer mixture.

As Carl searched the area for supplies that weren't destroyed, he bend down and looked at the tracks that covered the area. His tracker intuition took over. Tracing the outline of the track with his fingers, he noticed a hair found within one impression and picked it up. His eyes squinted as he studied the hair and rolled it within his fingers. The hair was short, thick, and coarse and came to a quick fine point.

Mick picked up a cooler, each side was cracked open like walnut and punched in as if a sledgehammer was taken to it. "There were bear tracks next to this cooler," Mick said, holding up what was left of one of the coolers, "so maybe it wasn't those teenagers. I can definitely see a bear breaking our coolers like this but not drunken kids."

"These tracks are wolf, the front end anyway. It has a paw print of a wolf, but…" Carl paused.

"But what? BUT WHAT?" Mick yelled,

annoyed with Carl's hesitation to what could have done this to their campsite.

"BUT," Carl snapped back, "but the back of the track is human. Almost as if the beast that trashed our camp is half man half wolf."

"Stop joking around Carl, this is no time for comic relief." Darren said.

"It's no joke," replied Carl, "Look at the tracks yourself; the front of the track is a paw and morphs into the heel of a foot."

Darren looked around the ground and saw tracks everywhere. "Maybe a wolf stepped where we stepped and that is why the tracks look like they are from one animal."

"I've tracked animals for too long, "Carl said, "I've seen overlapping tracks and these aren't that. There are no breaks between print to suggest they are a wolf's and ours. They are implanted at the same depth into the ground. These two tracks aren't overlapping into one track, they are one. I think we are dealing with a large wolf or a crossbreed or something."

As Carl searched about for other tracks that could explain half wolf half man anomaly, Darren picked up most of the trashed campsite. He didn't pick up the mess in an orderly way. Instead, he took what was left of his sleeping bag and filled it up with pieces the destroyed gear. When the bag got to the point where it almost had to be dragged, he approached his truck to load it into the back.

"Oh my God," Darren whispered, as his face flash froze in fear. His jaw dropped and quivered as if he was crying.

Behind him, Carl picked up a handful of dirt that looked as though was mixed with blood. Carrying it over to get Darren's opinion, his fingers spread apart releasing the dirt like an hour glass. Like Darren, he too frozen with his jaw dropped. "Mick, you better get over here!" Carl called out.

Mick approached to see what Carl wanted but unlike his friends his response was panic, "Holy, Jesus!"

Sprawled out on the truck's hood was the body Mick saw from across the lake. The body looked as though a bear performed an autopsy. A deep claw wound ripped the chest open down to the pelvis. All the organs inside showed signs that they were either chewed or eaten away. What was left of the ribcage had claw and teeth marks dug deep into the bone. The throat had teeth punctures on each side where the animal had crush the man's windpipe suffocating him to death. The man's arms and legs had smaller chew marks where much smaller animals, possibly skunk or opossum, had fed on the carcass after it served as a meal to its killer. The top of the skull was cracked open like an egg and hung off the side of the truck. Gravity worked on the skull's contents forcing a mushy pile of brains to slide out and plop onto the ground.

"Believe me now?"

"Shut up Mick," snapped Darren, "you're not helping the situation."

"Mick, I'll never doubt you again," Carl said as he walked around the truck examining the body. "Whatever did this was no bear."

"You think so?" Mick said, sarcastically. "No bear carries a dead body around a lake a places it on a truck's hood!"

"I think we are dealing with a rather large and dangerous wolf-human creature." Carl said with a shaky voice. Most of his life was spent in the woods and he has come across all types of animal carcasses. Nothing had ever scared him until now.

"That's what we were hearing last night. From across the lake those, screams and howls. That wasn't an animal being attacked by a wolf, it was that poor guy being attacked by a werewolf," said Darren.

Carl stood up. "If it's smart then that creature knows we are here. For all we know it could've been watching us all night long."

"Whoa, wait a minute," Mick said, raising his voice again in anger, "you two knew that this thing could have been out there watching us? Waiting to attack us and all you two did was ignoring that fact and put on waders and start fishing in the morning?"

Carl raised his voice back. "We didn't know what was out there, it sounded just like a wolf and that is all I figured it to be. I would say this was done by a rare hybrid wolf, or for all we know it is just a deformed wolf."

"A deformed wolf that carries a dead body around a big lake within thirty minutes, drops in on Darren's truck, trashes our camp, and runs back into the woods to let us know it's watching us? You're nuts! Whatever beast did this was a werewolf! That is plain to see," Mick yelled as he became annoyed and frustrated with Carl's guessing.

"I'm nuts, I'M NUTS?" Carl yelled back, "You're throwing around the word werewolf and you have the nerve to say I am crazy?"

"Both of you calm down and stop yelling!" snapped Darren. "If that beast is out there, then it is nearby and we don't need to let it know we are here for it to attack us next. We need to gather up what is left our gear and get the hell out of here in a hurry!"

Wanting to get out of the woods sooner, Mick grabbed the corpse by the arm and pulled it off the truck's hood. The body slide down the bloody hood to the ground with ease like a hockey puck gliding over ice. Not wanting to be the next victim, he jumped into the driver's seat and turned over the engine. "Get in or I'll leave you guys behind!"

Darren reached into the truck and turned the ignition off. "Get out and help us load the truck or you'll be walking back home through these woods."

"That monster is out there, stalking us and you want to pack up our gear, you two are crazy!"

Angrily, Carl pulled Mick from the truck, "We don't know what is out there, but just in case it isn't anything but a prank we aren't leaving our stuff behind."

"Pranks don't involve mutilated bodies!" Mick yelled.

"Damn you Mick, nobody knows what the hell is happening, just help us get the truck loaded. Stalling is going to get us all killed." Carl said, dragging Mick by the arm towards the camp. "Now help us load the truck!"

Over the next ten minutes, the men got the truck loaded and headed down the mountain. Darren drove slowly over the bumpy and rock-littered potholed road. At this rate, it could possibly take about an hour or more to get out of the woods to the main road. There he could make time and sped quickly down the mountainside. During the ride, Mick rocked back and forth in the backseat of the truck muttering obscenities and for God's protection. Carl shook his head at how annoying Mick became. Everyone in the truck knew Mick was an atheist. Repeatedly at every life threatening moment, he suddenly became a devoted follower of Christ.

"Whoa, whoa, whoa... stop!" yelled Carl.

Darren stopped, "What, what's the matter?"

"Back up about ten feet."

Darren stopped the truck and backed up.

"It's that campsite those teens set up, all their gear looks trashed too." Carl got out of the car and walked over to the camp followed close behind by Darren. Too scared to join them, Mick sat in the car reciting Bible verses, or what he thought were.

Looking over the camp, they noticed the same hybrid wolf-human foot prints. There were no signs the teenagers were killed or harmed in any manner. Both cars they drove up the mountain in were gone. Deep tire skid marks were found suggesting they left in a hurry. Carl and Darren returned to the car and continued the drive back down the dirt road.

"Well?" Mick asked.

"Looks as though they left in a hurry. There was no sign of foul play so hopefully they are safe."

Keeping a sharp lookout into the woods each of the men scanned nervously for the beast. With any luck, they wouldn't see the monster charging from behind a tree before they reached the main road. If the beast attacked, the slow moving truck would be a sitting duck. Seconds later, Darren reached the main road and accelerated, pushing the truck to its limit. The engine nearly blew a head gasket as the RPM's were pushed into the red. Burning engine oil could be smelled throughout the truck's cabin and every turn the tires squealed like hungry pigs.

"Slow down some, Darren, you're going to roll the truck and kill us all. I'd rather take my chances with that beast than your driving right about now!" Carl joked, as he held tight to the dashboard.

"If that is the case I can pull over!"

Mick said from the back, "Open the

door and jump, Carl, out I don't want Darren stopping for anything."

Darren sped around another turn and when he came around, he slammed on the brakes sending the truck fishtailing about twenty feet until it came to a stop. "I was just joking!" Carl said.

His comment was only responded with Darren pointing a shaky finger out the windshield. There, standing about ninety feet down the road was the beast.

The creature stood on its hind legs with its arm spread out from the sides of its body like a wrestler waiting for his opponent to lunge forward. Thick grey fur covered its chest; its hands were bare except for overgrowth of hair on the backside of the fingers as well as palms. Razor sharp fingernails were caked with blood and dirt and cut the air as the beast twitched its impatient fingers. Black fur covered the legs and arms, but not as think or patchy as the fur which grew out from the back and chest. Lean muscles could be seen pulsating underneath as the body lurched up due to heavy breathing. A plume of head hair hid its ears. Protruding from its face was a small snout with a black dog-like nose coming to a rounded point above long fangs projecting from its mouth. Saliva foamed from the mouth and hung off its fur covered chin like a St. Bernard after drinking from a watering dish. The feet of the beast were long, skinny and bare with chipped toe-nails. Swaying slowly behind the beast was its tail, long and nappy, full of grime from being dragged along the ground. Its overall appearance was mange, underfed but strong and fearless.

Suddenly, the beast darted forward on all fours and charged the truck. Darren yanked the shift stick, putting the truck in reverse and flooring the gas pedal, driving backwards up the mountain.

Carl and Mick yelled in fright, ordering Darren to do what he was already doing, drive. Gaining ground was the beast; every stride grew the monster inches closer until it was only twenty yards away. Darren slammed the brakes stopping the truck. The sudden stop caused the beast to stop as well and crouch close to the ground like a cat ready to pounce. Slamming his foot on the gas and shifting into forward drive, Darren rushed the beast. Carl and Mick yelled for Darren to turn around and escape but instead he continued to drive straight at the monster. The beast didn't flinch as the truck sped toward it. Closer and closer the truck came upon the beast and seconds before the moment of impact, the beast jumped forward at the truck landed on the roof. Swerving about the road, Darren tried to fling the beast off the roof to no such luck. For a brief moment, Darren lost control of the truck nearly flying off the edge of the road into the trees. When the truck was in his control, he slammed on the brakes screeching to a halt. All three men stared out the windshield hoping to see the beast fly off the roof rolling down the road away from the truck. All they saw was an empty road.

"I must have shaking that thing loose back up the road a ways," said Darren between heavy breaths.

Mick turned and looked up the road, "Unless it rolled off into the woods I don't see it anywhere in the road. Let's not find out and..."

Loud crumpling sounds rang through the truck cabin as the beast ripped open the roof with its arms. A flash of black and grey blurred into and out of the truck. The beast grabbed Mick's throat with its jaws and yanked him out. Fierce and hungry growls drowned out Mick's choking as his lungs filled with blood. In fright, Darren ran from the car into the woods. Carl was left in the truck, hopped in the driver seat, and sped away. The beast had dug its toenails into the top of the roof and ripped Mick's esophagus from his throat. With its claws, it tore through Mick's clothes gripping his flesh and then flung Mick like a maid snap dusting a rug. Mick's body slammed through the windshield causing Carl veer off the road and slam into a tree. During which time the beast leaped off and slowly walked on its hind legs toward the truck. The last thing Carl saw as he opened his eyes for the last time was the beast's mouth open and crush his skull.

Running faster than he ever had, Darren sped through the woods hoping the beast wasn't trailing behind. After about fifteen minutes of nonstop running, he stopped and leaned against a tree. He looked back and could no longer see the road, truck or the beast. As his breathing became normal he thought whether Carl escaped or not and how stupid it was of him to flee into the woods. Cursing himself for not staying behind and helping, he punched the tree nearly breaking his hand. Then he thought that maybe fleeing was for the best. If he could make it down the mountain safely then he could tell a park's ranger or police officer what had transpired at Harris Lake. Even though his legs felt like wet spaghetti noodles, he continued to run.

Hours past and Darren was now dragging his feet as he thought he had a safe and untraceable distance between the beast and himself. Thoughts of that very beast were few and far between as the feeling of thirst, hunger, and tiredness took its toll. Instead of wanting to get out of the woods for help, he could only think of stumbling along other campers, a creek or a cabin to replenish his body.

However, the only thing he came across on the mountain was trees and small animals that startled him every time they ran when he came too close. Soon he realized his wondering around for a stream, campers and shelter led him in circles. Three times in the past hour he had came across same large broken rock with a tree growing from the center. Darren was lost and the sun was setting, nightfall was upon him and soon it would be dark. He sat on the rock and regained his composure. His breathing returned to normal and his legs felt refreshed. This rest was exactly what he needed to clear his mind. Now he was able to ignore his need for water and food he shifted his attention back to escaping the beast.

# # #

Daylight succumbed to darkness and Darren was a good mile from where he rested. Instead of running full speed, he jogged to conserve energy. He would need it if the beast found him or if he stumbled upon it. From the corner of his eyes to the left, he thought he saw movement in the woods. At first, he thought they were tricks of light and shadow. However, tricks of light don't make panting noises, break tree limbs, and crush dead leaves on the forest floor. The shape of the figure, lean, tall and hairy was all too familiar, the beast had found him.

The beast was shadowing his movements waiting for the right moment to strike. Darren picked up his pace hoping he could somehow elude the monster in the darkness. In spite of this, he knew it was his scent that led the beast right to him. From horror movies he watched and stories read as a boy, he knew the monster had a bloodhound sense of smell. There was no room for escape unless he could shield or hide his scent. Every step he took as he ran made him perspire. His sweat was like a pheromone and the beast being half-human reacted to it. Darren's only option to do so was to find a water source and travel within it.

Thinking like his tracker friend Carl, Darren figured out the beasts hunting habits. It only pounced when threatened or if the prey knew the beast was there. Avoiding all contact and urge to look over his shoulders to find the beast he continued moving through the forest and soon he heard what he was looking for.

Just through a clearing in the forest, he could see the moonlight dancing off the breaking of water upon rocks. He found the water source he had been looking for in order to take a chance at escape. Sprinting, he took off through the forest as if a muscle car hopped up with nitrous, going zero to sixty in one second after skipping from first gear to third. The sudden burst through the woods alarmed the beast. It too blasted full steam through the forest breaking branches and uprooting ground growth with every step. Branches cut Darren's face, arms, and legs, leaving a fresh blood scent behind him for the beast to follow. Trailing not far behind, the beast was only a few body lengths behind when Darren came to a small rocky incline. Like a crawling baby, Darren clawed his way up the rocky slope on his knees and hands. Suddenly, he was stopped in his tracks by the beast. The monster dug its fingernails into Darren's shoe and pulled him down the slope. Kicking his feet at the monster, Darren tried freeing himself. By doing so, he slowed the monster down giving himself enough time to slip out of his shoe and kick the monster in the face, causing it to roll down the rocky incline. Darren got up on his feet and ran the rest of the way up the slope. When he reached the top, he ran from under the brush and screeched to a halt. He found himself at the edge of the cliff overlooking the steam below.

As Darren contemplated jumping into the water the beast gathered itself at the bottom of the slope. Charging in anger, it growled, sounding like two pit bulls engaged in dog fighting. The rock cracked and split open as the beast dug its claws in gripping the rock as it stampeded up the slope. Upon reaching the top, the beast sniffed the air for Darren's scent. Once the scent was zoned in, the beast looked in the direction it came and saw Darren stepping back away from the ledge. The beast dashed forward unleashing hairsplitting growls that echoed down the mountain. Salivating at the thought of sinking its teeth into fresh prey, the beast could taste Darren's scent lingering in the air. Tree branches broke off as the beast pushed through the brush and just as it leapt out onto the ledge, Darren had jumped into the stream. The beast sniffed the air for Darren's scent but all it could smell was the forest.

A football field length away, Darren floated along with the current. In the meantime, the beast turned and ran back down the rocky slope toward the stream. Like a hound after an escaped prisoner, the beast sniffed the stream bank hoping to pick up the scent.

Downstream, the width of the water narrowed and the depth lowered to ankle height causing Darren to continue through the water on foot. Turning a bend in the stream, he noticed straight ahead moonlight gleaming off a cabin window. Heading towards the cabin, he could hear the beast howling in the distance closing in on him. When he came upon the cabin, he knocked on the door, receiving no answer. Circling around the exterior Darren looked in the windows. The cabin was empty, except for wooden furniture, a gun rack above the fireplace, and an old oil lamp.

Darren kicked in the front door and began reinforcing the cabin. He placed the heavy oak framed bed in front of the door and the wooden dressers and tables in front of the windows. The only way in and out was the fireplace which he lit ablaze to keep the beast from climbing down.   After   he barricaded the cabin, Darren took down the shotgun from the gun rack and loaded it with slug shells. For now, this was his only plan of defense if the beast got in or it he had to make a dash from the cabin.

Not too long after Darren fortified the cabin, he could hear the beast outside scraping its nails on the log exterior, sizing up the dwelling. The beast let out bellows of anger as it slashed at the framework. The log frame was hard, thick, and would take hours to crave its claws through. Every slight noise the beast made on the outside Darren pointed the shotgun. Loud poundings could be heard up on the roof as the beast stomped and clawed about trying to smash through.

BANG!

The shotgun rocketed slugs skyward at the beast, causing it to jump back at every exit point exploding through the roof. One after another, the slugs shot up like antiaircraft fire trying to shoot down warplanes in battle. Slugs grazed the beasts hide knocking it off its feet.. With the fire raging within the chimney, the beast had no choice but to drop down from the roof and try its luck elsewhere.

All was quiet for the next few minutes. Darren listened carefully trying to hear the beast but all he heard was ringing in his ear from the loud gunfire.

Crash!

A loud startling bash fell onto the front door. Without hesitation, the shotgun swung around and pointed at the front door. The beast slammed its body against the door, forcing its way inside. With every slam into the door, the heavy bed skipped an inch across the floor. When enough space between the door and the frame was created, the beast wrapped its fingers inside the door. With all its strength, it pushed on the door trying to make its way inside. Darren's hands shook as he pointed the shotgun at the door and squeezed the trigger.

BANG!

Exploding from the shotgun barrel the slug tore through the door. Wood shrapnel exploded off the door scattering about the room. Outside the cabin, the beast let out a loud distressed yelp as the slug entered its left shoulder. The impact knocked the beast onto its back where it laid thriving in pain. Blood poured from the wound. The left shoulder blade was shattered when the slug exited, rendering the arm useless. Raising to its feet the beast swayed from back and forth and crept toward the cabin. The beast growl and slammed its good hand into the door trying to enter. However, the shotgun blast weakened the monster and it was unable to force open the door with only one arm.

As the beast paced the cabin perimeter like a guard dog, Darren broke open the oil lamp. He ripped curtains from the windows, tearing them into strips. With oil from the lamp, he soaked each strip. Next, he poured a portion of the oil about the cabin and dowsed the floor in an arced pattern around the corner in which he backed into. From this corner, he had a view of every possible angle if the beast tried to enter through a window or if it managed to once again pry open the door. Or if he had to, Darren would light the oil-soaked floor to slow the beast down so he could fire off more rounds. With shotgun in hand, he was ready for the inevitable show-down. There was no escaping the beast down the mountainside and he knew what he had to do next, wait for it to enter and kill it.

Silence surrounded the cabin as the beast stalked the foundation looking for easy access inside. The only way in was through the windows. Thick walls, a raging fire, and only one good arm to climb on top of the roof prevented the beast from using those options of entering. The beast would have to jump through with enough force to topple over the dresser or table propped up as barricade.

Startled, Darren jumped to his feet as window glass shattered followed by the bang of the dresser falling to the floor. The beast bounced back off the dresser and re-mained outside. Darren aimed the shotgun at the window. His finger on the trigger twitched nervously accidentally firing off a round, which blew through the cabins wall under the window. Not knowing if he hit the monster he again pumped the action and aimed at the window. The beast didn't rise into view and all was quiet.

Minutes went by; Darren never low-ered the shotgun until suddenly…

CRASH!

…a second window shattered and the force from the beast jumping through knocked over the barricade. This time how-ever, the beast fell through the window and upon impact it rolled across the floor.

BANG, BANG, BANG, BANG!

Muzzle flash from the shotgun lit up the cabin like fireworks. Each shot blasted through the beast's body. However, it kept inching forward.

Darren unloaded the remaining shells.

BANG, BANG!

But each round missed its mark. Panic set in as he tried to reload, his hands shook in fear causing him to drop the shells.

Growling, the beast staggered like a drunkard while reaching out with its claws. Darren pulled matches from his pocket, struck one on the side of the box and dropped it to the floor. A quiet popping whoosh fol-lowed by a wall of flames shot up like a lit stove burner as the oil ignited. The beast jerked back covering its eyes as the flash mo-mentarily blinded it. The beast shook off the surprise and inched forward. With every bit of remaining energy, the beast leapt through the flames tackling Darren to the floor. Push-ing his hands up on the beasts jaw Darren used all his strength and rolled over on top of the flames. The beast bellowed, released Darren and rolled about the floor in pain as it burned. Unable to smother its flaming body, the beast rose to its feet staggering about the cabin. Melted flesh dripped like candle wax spreading the fire about the cabin. Embers of fur floated about sticking to the ceiling caus-ing sporadic fires to burn through to the roof. The cabin became engulfed in flames. A wall of flames blocked every exit. The fire inside the fireplace spread out across the floor.

Catching site of Darren through the raging flames, the beast lurched forward as its charred body crumbled like snack chips. Darren wrapped the oil soaked strips around the shotgun barrel held them over the flames igniting them. The rags lit up like a torch. Waving the burning rags between the beast and himself, he kept the monster at bay. Soon however, the rags burnt away and the beast again found the strength to lunge at Darren.

The beast tackled Darren to the floor.

Hot molten flesh of the beast sizzled through Darren's clothes setting him ablaze. Unable to extinguish his burning clothes as he fought off the monster, he felt his skin start to blister and melt. He yelled out in intense anguish but was soon silenced as the beast's jaws crushed his windpipe. Weakened from the violent cabin fire the roof collapsed. Blazing ceiling beams and shingles fell, crushing to death what little life the beast retained.

The fire spread across the mountainside burning all trees, plants and animal life trapped within the blazing path. Days went by as the fire burned uncontrollably. Fire departments, volunteers, and the National Guard fought the fire. Members of each perished trying to control what was now classified as a wild fire. Nearly two weeks went by until the fire was finally under control in part to the efforts of man and a rainstorm that swept across the mountain. As fire investigators and cleanup crews worked the area, no signs of the cabin or Darren were found expect ash and bone fragments. Only small fragments of the beast were found. Investigators wrote those remaining bones off as human.

Decades later the forest recovered and the beast's allure remained a tall tale started by teenagers. Every so often, a group of crypto-zoologist and monster hunters would trek about Harris Lake looking for the beast. The monster seekers' only evidence are stories and eyewitness reports that rose every so often over the years. Skeptics write these reports off as hoaxes and misidentification of local wildlife. No signs of the monster or anything like it have yet to be found. As for the wildfire, its cause was contributed to a truck accident that occurred on the mountain. Two badly burnt bodies were found inside the truck. The truck in question was registered to Darren.

The End

Adam P. Lewis lives in upstate New York. He is inspired by modern and classic horror fiction and movies, which translate into his written work. His short stories appear in anthologies and online zines since his emergence in late 2008. If you dare to venture deeper into the frightful mind of Adam P. Lewis, please visit, www.adamplewis.com, for more information, fiction and frights!

An Idyllic Mission

By Edward Rodosek

I'm gazing spellbound at the holographic scene.

A broad white staircase goes up somewhere into a translucent blueness. A slender, frail woman's figure is on the front landing. Her sad, pale face touches me; I notice a dumb appeal for help from her large green eyes. The scene dissolves slowly and the commander's voice puts me back into reality.

"You know Lady Grace is one of our most loyal allies on the Attar II; and what you see is the last holo record of before the video connection went off. Yet, we know she's still alive for we get occasional audio signals with her voice. And now, Lieutenant Peck, let me hear again, what the purpose of your mission is."

"The unknown monsters on the planet Attar II besieged the castle of Lady Grace for several weeks and many of her faithful subjects have fallen. Because the situation became critical you sent Lieutenant Crawford on the rescue mission three days ago. He'd reported he succeeded in arriving at the castle, but then we lost any connection with him. My primary task is to land on the planet, drive my armored car to the castle and free Lady Grace by force if necessary."

I tried to hide my excitement—what a glorious task! A helpless beauty and a fearless knight who'll rescue her...

"Very good, lieutenant. And your second task?"

"To find out what had happened to my comrade-in-arms and fetch him or his dead body."

"Excellent. I wish you good luck, Lieutenant Peck."

# # #

The first thing I feel is the salty taste of blood in my mouth and then a blunt pain at the nape of my neck.

Now I recall the sequence of dramatic events exactly at the moment when I noticed the plateau on which the castle of Lady Grace stands. A huge explosion that meant an instantaneous breakdown of my spacecraft module engine—my spasmodic efforts to slow down my too fast approach to the uneven surface of Attar II—the angry thundering of the emergency jet drive—the violent thrust of the module parachute—and, finally, the brutal impact a split second before I lost my senses.

I'm hanging upside down and when I try to untangle my seat belts I groan with pain; most likely a couple of my ribs are broken. Awkwardly I slip onto the floor, shaking my head. All around me there are smashed electronic apparatus, a heap of spare equipment changed into a useless junk. And the worst of all—the passage to my armored car is hopelessly blocked. I have no weapons on me except the paralyzer hanging on my belt.

Suddenly, a strong smell of smoke fills my nostrils—oh my God, something is on fire! I try to climb over the ruins to the exit and now I see flames are blazing in one corner of my module. My equipment is being swiftly transformed into a glowing furnace.

I must get out through the exit trapdoor, which is now nearly above my head. The knob for automatic opening is right in front of me! But it's useless now so I try to pull the lever—it sticks. I pull it again with all my strength; the trapdoor opens abruptly and I fall over the heap of equipment. A sharp, violent stabbing pain rips through my thigh—but there is no time to look at my wound.

The fire is approaching fast, the suffocating smoke makes me cough and my eyes are brimming with tears. I must find something useful—oh, here it is, my laser, the most powerful personal weapon I know of. I swing it out through the trapdoor and then, with the utmost effort, I manage to lift my sore body, twisting my way through it and, finally, I fall on the stony ground.

I gasp for breath; I'm dizzy, my pulse quickening. A blue-white sun glows from the violet sky, its sharp rays dazzle my eyes and pricks sting every part of my uncovered skin.

All around me is an endless, glittery white plain. Only in one direction, on my left, a silhouette juts out of the flat surface of the plain. Is it possible that's the Lady Grace's castle? If so, then—

My musing stops for I catch sight of a monster.

A freak, an unbelievable mis-creation from a nightmare—it's a beast fifteen feet tall and equally wide, a real Gorgon with undulating margins within which a sort of jell-o is flashing with interchanging colors. I'm staring in horror at its changing contours, at its form which is a negation of all possible forms. The monster is growing bigger—and only now I realize it's approaching me, slowly but inexorably.

Reflectively I aim my laser at the center of that horrifying bulk and convulsively squeeze the trigger. I watch with a wicked satisfaction as the ruby-red laser beam penetrates deep into the monster's body.

But, how in Space is it possible that nothing is happening?

Why doesn't the enormous heat of the laser beam—several thousand degrees—burn a hole in that disgusting bulk? Why can't I smell the offensive stink of burning flesh? The monster pays no heed to my lethal weapon; the waving jell avoids the beam in a strange way and in the next instant comes back, undamaged. There is no wound in its tissue, no scorching scratch at all. Instantaneously, the ruby-red beam pulses two, three times, then stops.

My laser is empty now and the Gorgon is still coming nearer to me, in no hurry, self-confidently, as if it knows I can't escape.

My useless laser slips out of my hand. Now, nothing remains but to run for my life.

I try to sprint but my left leg refuses to obey me; I stumble and fall on the dusty ground. What's the matter with me? At the moment my brains are useless but my ancient survival instinct doesn't let me down. With utmost effort I manage somehow to stand up, but my left leg fails again. For the first time, I look down. The left trouser leg of my flying suit is thoroughly soaked with my blood and at every step a tiny trickle of crimson pours out of the wound.

For heaven's sake—I must have nicked an artery!

I know how lethal that wound is; if I don't stop or at least reduce that bleeding at once, I'll soon be too weak to run away. I press hard on the wound with my thumb. I try to hop on my right foot, but that doesn't work, I must lean on my left leg and every time I do more blood trickles under my thumb.

I realize I'm running away at random, just away from the beast, and that's foolish. I have to run more to the west where the plain with Lady Grace's castle is. Only there do I have a slight hope to find some help or at least to conceal myself.

I'm trying to turn to the left, but my wounded leg won't allow me; I fall on my knees and hands, then I stand up again, pressing my thumb on the wound and staggering like a dead drunk boozer. Oh God, let me reach the castle! Now I'm just a stone's throw from it—but the Gorgon is even closer to me. I'm breathless, dripping with sweat, my mad pulse trying to blow up my chest; my strength is ebbing for the life is still fleeing out of my wound.

The Gorgon is so close to my back I can smell its disgusting stench. I'm only a dozen steps from the huge gate of the castle—only eight, five, two... But all my effort is in vain for the gate is closed and an enormous bolt hinders my way.

Everything is over.

The Gorgon is next to me, nearly over me. I turn around, wrathfully, for I've nothing more to lose. In these last seconds of my life, I'll look directly at my executioner; it mustn't know I'm frightened to death. I stand upright and my hand feels my paralyzer hanging on my belt. Wait a second, you damned freak! I'll show you what I'm capable of—I'll burn your bloody guts before you finish me!

I grab my paralyzer and stretch both my arms out into the Gorgon's varying bulk and squeeze the trigger.

I hear the frightful high voltage buzz and see the dark emptiness emerging around the crackling sparks—but just for a few seconds and then the mass returns in its earlier intact form. The Gorgon is invulnerable, indestructible...

The paralyzer slips out of my powerless hands; my knees are weak so I have to lean against the gate. I close my eyes, waiting for death to come—for the fatal strike, for the bite of sharp fangs, for the ripping of giant claws or for something even more fearful...

Suddenly, the gate behind my back opens, I lose my balance, falling backwards, and an unbelievable scene appears before my astonished eyes.

A broad white staircase goes up somewhere into a translucent blueness.

On the front landing, a slender woman with a pale face and large green eyes is sitting in an armchair. Yet there isn't any trace of helplessness in her self-confident poise and her gaze shows a cold, steely determination.

But... but what is that near her?

A few steps from her is something—something so odd that I can't, at first, recognize what it is. When I see its nature, the discovery freezes me on the spot.

A uniform with lieutenant epaulets is lying on the ground; a few steps further there is a huge rotisserie over the extinct embers. And on the skewer is impaled ...

I feel nauseous, so I have to sit down on the ground.

Lady Grace looks me over from head to toe.

"Well, two delicacies in three days—that's not bad at all." A broad smile appears on her face as she turns to the Gorgon.

"Good job, lad. Take tomorrow off."

The End

Edward Rodosek is a Construction Engineer and Senior Professor at the Univesity of Ljubljana, Slovenia, European Union. Aside from his professional work he writes science fiction. More than sixty of his short stories have been published in SF magazines in the USA, UK, Australia and India. Recently he published the collection of short stories *Beyond Perception* in the USA.

Peanut Butter

By Linda Lyons

I'm not quite *The Man in the Iron Mask*, but from behind my veil I watch Tom put the mail where he always does and pick up my NetFlix to return. He's a good neighbor. Flora will be over later to put away my groceries. She's a big help. I know she'd like nothing better than to sit and have a coffee and chat, but she understands I can't do that comfortably, so she chirps away and tries not to stare and then leaves and locks up.

It's Saturday and the stock markets are closed. My friends are busy so other than Floyd delivering the groceries, I have nothing pressing to do. I've got the usual junk mail to ignore and recycle and a new movie to watch. This is one I didn't request from NetFlix. If it's not what I'm expecting, I can watch something from the satellite feed or unearth an old favorite from my collection.

I've grabbed the spoon and the peanut butter jar, ready to let a generous dollop melt in my mouth while I semi-recline and check out the movie, but right away I know there's something different happening. The image is shaky, the camera held by an unsteady hand. The video is grainy and amateurish. The title flashes on my screen: cut-out letters from newspapers like ransom notes in *Thin Man* movies. Nick and Nora Charles would take this seriously.

WHO THE HELL DO YOU THINK YOU ARE?

#

There's a scene in *Field of Dreams* where Kevin Costner tracks down Thomas Mann and finds him secluded in an apartment, his privacy guarded by protective neighbors. Costner has to be his most persuasive and persistent to get in.

I'm no Thomas Mann, but I do live a solitary life. If Kevin Costner tried to get in to see me, I don't know what I would do. On the other hand, my door is always open for Denzel.

I live in a seniors' community: cloned bungalows plopped on a former tobacco farm and packaged as "the ultimate in retirement living". There's a doctor from town who sets up shop in the Rec center every Friday morning, dispensing arthritis meds and trimming woody toenails. For me he makes a house call. My next door neighbor, Flora, sends her husband Tom to the community mailbox every day for my NetFlix fix and whatever legal papers trickle in.

Flora is like the others around here: curious but respectful of my privacy. Our houses are far enough apart that we can't exchange that neighborly cup of sugar by opening our windows and reaching across the gap, but close enough that I can smell roasting meat and hear clinking beer bottles on warm Saturday nights.

If disaster ever struck, I know I could count on her. Tom keeps an eye out for me too. When the yard maintenance guys come, Tom wanders over to the fence and makes sure nobody tries to peer into the windows.

Everybody knows about me and wants to brag they've seen me – it won't happen. The details they imagine might be far worse than the truth. Probably not.

Tom's the one who opens my door for the electrician or plumber to come in and repair whatever needs repairing. I trust Tom and Flora with a key to my castle, but I'm the only one who can command my throne room.

I'm 27 years old, surrounded by an outer ring of pseudo parents and grandparents. I live here thanks to the largesse of a huge trust fund and a generous monthly income established for me by a well-insured drunk driver and my very competent lawyer. My lifeline to the other world, the world past Tom and Flora, is my computer.

#

Whatever, this is, it's no joke. It's a silent movie, no talking or music, but I detect a whirring tinnitus, the sound of revolving mechanical parts, underscoring the video. There's a montage of destruction flowing across my screen. Tsunami waves crash with apocalyptic force against beach huts and breakwalls and then the image cuts to bodies hanging from trees and lying on beaches, calm waters lapping at the edges.

The twin towers crumble and fall over and over and over. The debris cloud builds up and turns into an atom bomb flash. Wide-eyed stick children, too weak to cry and covered in flies expire in front of my face. The terrorist aftermath of Barcelona and London invades my sanctum and mocks me.

I pause the video and grab the package. It's got my name and address and account number, just the way it should. Someone who knows me has made this monstrous film. Someone I know wants to create fear.

My castle has been breached and I know what to do. I punch in the code on my speed dial and pray, "Please, please Colleen, pick up."

#

Jimmy Stewart has wise-cracking Thelma Ritter, gorgeous Grace Kelly and murderous Raymond Burr to spy on through his *Rear Window*. I've got Tom and Flora, this really great chair like a reclining waterbed on wheels, and computers. Flip a switch and I'm Captain Kirk voicing text and commands to "computer" on the bridge of the Enterprise. Flip another switch and I'm reclining on an air mattress floating on a pool in some exotic locale, Esther Williams and the girls performing water aerobics around me. I make the best of what I have, and when I lose perspective and start to feel sorry for myself, my shrink sets me straight.

Colleen isn't really a shrink – not even close – but she was the first non-medical face I remember seeing after the accident and she's stuck by me ever since. She's in her fifties, plump, bossy and smart. No one can be all things to all people like Jane Fonda in *Klute* but Colleen comes close to a favorite aunt or a godmother.

I don't have an aunt, or a godmother, or even a second cousin once removed. I'm a total orphan, so my relationships, even virtual, are more precious to me than you can imagine.

Mom and Dad were both only children, children of only children. I was an only child for a long time too. When they told me I was going to have a little brother or a little sister, I remember thinking I must have failed them somehow. *Little Man Tate* wouldn't have liked Jody Foster producing a sibling

169

either.

My brother was in his car seat, in the rear on the passenger side. At 5, he was big enough to sit strapped into a booster, but my parents were super protective. They bribed him with Game Boy time. My mother was beside him and my father sat beside me in the front. It was my first time driving the family. Dad and I had just returned from the DOT office where I received my license and I was driving us to Applebee's for a celebratory lunch. I remember hearing the beep beep of 12 noon on the radio and then a big bang and everything went black.

Colleen was the junior clerk (read go-fer) of my Court-appointed Trustee. She volunteered to go to the rehab center to see the "poor little thing in the coma". The staff had informed the Court that I was sort of in and out, so Colleen just happened to be there when I was finally out.

I guess she must have been there for a while, watching me flutter my eyelid, mumbling and shifting in my skin straight jacket. I didn't see any horror or revulsion on that freckled face, just a bit of moisture welling in her eyes. I remember her hand was warm, and for some strange reason she touched the side of my cheek.

I was thirsty, very thirsty but my mouth didn't move right. I heard myself wheeze out a word that was supposed to be "water". My mind heard "water" but my ear heard "huh". But Colleen understood. She leaned over, soft puffs of warm breath fanning my cheek and maneuvered a straw into the corner of my mouth. There were nurses fussing around behind her, but Colleen just looked into my eye and bent over, urging me with her body language to sip.

She visited every week. She smuggled the mirror in and held me while I sobbed. She walked beside my gurney down yet another fluorescent hallway in predawn dusk and held my hand when the bandages were removed. It was Colleen who empowered me to say NO to more reconstructive surgeries. She liased between me and the dipsomaniac's doctors. If I wasn't up to having another troop of gawkers gag, Colleen would blockade my door until they went away.

# # #

Colleen is coming. She had a date but she cancelled it. I counted on that.

"Stop watching the damn thing right now. Call my Dad if you need to, but stop torturing yourself. I'll be there by 6. Will you be okay?"

"I'm sorry Colleen. I'm so sorry to bother you. I don't know what to do."

"And stop apologizing to me. Friends do this for friends. I'm calling my Dad and telling him to get over there right now. Grab your hat, honey, the cavalry is coming."

"Please Colleen, leave Tom and Flora out of this. I just need you to tell me what to do."

"I'm telling you. Turn the damn screen off. We'll figure this out together. Go in the kitchen and eat something, or take a shower or get in one of those damn chat rooms and flirt with somebody, but stay away from that film. You understand?"

I understood. Colleen is coming. I have things to do. I wish I could smile.

# # #

I live in Three Oaks because Flora and Tom live here. They're Colleen's parents. When Tom retired, he and Flora looked all over for a place to settle, and Three Oaks was the best they could afford. I can see one oak tree from my throne room. Tom tells me the other two were cut down because of disease and old age. How lucky for the trees that someone who cares decides when they stop suffering and affords them a dignified removal.

Colleen bought me this really cool hat. It's a beekeeper's pith helmet with a Velcro mesh veil. She found some extra dark fabric and concocted a new veil that hangs down covering the center part of my face and goes all the way around the left side to behind my right ear. We tried a bunch of wigs, but to stay on straight they had to be so tight they rubbed against my scar tissue and drove me nuts. I don't have a lot of mirrors, for obvious reasons, but if I do catch a glimpse of myself whirring around my castle, I kind of like the way I look, from the right side. Sort of early Mia Farrow without the ½ inch of hair. If Tom or Flora come over for some reason, they wait for me to get the hat on before they open the door. My "iron curtain" protects everyone.

I was very lucky to survive the accident. It took a lot of no-nonsense buck-up lectures for me to get around to that, but I'm there, most of the time. The burns are not from an exploding gas tank or anything. I somehow ended up on my side in a pool of battery acid pinned under the car. I don't remember any of that, just the beep beep and the bang. The scar tissue than runs up my left side from my knee to my temple pulls me over, so even though I can transfer myself into a shower chair and rinse off whenever I want, I'm not the steadiest walker on the planet. It's easier to glide like 3CPO from room to room and sleep on my customized waterbed.

Colleen hired an occupational thera-pist to redesign the kitchen and the bathroom so I can fend for myself, on foot or from the chair. She co-ordinated all the renovations and dealt with the contractors. I've got one of the first "smart houses", before there was such a thing, but it was me who insisted in painting the whole place cherry red. After all, to malaprop, *Who's Eye is It Anyway?*

I'm not a big eater. I like to snack. If I could hire Cher from *Mask* to fix my meals I would. All those little things on sticks. When I have a Big Mac attack, I call and arrange for a cab to pick-up the food. Floyd drives one of the two taxis in town. I've got his cell-phone number and he's happy to run little errands. He doesn't mind the long trip, or the big tip. Floyd is older than Flora and Tom. I think he drives taxi to keep himself busy, and because he likes people. It's only the older people who don't drive anymore who use cabs around here. This is farm country. From my window I can see a lot of pick-ups and SUV's out on the main road near the oak tree. So far, no sign of *Thelma and Louise* blasting down the highway in that convertible.

It's a good thing we are a bit too far out for the kids to bike. Small towns have a lot of tongue-waggers and they delight in speculation, especially about newcomers. Three Oaks has been here for a few years, so most of them and us have arrived at a cautious acceptance. Of course, I am not exactly an "us". I'm a square peg in a round hole. I have an alarm system built into my fence. I'm finished with being a pathetic victim. I take care of myself now.

Right after I moved in, some bored kids out crop checking (which means drinking beer in the boonies) decided to get a closer look. They walked through the corn field between my yard and the road and tried to hop the fence. My outdoor spots came on and the alarm woke up the entire population of Three Oaks. The whole thing scared everybody half to death, and some of "us" are already pretty close to that.

#

It's hard to flip switches when my hand is trembling, and nothing responds to my voice squeaking an octave higher than normal. This is a lesson to be learned. I need a back-up system installed. There's an idiot savant type I met on line. He's no *Rainman* but he can make a watermelon play the tuba. I'll pose a hypothetical to him and see what he recommends. Or he may be Lex Luthor, I don't know him well enough to be certain, in which case I'll need someone new to seek him out.

Until a few weeks ago I trusted my judgment about people and I trusted myself. I need to be strong. Evil can invade my house, but I can't let it violate me. I have a resolve and a purpose to my life now.

Nobody has ever suggested that I was the crispest chip in the bag academically, but I am a well-informed, analytical thinker. There are a growing number of people who value my wisdom and knowledge. I am self-sufficient. I am a fighter. I will not let anyone victimize me.

Please hurry Colleen. You need to be here.

#

I love Audrey Hepburn in *Wait Until Dark*. She is so amazing, foiling the killer by using her own heightened perceptions to disadvantage him. I wonder how she didn't sense there was a dead guy hanging on the back of her closet, but not too much. It would spoil the movie for me if I dwelt on the little inconsistencies. I love her in *Nun's Story* and *My Fair Lady* and *Sabrina* too. She's gorgeous and believable no matter who she portrays. I use her body type for my avatar in the alter-world reality I live.

Colleen was a little dubious about my wish to live independently. I didn't even have a high school diploma, no life skills, unless you count willing yourself to live, and no clear direction for the future, so we made a deal. She'd facilitate everything – more like move mountains – if I could graduate from college on-line. I found a tutor on Craig's list willing to guide me through algebra and pre-calc in a chat-room/blackboard and paid the ward clerk's unemployed son to read cultural anthropology texts onto discs. An ear bud became my virtual professor, excluding the "Wow dude, this is crazy" comments that slipped in, and my physio sessions became commands and responses in French. When I reached cent I knew I had done enough leg stretches.

No one offered me a Rhodes Scholarship, but I passed. I have a general degree in nothing, which is my personal ticket to everything, which is why I am trembling and waiting.

#

Floyd just scared me out of my skin. He forgot to call and tell me he was on his way, and I forgot he was coming. The groceries are in my entry and Flora is on her way over. I won't eat or drink in front of Flora, but maybe I could offer her a coffee. It would be nice to have her sit in my kitchen for a while – almost like having Colleen here. I hope Colleen didn't call her parents. No. She couldn't have. Tom and Flora would have been over here in a flash and for sure caught me without my hat. It would be a toss-up as to who would be more frightened. I think I'll keep my hat on until Colleen gets here. It gives me the element of surprise to use as a weapon if there were a homicidal maniac stalking me.

#

My throne room is like nothing you've ever imagined. We took the breakfast nook and adjoining family room and opened it wide up. I have voice command lighting systems, surround sound, a home theater above the gas fireplace (which also ignites at my voice) and an awesome computer set-up. I've got digital clocks mounted on the wall above the computer stations showing the times in Europe and Asia where I have virtual friends. It looks like the set from Network without Peter Finch and the newsreaders' desk.

I've got a daily routine going, or nightly depending where you are in the world. The scar tissue seems to contract when I sleep, so I catnap off and on. When I am awake and engaged I don't notice it so much. In odd moments I update my digital diary, a pixilated narrative of what I do, who I am – what I wish. It's a one-sided conversation with a one-sided person – ha ha.

I met my friend Manos in an on-line game site. He's an accountant in Athens and a real hunk. I've seen his Facebook pictures. Manos has two daughters, teenagers he can't relate to at all, and a passion for Scrabble. He and I play every evening after his dinner and solve the problems of the world. His English is excellent, but I think he cheats. There's no way a Greek accountant knows the word 'oyez' without using a dictionary. It doesn't matter. Manos thinks I am a retired anthropology teacher, male, widowed and childless.

He treats me with the respect he would offer any distinguished gentleman, and sometimes tells a saucy story or two. Two men of the world bonding.

When Manos signs off, I snooze and have a light lunch and check into a chat room in Japan. There are a lot of Japanese with very fluent English, but their metaphors need work. Miko is an interpreter, so she says. I say she's a hooker, but it doesn't matter. She thinks I'm an insomniac in Leeds, England, with an abusive husband and a problem with alcohol. I've got dozens of tales of woe for her and she has a wealth of experience dealing with dominating men and passions . I use bad movie plots for my side of the conversation and she uses pragmatism for hers.

#

Panic over. Flora rattled around stowing familiar goods in familiar places, bitching in her chatty way about Tom being underfoot all the time. It's plain to see they adore each other, but they need space. I suspect that's one reason both of them jump at the opportunity to get over here where privacy is queen.

While Flora talked and bustled, I got into my mental groove. By the time she left I was ready with rational analysis of the situation for Colleen.

A) Someone is pissed.

B) Whoever the unsub is, as they say in *Criminal Minds*, he knows how to find me.

C) He's sending me a message but he's basically a weenie. A few spotlights and an alarm rousing an army of octogenarians wouldn't stop a respectable maniac.

D) This is a plausible hypothesis. Things will be resolved.

MSNBC streams into the computer on my lap table all day. I follow the Dow with a passion. My future is invested in those little ticks. My financial advisor emails me daily reports and I know exactly what they should say before I even receive them. Bernie Madoff and company won't ever pull the wool over my eye.

When there's no movie playing at the theater near me, and that's not often, there's music at a companionable volume flooding the house. I'm in a bit of a time warp on that. I was ga-ga over the Backstreet Boys before the accident and missed much of the next 5 years or so. C&W, with all the moaning and wailing doesn't do much for my disposition, but Patsy Cline's "Crazy" hits the spot some nights. I've developed a fondness for baroque chamber music. I first heard it in period black and whites from the 50's – B movies based on a historical grain of truth and developed into vehicles for dreamboats and pin-up girls. Tights, cleavage, exquisite manners et al. Leslie Howard's *Scarlet Pimpernel* is one of the worst movies ever, but I can relate to the justice in it. He was a real wuss in *Gone With the Wind* though.

I'm convinced that most elected officials begin to run for re-election the minute they are installed in office. I've got high hopes for Obama, but he's got to deal with that congressional collection of weenies. Not a *Mr. Deeds* in the bunch. Politics gives me a headache.

My *raison d'etre* these days is my financial newsletter. It started as a joke. I was monitoring this blog out of England, all pip pip cheerio and blah blah blah, where the expert was commenting on currency traders and puts and derivatives, stuff I can't and don't want to understand. Give me a company that makes a product that I know and I'll give you an opinion, but this other junk is for the birds. Watch the bigwigs testify before governmental subcommittees if you don't believe me.

Anyway, I wondered how many panicked people follow this line of crap and react instead of act. I created my own blog called Archer's Arrows. I wrote a blurb a 2-year-old could comprehend and posted it for the world to see. It was basic common sense. Don't buy it if you don't know what it is. Don't risk the money if you can't afford to lose it. I stuck smiley faces and emoticons all through it so no one would think Alan Greenspan was ghost-writing and sent it off into the ether.

#

Colleen is here and I need to stay focused because:

A)   Colleen is pissed.

B)   Colleen is pissed at the unsub

C)   Colleen is pissed at me. I told Colleen about my alter-egos and my avatars. I want her to know how smart and resourceful I am. I want her to understand how far I've come.

I think part of her is proud of me and part of her is disappointed too. She can't believe what I manage to get up to here in my little world. I have a life, or lives, she knew nothing about. She has her own spoon for the peanut butter and we are mulling the situation over. We'll watch the movie together. I knew I could count on Colleen. I'll miss her.

#

Hot damn! Some people will read anything. They told other people who told other people, yadda yadda yadda. My financial advisor, who thinks I'm more naïve than I seem, even quoted it (unattributed of course) in his daily report. He's another prime weenie, but he's honest.

By the end of the first week I had 12,000 hits. TD Ameritrade wanted to buy ad space, the Wall Street journal requested an interview with "Mr. Archer" (sexism abounds in the old boys club) and the hits kept coming. I was going platinum in Phil Spector parlance. Every day I took ten minutes from my busy schedule and composed a quick paragraph on basic money matters and people who know more than me lapped it up. Suze Orman's publisher asked for permission to reprint my treatise on basic interest.

It was amusing at first and then intriguing. Manos had just scored a triple word on "scissors" —I swear he manufactures S's when he needs them—when he asked if I'd ever heard of Archer's Arrows.

"What's that?" I responded. "A new beer?"

"No my friend. This Archer fellow from America writes an investment newsletter. The business channels here are quoting it. Is Archer famous in America? Does he have his own television show?"

"Manos, the only Archer I know is Geoffrey Archer, the fiction writer embroiled in some sordid scandal in Britain. There was a radio program back in the 40's about a dysfunctional family called the Archer's. I'll have to look into it."

# # #

The movie is really lame. Just more of the same shocking pictures and revolting slo-mo's. Spielberg would be embarrassed but there is a certain *je ne sais quoi* about it—like *The Invasion of the Killer Tomatoes*. After a while even Colleen became inured to the violence and it lost the desired impact. She wants to call the police but I say no. This is the act of someone with no power, a sad tortured soul lashing out at a perceived injustice or injury.

It's important to have Colleen here. She's going to spend the night and go visit with Tom and Flora before driving back tomorrow. It's been a few months since we've seen each other. We've both been busy in our own ways. Her health is not good, but she has a boyfriend, a bailiff, widowed, 3 kids. Colleen needs someone to nurture. This little chick is all grown up now.

Colleen never talks about her first marriage, but I know it left scars. Not all scars are on the surface for everyone to see—the worst ones are always down deep and hidden. I'm not the only one who wears a mask.

# # #

One thing I am very careful about is giving financial advice on specific stocks and companies. There are enough mea culpa's echoing on Wall Street without adding my little warble.

I don't know any more than the next guy about which company to invest in or which is a bounced check away from bankruptcy. This is why big banks and investment firms pay huge sums to analysts, who also don't know but get paid to say they do. The closest I ever get to giving advice is to send an automatic response to email inquiries advising them that I do not respond. I only pontificate. I don't name names, I talk in generalities and parables like Chance Gardener in *Being There*.

If every kid on your block has to have

the latest whatever, and every kid they know has to have the same thing, there just might be a demand for that specific whatever to keep the company who makes it busy for a long time. And if you think the thingy is over-priced, all the better. Chances are the company is making a pot full of money on each unit. Get it? Basic common sense—not astrophysics.

And yet, Archer's Arrows was like a resurrection of the Dead Seas scrolls. One total unknown had the nerve to say "cut the shit" to the high paid snouts and people started to wake up and think for themselves. When I think about it, it really is rather brilliant.

#

Remember Al Pacino kissing his bother Fredo at the Cuban nightclub in *The Godfather*? Colleen went to bed thinking somebody lost a fortune on what they think I said and is trying to strike back. She's wrong. It isn't that.

We stayed up until midnight, catching up, finishing off the peanut butter, and then she went off to the bedroom, She takes a lot of pills and needs to sleep. I have places to go and people to meet, virtually. I've got a flirtation going with a nice young man in Canberra. He's terminally ill and confined to bed. It isn't *Love Story* or anything. If it were, he'd be Ali McGraw and I'd be Ryan O'Neal.

He's 18 and knows what sex feels like, but I don't. We are virtual lovers. He thinks I'm 17 and paralyzed so he describes to me what we do and say to each other and how it makes us feel and I forget the pain and drift with him somewhere else and get a taste of forbidden fruit. This is the most I can ever

hope for and the best he can achieve. Some day soon he will not be waiting at his laptop for our encounter. I like our intimacy. I'll need to find another friend.

I need to send a thank you to Miko. She really does interpret when there is work, writing voice-overs for documentaries. She found some great footage that a Japanese production company re-mastered for their version of *Frontline*. The girl is a whiz at editing too. She does do favors for gentlemen friends, and me, for a price, so I haven't lost my touch.

#

I'm not good at good-byes. I've asked Tom and Flora not to come over. They are still grieving. I have enough pain. I can't take on any more. *Terms of Endearment* is playing on their screens for the rest of their lives.

My new agent found a loft for me in Manhattan. It has 4 exposures with a wraparound terrace. I'll miss my oak tree, but I'll overlook Central Park. Archer's Arrows is by subscription only—at an outrageous price. I limit the number of subscribers and the fee guarantees they guard the information like Fort Knox. I do virtual interviews on all the major networks and retain my privacy. The Matt Drudge of finance.

I still play Scrabble with Manos and gossip with Miko, but I'm too busy writing my blog and my books to watch many movies these days. "Amy Archer" is a cult persona in the financial world. She has the talent to ferret out details that provide astute investors with an edge, for which she is amply rewarded.

It was research that got me to the big time, and as long as there is an internet and public records, it will be research that keeps

176

me here. I've got assistants working in all the major markets and a system of incentives for inside information that rivals none. I still don't dispense investment advice, just facts and common sense for which people are more than willing to compensate me.

I threw out my copy of *Beaches*, but I underestimated how much I would miss Colleen. She was the only person who didn't turn away. I knew there had to be a reason. I found it.

Colleen's ex was the well-insured drunk driver. He was only driving because she had passed out seconds before they hit us and the drunken bastard reached over and grabbed the wheel from her. Flora and Tom lost their home and their savings helping Colleen out of her mess. I think they really do care about me, but emotions covered in guilt and pity are hard to read. It's not fun being piggy in the middle when everyone knows the truth but you.

I did my research well. Colleen always ate more peanut butter than me, but I took a purgative that night, just in case. My liver is one of the few things that isn't destroyed. Colleen, the bitch, just passed out for the last time.

The End

Linda Lyons studies Creative Writing at the University of Arizona South. Her short fiction and memoirs have been published in *Nota Bene*, the Phi Theta Kappa Literary Magazine and by Silver Boomer Books. She is currently revising her first novel and working on a collection of memoirs.

www.ingramcontent.com/pod-product-compliance
Lightning Source LLC
Chambersburg PA
CBHW080901120626
46555CB00008B/2904